Caffeine Nights Publishing

E

B.A. MORTON

Fiction aimed at the heart
and the head...

Published by Caffeine Nights Publishing 2015

Published in Great Britain by
Caffeine Nights Publishing
4 Eton Close
Walderslade
Chatham
Kent
ME5 9AT

www.caffeine-nights.com
www.caffeinenightsbooks.com

British Library Cataloguing in Publication Data.
A CIP catalogue record for this book is available from the British Library

ISBN: 978-1-910720-10-3

Cover design by
Mark (Wills) Williams

Everything else by
Default, Luck and Accident

Born in the North East of England, B.A.Morton writes across a number of genres including crime, romance, horror and historical fiction. After a twenty year civil service career, she and her family escaped the rat race and relocated to the remote beauty of the Northumberland National Park. She now lives in a cottage built on the remains of a medieval chapel.

A member of the Crime Writer's Association, she is a self confessed crime fiction addict. In 2011, her debut novel "Mrs Jones" a crime thriller set in New York, took second place in the international literary competition, The Yeovil Prize, and launched her writing career.

Website: http://bamorton.weebly.com/

Bedlam

B.A. Morton

For Peter

Fear

A primal reaction unfurled from a slender thread.

A shiver etched with icy claws upon skin stretched taut with dread.

One

Fear is subjective. I know this to be true. In my time I have faced them all. The scuttling arachnid, the hissing serpent, even the searing heat of the pyre has left me unbowed. But, when I stand toe-to-toe with the wide open space, the plummeting depths, the void at the edge of my world, the panoramic vista draws me, seduces me, entices me to take that final step back into Bedlam.

I'm shaking now, deep inside. My organs rattle like poppy seeds in a desiccated pod. No warm flesh to cushion them, I am but a dry shell. Yet I feel perspiration, cold against the back of my neck, hot on my face, and I force my eyes to remain open. This time I must see what lies before me. This time nothing will stop me.

I hear him coming softly through the darkness, his measured step as he circles ever closer. I feel his presence. The subtle movement of air around me as he moves disturbs my fragile being. I must retain focus, but I have not the power to resist as his warm breath whispers against my ear, taunting, teasing. He knows I will succumb, as I have for what seems like an eternity.

This time is different. I must overcome, I must succeed.

I inhale. The simple act of breathing causes my chest to burn. My heart beats a warning, my senses buzz. I clamp my mouth shut, hold my breath. He is all around me; he is poison – and yet my lungs yearn for release. My body betrays me and my lips part with a soft sigh. The threat is real. I know it. I cannot help myself. I step forward.

My toes are bare, scuffed and bloody, but I feel no pain, merely the cold steel beneath my feet. I have travelled far. I am nearly there, almost at my destination, the point of no return.

Sadness seeps from my pores. Melancholy hums gently in my head. I curl my toes over the edge, feel the roughness of rusted rivets, and steady myself against the night breeze.

He smiles. I feel it against my skin in the same way I hear his laughter in my head, harsh and mocking. He is letting me know that my actions are his and I am powerless. I seek out the rage that lies hidden in the depths of my used and abused excuse for a soul. It evades me.

I inch forward. Now my toes are free of the rusted metal and I pivot precariously on the balls of my feet. Cool air, an updraft of sweet intoxication, beckons, and I am tempted. Behind, he urges me on, whispers his jibes, like lyrics to a favourite song, over and over until the chorus threatens to overpower me, to push me over, to pull me in.

I know what must be done. In my head, in my waking dreams, I have argued and reasoned with my doubting, lesser self. In my dreams I am strong, but now as I stand at the brink, at the beginning of the end, I am shaking, and he crowds my thoughts with his own.

He's closer now, almost upon me. I feel his coldness where others might imagine warmth. I risk a final breath through pursed lips, and it is my undoing. The heady scent assails me. That coppery tang is love and life and all things to me in my twisted perpetual world. My senses are bombarded. My brain is awash, alive. I clench my fists, curl my toes, and plead with myself.

He laughs now, no longer in my head, but out loud, so all can hear the chilling sound. His venom anaesthetises my feeble revolt. My mind is numb with need. My nerve endings tingle. I begin to salivate.

It is almost time. I feel the approach of midnight as strongly as I feel him. I am torn, pulled by twin temptations. His hand reaches out and caresses my arm. His icy touch penetrates my skin through dermis down to bone. I incline my head, weak and helpless, as he reaches my neck. I am done for, beyond help. My futile plotting, my longing for the end, is all for naught.

Raising my eyes, I see the clouds which shroud the night sky move gently, and the moon, serene and all-seeing, is released from darkness. All Hallows is upon us. I hear his gasp, the catch in his throat, and, finally, his weakness is revealed.

I have but a moment. The risk is great, yet I am suddenly energised, reckless in my naivety. I feel his bite, sharp and cold, and my body reacts, as I know it will. Iciness transforms to burning heat. Capillaries swell and throb as I come alive. My blood rushes to navigate every shrunken vessel, my organs rejoice. For one brief moment I have the power and he has naught but need.

I pull him close; he shares my precarious position on the very edge of nowhere. Bedlam beckons. The boiling maelstrom reaches out its welcome. This time I will not step out alone, I will not suffer the torment of another tortured existence, continually seeking redemption and finding nothing but trial and defeat. This time I will take him with me and he will finally know what it is, this half-life he has gifted.

The blade is sharp. I feel it against my palm. The silver glints in the lunar glow. It sings to me – a song of hope. His voice in my head is receding. My mind becomes free, filled with the joyous sound of the blade as it punctures his flesh. His confusion is overwhelming – betrayal and disbelief. But I have him in my embrace, and he is lost.

I step out into the void, and this time we make the final journey together ... back to Bedlam.

Two

The phone roused him from the pit of oblivion where he'd settled when both booze and willpower ran out. He lay naked amid tangled sheets, alcohol-infused sweat leaching from his pores. Struggling to focus, he joined the dots, connected the shorted wires in his brain, and re-established contact with the real world.

He winced at the repetitive buzzing, a dentist's drill seeking out cavities in a brain where common sense had long since succumbed to decay, and, with a muttered curse, he reached out blindly to silence the racket. The contents of the nightstand crashed to the floor. His stomach heaved. He felt like death.

"Huh!" he grunted into the phone, scraping the guttural sound past a sandpaper throat. His whole body ached, his nerve endings screamed for mercy, and all he could think about was more of the same. When his hand touched upon an empty bottle rolling on the floor, he swallowed painfully, took a long steadying breath, and turned his attention back to the caller.

"Joey, 'bout bloody time. I've been calling for the last half hour. Get your arse in gear. You need to get down here."

"What time is it?" Joe McNeil slumped back against the pillow and risked first one eye, then the next. He tried to think, to put things in the right order, but failed. It was one thing knowing where he was, quite another recalling how he'd got there. He turned his head and a tiny spark of hope was instantly extinguished as he confirmed he was alone. The side of the bed where she had lain was empty.

"Time you were out of your bloody pit and down here working. You're late – again." The words jumped with impatience.

It was well deserved. Lately he'd been stretching things to the limit. People he'd known before, when times were good, had been covering his back, looking out for him, clearing up his mess and making his excuses, but irritation at his behaviour had seen them dropping off, one by one, until only Dennis remained. Now even he was getting leery, anxious at just how far McNeil could possibly fall, and, more crucially, who might be dragged down with him.

Switching the phone to the other ear, he squinted at his watch. Eight thirty, Saturday. First day of the weekend, only he'd started his the night before with a lock-in. He hadn't intended it. He never did. He'd begun the evening with good intentions, a name, a meeting and some information, if he was lucky, but it had spiralled out of control. Not that it mattered. Drunk or sober, his days were all running into one. Each day a replica of the one before: work, boozer and bed, the exciting life of an almost ex-detective. The way things were shaping up, it wouldn't be long before the 'ex' became permanent.

"Piss off, Dennis," he muttered. "It's Saturday."

"DI Todd, to you."

"Piss off, DI Todd. Like I said, it's Saturday."

"And that makes a difference? When I call, you come running, DS McNeil. Perhaps you missed that page in the handbook? We're picking up the mess from Friday night, or did you forget? So, like I said, get out from beneath the sheets."

"Who says I'm in bed? I was lifting weights while you were on your first coffee of the morning."

"Oh, yeah, pull the other one, Joey. You sound like shite. We both know you were down at Minkey's until well after closing."

"You checking up on me?"

"People talk."

"Who?"

"People with poor regard for the individuals you've been hanging around with lately."

McNeil swung his legs over the side of the bed and rested his elbows on his knees, his head in his hands. "Yeah, well, people should mind their own damned business. I keep telling you, I'm undercover. I'm meant to hang with the tossers."

"Of course you are, Joey. Just keep telling yourself that. I think his nibs might have misjudged you, mistaken you for a waste of space who spends more time enjoying the company of low-lifes than he does locking them up."

McNeil smiled sourly. The guv was on the money; he had indeed gravitated to the gutter. "Hey, you know what they say, it's a shit job but somebody's got to do it, right?"

"Wrong. I'm just looking out for you. Sticking my neck out, as it happens. You want to invest all your hard-earned keeping Minkey's missus in the manner to which she's become accustomed, go right ahead. Just don't let it mess with your job – right?"

McNeil lifted his head wearily. He didn't need a lecture on top of a hangover. "For Christ's sake, Dennis, so I had one too many. What's the big deal?" He counted out the pause that followed and got to five before he heard the sigh. He knew why Dennis was pissed but was powerless to do anything about it. Okay, so he wasn't undercover, not officially anyway, but he was on self-destruct. Not the gun to the head finality, but the slow malignancy that eats away until nothing is left but regret.

"We got another one ..." continued Dennis in the tone he dragged out especially for sombre occasions and shit jobs. "Mather's in a ruddy spin. He's got that bird from the 'Herald' on his case and I've copped for running the investigation."

McNeil pulled himself back with a shudder. He knew without asking, but the words were out before he could stop them, "Another what?"

"Situation, Joey, another bloody situation, and, as usual, I'm a man down. That man being you. I've covered your back so far, but Mather's just arrived to rally the troops and I can see him now doing a roll call, counting heads and bodies. You'd better make sharp before he runs out of fingers or you'll be squaring up to him, not me. You need to be here doing your job, Joey, or you need to admit that you can't."

Already on one warning, behaviour unbecoming in a police officer, McNeil wasn't stupid enough to make it two. He needed this job, and not just because it paid the rent. This job that he hated gave him access to people he'd rather not know and places he didn't want to be, and right now that access was more important to him than life itself.

He kicked off the duvet and fumbled for his clothes, discarding a shirt with a grimace when the stink of sweat and booze made his stomach roll. He stood for a moment, wavering, with one hand on the nightstand, while he recovered his fragile equilibrium. He'd overdone it last night, even by his own standards. The game had, quite frankly, gotten out of hand, and he wasn't quite sure how to pull it back.

"Where are you, Dennis?" he asked as he stumbled to the shower, hopping from one foot to the other on the chilly linoleum floor.

"You need ask? Where do you think? Murder Central. There's been a bit of a party."

"A party?" McNeil closed his eyes briefly as the room began to spin. He steadied himself with a hand on a freezing radiator. The whole flat was an icebox, the direct result of ignoring the growing pile of unopened mail and bills. He shivered. He was done with the cold and the booze. He had an unwelcome flashback of an amply endowed girl, a tattooed man, and a brawl in which he'd come off worse. He raised his right hand; the knuckles were grazed and swollen. Maybe he'd managed to land a few before he went down.

"Seeing is believing, Joey. Talk about painting the town red. Whoever did this bought a job lot from Dulux. It's like the Tate Modern down here. All we need is a sheep in formaldehyde and we could charge an entrance fee."

"You mentioned a body?" He sucked in a breath and let it out slowly, oxygenating his brain in the futile hope that it might improve his cognition. It merely focused his attention on his churning stomach instead.

"Bodies – plural."

McNeil didn't need parties, and he didn't need bodies. He needed to switch off the phone, climb back into bed and sleep for a week.

"Okay," he sighed. "I'm on my way."

Three

McNeil was used to messy crime scenes, but today he felt the need to stand back and survey from a respectable, post-hangover distance. The space beneath the viaduct, a no man's land of decay, was a notorious spot for jumpers, flyers and druggies; a haunt for the city's weirdos and no-hopers.

Beneath his feet, the ground was littered with the detritus of a drop-out subculture. Mud oozed with discarded needles, beer cans and vomit. Above his head, giant iron pillars, daubed in anarchic profanity, leached rust like an open wound. He took a shallow breath. The air was thick with the fetid stench of putrefaction. His head hurt just looking at the desolation, but he'd spent too long working amongst the dregs to be shocked. This was just another day down here in Undesiraville.

What made today stand out from any other wasn't the fact that someone had ended up dead, but the fact there were three of them, which was excessive even by McNeil's standards. Two were suspended from the ironwork struts by their throats, not neatly with a rope around their necks, but brutally impaled on the point of a meat hook. Homeless and lifeless, they hung like abattoir carcasses, their ragged, lice-infested clothes flapping gently in the breeze. The pool of congealing blood on the ground beneath their feet, and the broad blackened splatter on the steel structure behind them, gave more than a hint as to the cause of death. Flies gorged on the unexpected bounty and subtle movement in the murky undergrowth announced the arrival of opportunistic rats. A plastic sheet had been draped temporarily over the third victim, who lay half submerged in the stinking slurry.

The crime scene was already a hive of activity, photographs taken, areas taped and marked for evidence, the mortuary van standing ready and waiting for the off.

McNeil nodded a stiff greeting to the other members of the team as he signed in and donned a flimsy protective suit. He ignored the questioning looks at his late arrival and concentrated on trying to don gloves with hands that shook and fingers that wouldn't oblige. Like a child who hadn't progressed beyond mittens, he gave a frustrated scowl, stuffed the proffered gloves up his sleeve and took a cautious step forward.

Hastily laid boards mapped out a line of access to preserve the scene. One step either side would have pitched him into the mire. McNeil glanced sceptically at his protective overshoes. He'd left his Wellingtons in the boot of the car, parked beyond the outer cordon. He'd already run the press gauntlet once, and wasn't about to retrace his steps and have to go through the whole rigmarole again. He sighed and kept to the centre of the path.

"So, what do we have, Dennis?" A reluctant question, and once it was asked there was no going back. He was hooked, unable to step away, even if he wanted to. There was something in his crazy, mixed-up psyche that kept drawing him in when he should have turned around and headed back the way he'd come. Death had that macabre effect on some people, but on a murder squad detective it was viewed with more than a little suspicion.

Dennis Todd shrugged noncommittally, delaying his reply as he studied the younger man through narrowed eyes. "Are you fit, Joey?"

"Fit for what?"

"Work."

McNeil shrugged. "I'm here, aren't I? What more do you want?"

Dennis partially unzipped his overall and fumbled in his jacket pocket. He withdrew a packet of mints and held them out. "Lord, save us from whiskey breath. Just pray no one lights a match or we'll all be buggered."

McNeil's lips twitched. He wasn't up to a full smile, that would have required a sense of humour, and he'd left his at home along with the empties.

"You look like shite," sighed Dennis.

"Thanks."

"Don't you own a razor?"

19

"Hey, people pay good money to look like this."

"Joey, stop kidding yourself. Slow down and start looking after yourself. I'm being serious here. Take some time off if you need to, but this ..." he gestured to McNeil's dishevelled appearance, the grey skin and bloodshot eyes. "This isn't designer, and it isn't right, and I'm not the only one thinking it."

McNeil scowled back at him. "Give it a rest, Dennis. I had one too many on my night off. Big deal."

"Is that a black eye?"

"Shit, no." It was all coming back like a ropey Vindaloo. The tattooed man with the meaty fists and the heavy skull ring – he'd packed a punch for sure.

"No? Then your mascara has run, DS McNeil."

"It's nothing, a misunderstanding."

"Please yourself. I'm concerned, that's all." Dennis gave an impatient shake of his head, like he was weary of playing nursemaid, but he sidled in close nevertheless and dropped his voice. "I know you're dealing with a lot at the moment, Joey. I wouldn't want to be in your shoes, nobody would, but you have to be realistic. Kit's gone, and no amount of booze is going to bring her back."

McNeil looked away. He didn't want to have this conversation, not with Dennis, not with anybody, and particularly not in the middle of a stinking crime scene. He scuffed at the dirt beneath his feet and inhaled slowly.

"Do you hear what I'm saying, Joey? Look around you, life goes on, bad things happen, and it's our job to try and put them right. If you can't deal with it, that's fine, I understand, but you need to make a decision. You're either with the living or the dead. Kit wouldn't want this. She wouldn't like what's happening to you."

He felt it then, deep inside, that twist in his gut that grew tighter every time her name was mentioned. He wanted to tell Dennis to shut the fuck up, that he'd no right to speak about her as though she no longer existed, but instead he kept his cool. As well as being his senior officer, Dennis was just about the only friend he had left.

"I'm telling you, I'm fine. Just got up in a rush, that's all. Some bloody nonce kept ringing my phone." He tried for a smile and failed. He didn't like what was happening to him either, but it wasn't something he could control. He'd made a promise and would make good on it, regardless of the cost.

"You'd shout up if you needed help, if you wanted to talk, wouldn't you?"

Dennis was the last person he'd burden with the crap currently going on in his life. He was a good guy, the rock in an otherwise stormy sea, but, despite that, or perhaps because of it, he wouldn't understand. No sane person could possibly comprehend what fuelled him night after night to keep searching when failure snapped at his heels.

"If I need a shoulder, I know where to come. Satisfied? Now, what's the story down here?"

Dennis didn't look convinced. He opened his mouth as if to add something, then changed his mind with a shrug and turned back to the crime scene.

"Three deceased, Joey. Two homeless white males and a twenty-something slip of a girl. That's as much as I'm prepared to say until I've got the pathologist's report, but something's not right, I mean, apart from the fact we've got bodies hanging like washing on a line. How on earth did they get up there, anyway?" He gestured to the crow bait dangling twenty feet from the ground. "We'll need a cherry picker or a friendly fire crew to get them buggers down."

McNeil shot a quick glance at the suspended corpses. His stomach heaved. He dropped his eyes and focused on Dennis instead.

"Who called it in?"

"Community Support Officers were first on the scene. Did a bit of trampling, as you might expect, but fair dos, they secured the area as best they could. It's a bit early for sightseers, but they kept the press at bay and the dog walkers on the leash, which is just as well considering the amount of fresh meat lying about."

"What alerted them? Who in their right mind comes down here?" McNeil shuddered. If ever there was a gateway to hell, this was the tradesman's entrance.

"Kids, down here messing about, hoping to score a half-done hypo, no doubt. 'Course they hightailed it without giving names. Bloody typical."

The breeze picked up. The bodies swayed ghoulishly and McNeil hugged himself. Despite the cold, sweat coated his skin. Despite promising never to touch another drop, his body screamed for a refill. He contained the tremors and the urge to vomit with difficulty. He felt all eyes upon him, some sympathetic, some hostile, all waiting with varying degrees of anticipation for him to slip up or crack up. Expectation was a heavy burden. His shoulders sagged in response.

He drew a steadying breath and squinted back up at the first body. He recognised the oversized boots and fatigue trousers, and settled his eye on the ginger beard. "Is that Popeye?" he asked as he raised a hand to shield his eyes from the ominous glare of a sky thick with cloud. Popeye was well known amongst those who lived on the streets and slept in doorways.

"Unless he has a stunt double."

"Reckon his line dancing partner is Jaimsey?"

Dennis nodded. "It looks like him, though until we get them both down we can't be sure. It makes sense, though. The local boys cleared the pair of them out of here on a number of occasions. Personally, I can't see what the attraction is." He swung his gaze from the hanging cadavers to the piss-pot of a makeshift camp. "I mean, just look at it. What am I missing? Who wouldn't rather be holed up in the Dog and Anchor on a Halloween night, or curled up at home in front of the fire? I just don't get it."

"You've got to be *local* to enjoy the local. Somehow I can't see that pair of tossers propping up the bar in The Dog and supping real ale. And as for keeping the home fires burning, not everyone's that lucky. Popeye and Jaimsey were outcasts." McNeil tapped at his head. "Lost their wits way back in time. Popeye was thrown out of every shelter in the vicinity. Jaimsey, being his point man, just had to tag along. Looks like they stood back-to-back until the end."

"You could be right. We'll get some foot soldiers on door-to-door, checking out the shelters, the usual haunts, and see if anyone saw anything, knows anything."

"You're wasting your time. Supposing they were sober, they wouldn't talk to the police."

Dennis shot him a glance. "Maybe not, maybe they'd rather talk to you. The way you look today, you'd fit right in."

McNeil ignored him. "What about the one on the ground?" He swung his gaze to the last body, inexplicably drawn to the surprisingly small mound beneath the plastic sheet. *Please God*, he murmured silently, *don't let it be a child*.

"Nothing like the others. In fact, we almost missed her, what with the puppet show above our heads. I don't know what's worse, strung up like game birds at a shoot or face down in a city's effluent."

"Mind if I take a look?"

Dennis scanned him with a worried glance. "Are you sure you're up to it?"

"I wouldn't be here if I wasn't."

Dennis shrugged his disbelief. "Joey, let's be honest. You're only here because I dragged you. But while you're here, better make it look as if you're doing your job, otherwise Mather will call time on you. He's been sniffing around, making noises you don't want to hear."

"Stop worrying, Dennis. Just tell me what you know and I'll play the good little Sherlock for Mather and the boys." He shot a quick glance in the direction of the DCI and felt a flicker of irritation at the falseness of the whole situation. Oh, sure, they were all going through the motions, doing the job they were paid for, but, despite the collective years of experience gathered together, he was the only one who knew what it was really like to be on the other side of an investigation. Every hour spent digging around in the grief of others was time he could have spent searching for Kit.

They all thought she was dead. He knew she wasn't.

It seemed there wasn't a minute of the day when he wasn't thinking of her. He knew it wasn't normal, knew the guys thought him obsessed and crazy, and they were right. He gave himself a shake. This was one place where he didn't want to remember her.

"There's nothing much to see, Joey. It looks like the girl's had a bloody good hiding, but I've seen worse. Roger declared life extinct at 0800 hours."

Dennis' voice dragged him back, and McNeil glanced up. It was two hundred feet or more to the parapet. "Could she have fallen?"

"Nah, too bloody high. If she'd dropped that height, we'd be scooping her up with a shovel."

McNeil winced. "Nice image, Dennis. I thought I was bad cop today." He turned and scanned the area. Ignoring the viaduct, his gaze was drawn to the water running through the site. He'd have called it a stream if it had been capable of sustaining life. As all vegetation adjacent to it had long since given up and died, he figured it was more likely a run-off from one of the industrial buildings at the top of the rise. "What about the sewer pipe? Dumped and washed down here with the rest of the crap?"

"I don't think so. There's a substantial metal grill over the outlet."

"Do you reckon there's a connection between the bodies?"

"Well, in the sense that they share a crime scene, yes, but in terms of how they met their maker, nah. I'm betting on the bus theory."

"Huh?"

"Wait long enough and three turn up at once."

McNeil ignored Dennis' gallows humour, squatted down in the mud, and fumbled the latex gloves from his sleeve. Cursing as they landed in the quagmire, he gave a quick glance over his shoulder, checking that Dennis had stepped away before easing back the sheet between finger and thumb.

He knew he should have waited, picked up some replacement gloves from the SOCO, but he was avoiding the super cool bitch in the white overalls who was solely responsible for his current warning. He'd seen her dismissive look when he'd arrived on site. She believed he shouldn't be here, shouldn't have kept his job. Maybe she was right. After such a promising start to his career, he'd turned into the problem child that everyone frowned upon and no one understood. Everyone was waiting for his next tantrum, but today it seemed the SOCOs had problems of their own to contend with, and maybe that's why Ms Mary Cameron had a face like a smacked arse.

The access boards had run out short of the body, and the tent that should have protected it while forensics did their bit lay half-assembled. He obviously wasn't the only one with hand-eye co-ordination problems this morning. Heads would roll, and the thought that someone other than him was in for a bollocking caused a flicker of a smile. Anyway, gloves or not, he wasn't about to get close enough to compromise evidence. Just a quick look was enough to be going on with.

Between the mud and the blood, it was hard to make out anything but the fact that she was young and naked. She hadn't come off the viaduct, that was for sure. Yes, she was beaten up, but just like Dennis, he'd seen worse, far worse. He wrote off the sewer theory just as quickly. Maybe someone had tipped her out the back of a car and she'd tumbled down the embankment. Then again, he wasn't one for coincidences and, as Dennis had already suggested, something weird had gone on, so there had to be a connection.

She was laid on her front, her head to one side, kind of serene in a morbid way, like she was sleeping at home in her bed, not splayed out naked amongst the nettles. He reached out a hand and gently brushed the tangled hair from her face. She was ice cold. Blood trailed from her ear, slime leached from the side of her mouth. She'd likely lain in the filth all night with no one to miss her. He felt anger and frustration curdle inside. Guilt gnawed at him as he realised that, while he'd been at Minkey's getting hammered, she'd been laid out, dying in the shithole known as Bedlam.

His fingers lightly skimmed her blemished skin. For the first time in a long while, he felt a stirring of compassion and sadness at the waste of life. He'd been too caught up in his own nightmare to care much for anyone else's, but the sight of the young woman lying discarded and broken hit him. He felt the lid on his emotions unscrew just a little, releasing a fraction of the hurt to dissipate. He swallowed, steadied his nerve, and resisted the urge to step away and never come back. It would be easier to give up, to admit he was a wreck, as broken as the body before him, but something stopped him, and sheer determination kept him where he was. He reached out tenderly and tucked her hair behind her ear, was about to replace the sheet and withdraw, when, unbelievably, her dusty lashes quivered and her eyes flickered open.

Fear and horror had him scrambling back, slipping in the mud, heart racing, stomach churning. Corpses did all kinds of crazy things, he knew that. It was all down to body gasses and decomposition, but he'd never seen one open its eyes, except in his dreams, his nightmares. Dennis should never have spoken Kit's name, not here in this place of the dead. In that moment, he hated Dennis and despised himself even more.

Unconvinced that he hadn't imagined it, wished it, conjured it up in his hung-over, messed-up brain, macabre fascination drew him back through the foul-smelling ooze. He leaned in closer. His hand hovered over her skin as he waged an internal war between what he'd been trained to do and what he felt compelled to do. His gut tightened one more excruciating notch. *I hear you*, he murmured softly as he placed his palm hesitantly against her cheek, felt warmth where there had been ice, and watched as her eyelids flickered once more and her lips parted with a gentle gasp. *Jesus!*

He rolled her over roughly. The plastic sheet caught by the breeze fluttered free and her slender arms slapped softly on the wet ground. Protocol forgotten, he placed the heel of his hand on her chest and his lips to hers ... "Breathe ..." he demanded frantically.

Behind him heads turned in shock following the flight of the mortuary sheet as it skimmed the scene. Lifted by a sudden updraft, it soared toward the suspended corpses, settling like a shroud around the shocking spectacle. All eyes swung with horror at the sight of McNeil kneeling in the mud, his hands on the dead girl's body, his mouth on the dead girl's lips, his DNA all over the crime scene.

"What the fuck is he doing?" yelled Mather. He began to run. His men followed, close at his heels.

McNeil ignored the shouting, the sound of running desperate men, feet skittering on the inadequate boards and slipping in the mud. Adrenalin shot through him. "Breathe ... come on ... you can do it." He wiped the slime from his mouth, spat out the taste and tried once more. A final hot desperate exhalation and, beneath his hands, he felt her chest rise and her heart begin to beat.

"Dennis! Get hold of that fucking idiot," Mather bellowed. Close by, but not close enough. "He's finally lost it."

Rough hands grabbed at his shoulders, yanking him away. He resisted, pulling back, throwing off his attacker, slipping from his grasp and scrambling back to her side, frantic now that he shouldn't stop, that he continue what he'd started, that he didn't let her down. Until, suddenly, there were more than just Dennis, and try as he might, he couldn't fight them all. They hauled him off, Dennis taking the lead, grabbing him by the collar, pushing him backwards through the stinking slurry until he was slammed against the cold iron legs of the viaduct amidst the poisonous graffiti.

"What in God's name is wrong with you?" hissed Dennis, breath hot in McNeil's ear, his weight squeezing any attempt at retaliation right out of him, his hand tight at his throat.

McNeil fought for breath of his own. Hot tears of panic, shock, and confused relief streamed down his mud splattered cheeks. "She's alive ..." he stammered. "She's still alive!"

"For pity's sake, Joey, just stop! Get back to the real world. Kit is dead. Get that into your head once and for all, before you fall so far no one can help you."

McNeil struggled against him, "No, you don't understand. I'm telling you, she's alive ..."

"You need help, Joey. Professional help, and, I'm sorry, but I can't give it. I'm done with you." Dennis released his grip, leaving McNeil to slump to the ground, defeated. "Go home, Joey. That was your last chance, and you just blew it." He stepped over him, his attention drawn by a sudden shout from one of the DCs stooped over the body.

"Bloody hell, guv! Joey was right. She's got a pulse. Quick, where's Roger? Where's that bloody doctor when you need him?"

McNeil raised eyes blurred with tears and caught the look of shock on Dennis' face before it was quickly masked.

"What did you do?"

McNeil was shaking, his whole body going into shock, stomach clenched tight with nausea, head a blur of confusion and fear.

"What did you do?" repeated Dennis as he swung his gaze from the frantic scene back to McNeil. "She was stone cold dead. What the fuck did you do?"

"What did I do? ... I'll tell you what I did," stammered McNeil. "I didn't give up ..."

Four

I feel his presence long before he touches me. His sadness breaches my shell. It tugs at my inner self, that tiny seed of curiosity that is my greatest flaw. Gently at first, then, as his attention is drawn from the horror that is death to the futility of life, his sadness blooms and, in turn, so do I.

Emotions are unpredictable, as I've found to my cost. Complicated, and with a mind of their own, they use us like playthings, and, when exhausted and bored with the game, they leave us spent, like litter on the playground floor. I know their power, but I am still at their mercy.

Softly, tentatively, his fingertips skim my brow. His skin connects with mine and suddenly the fuse is lit, his energy is zipping hot and furious throughout me, igniting my nerve endings. There is pain ... such terrible pain, but, just as before, I am unable to resist. I long to scream, to yell out a warning, to plead with him to leave me alone before it is too late. I'm not worth it, as he will discover. But, for the moment, I cling with shameful desperation, content to savour the salve of another's compassion.

I open my eyes and see shock on his face, his disbelief and fear as he pulls away from that which he believed dead and now is alive. I reach out to him. My mind, heart, and soul willing him back, embracing him with my silken threads of need and want and longing. Then his lips are on mine, his breath is within me, and the connection is made.

He is the one. I know this is true. Soon, he will know it too.

Five

She came to him that night in his dreams, sweet, beautiful Kit, with her golden hair and angelic smile. He felt her warmth, her slender fingers entwined with his, and he clung on desperately – a drowning man with no rescue in sight. He basked in her soft laughter, the taste of her sweet breath as her lips skimmed his. Her delicate scent wrapped around him and held him in the closest embrace, until he felt her heart as it beat in time with his. His body reacted. His heart swelled almost to breaking, filled to capacity with every precious moment they'd shared. He murmured her name and was instantly soothed as she whispered his. He lived for this, this brief remission from a life with no purpose other than his unending search for her.

This time, though, his place of sanctuary, his balm to a life without her, was breeched, marred by fragmented images of the real world. The tattooed man, the bar room brawl, the girl he'd dragged back from the dead, and an overwhelming sense that he was damned, lost, and incapable of finding his way home.

He woke once more in a sweat. This time, alcohol was not a contributing factor. Instead, his mind was filled with past and present, sorrow and regret – and a bizarre image which would not be shifted, no matter how hard he tried to replace it with Kit's sweet face.

A two-headed serpent. Black and white. Yin and yang. Life and death.

***

"You're a liability, Joey. Get some help or forget about your career."

McNeil nodded slowly, accepting that, under the circumstances, there was little else that could be done with him. He was unpredictable, unreliable, and, yes, he did need help.

But not the kind that Dennis meant. All the same, the unfairness of the situation rankled deep inside.

"I saved her life, Dennis. She'd be lying in a mortuary drawer with a tag on her toe if it wasn't for me. Does that count for nothing?" He wandered into the kitchen, pulled two mugs from the sink and spooned coffee into them, instant crap. Kit would have had the best. The flat would have hummed with the aroma of fresh coffee beans instead of booze and dirty laundry. "Anywhere else in the world and I'd be looking at a commendation."

Bracing his hands on the edge of the bench, he turned his head and watched as Dennis took a seat. He hadn't invited him, but hadn't been surprised by the visit. Dennis was spooked but curious. McNeil had seen the look on his face down there under the viaduct. Dennis wouldn't rest until he knew exactly what he'd done. Trouble was, McNeil didn't have any answers.

Usually they rubbed along okay. Dennis pulled rank when he needed to, but basically they got along and an unlikely friendship had developed. Dennis reckoned they complemented each other and generally kept him close, accepting the value of his uncanny instinct and terrier's tenacity. But that was then, before he lost Kit and turned from good cop to bad drunk, from most likely to least likely. Now McNeil reckoned Dennis kept him close as a matter of damage limitation, keeping him straight, hauling him up when he threatened to fall. Recent events had tested the relationship and the last twenty-four hours had further compounded the fractures. Being pounded into the ground by Dennis and the guys hadn't helped. They'd all thought he'd flipped out there, beneath the viaduct, and knowing the whole squad were on tenterhooks waiting for his next wrong move left him uneasy and irrationally paranoid. It was little wonder that Dennis was here in his kitchen, drinking his best-buy coffee and checking him out.

"Are you going to explain to me what happened out there?"

McNeil shrugged. "Roger messed up, declared life extinct when it wasn't. I expect you've paid him a visit as well. No? Now why does that not surprise me? What's one more body in the grand scheme of things?"

31

"Roger didn't mess up, Joey. The paramedics didn't even bother with resuss. She was dead."

"Sure she was. So what are you saying? I sprinkled fairy dust and magically brought her back to life? I know we just had Halloween, Dennis, but that's shite and you know it. If you want to cover up for Roger, that's fine. I mean, let's be honest, I'm the expendable one here, aren't I?"

"I'm not covering up for anyone."

McNeil ignored him. "Does it matter, anyway? She's alive now because of me. I'm the fucking hero. So why are you here giving me a hard time when you have your key witness? You should be out there cracking the whip with the rest of the team, knocking on doors, casting your net, catching the guy who did it."

"I'm here because I'm worried about you."

"I thought you were done with me. Wasn't that what you said? I mean, I could be wrong. You did have your hands round my throat at the time."

"Do you blame me? Christ, Joey, you're a bloody disgrace. You turn up on scene half-cut, ignore procedure and contaminate evidence. You see ghosts and shadows at every bloody turn. Is it any wonder we all jumped to the wrong conclusion when you decided to lay one on a corpse?"

"Ghosts?"

Dennis sighed heavily. "This whole business with Kit. You need to sort it out, Joey. It isn't healthy. It's affecting your judgment, your behaviour. There's only so much grief a body can take."

McNeil took his time pouring hot water onto the coffee, concentrating hard to make sure the water ended up in the mugs and not all over the counter top. "This whole business, as you put it, has nothing to do with you, Dennis. But since you don't seem able to leave it alone, let me explain. Grieving is for the dead. Kit is not dead."

"We've been through this so many times. I wish things were different, too, but they're not. She's dead, Joey. You just have to accept it."

"You show me the evidence and I'll accept it. That's what we work on, don't we, hard evidence? I've seen nothing that convinces me that she's not out there somewhere."

"You want evidence? We have evidence, Joey. The abandoned car? The blood at the scene? The broken bracelet?"

McNeil slammed his mug down. Scalding liquid seared the back of his hand but the pain didn't even register. "Evidence of a crime, not a murder."

"Joey, you know as well as I do the number of cases where we never find the ... victim. It's about balance of probabilities."

"Hey, don't pull any punches on my behalf, just say it, Dennis – the body. That's what you think, isn't it? That whoever took her killed her and dumped her body. Well, I'm sorry if it messes up the bookkeeping, but I don't accept that. I'll never accept that."

"The case will stay open until we find her, I can assure you of that."

McNeil's face twisted angrily. "Yeah, and how many officers are working the case?"

Dennis shook his head wearily. "Okay, let's say you're right and she's still alive. Would you rather that she'd walked out on you, left you for someone else, someone better perhaps? Is that more palatable? Because I'm telling you now, Joey, if that's the case, she did a bloody good job of making sure she couldn't be found, and that begs the question ... why?"

McNeil closed his eyes and counted back in his head. The only thing he wanted was Kit. She wasn't dead and she hadn't left him. Both options were equally unpalatable. But the alternative, that someone might be holding her against her will, was unbearable. When he spoke the words, they came out strained, his voice barely audible. "Dennis, I can't do this today."

Dennis considered him a moment longer before pulling out his wallet and extracting a card. "You won't listen to me. Maybe you'll listen to the shrink. I hear he's very good. You have an appointment Monday morning. Don't be drunk and don't be late."

"And the investigation ...?" McNeil let the card fall to the table. "What has the girl said?"

"I told you, you need to sort yourself out. I'm not prepared to discuss the case anymore until you do."

"Sure. So, basically, she's said nothing and you're no further forward."

"Something like that."

"But she is okay? I mean, physically, mentally. Is she able to communicate?" He recalled the state she was in when he'd first seen her. Some people weren't meant to be dragged back.

"You sound concerned."

"Shouldn't I be?"

"Like I said, I'm not prepared to discuss details. I will need a statement from you, though."

"A statement?" McNeil snorted derisively. "Like I performed CPR and, bingo, she revived. That'll be an interesting read. Maybe I should add, 'And the guys all think I'm a fucking freak!' Do you want me to come down to the station to make it, or shall I just write it on the back of an envelope and save some departmental time?"

Dennis took a sip of coffee, twisted his face at the bitter taste, and replaced the mug carefully on the table. "No, I mean a statement detailing your prior involvement with the victim."

McNeil paused, coffee in hand. "*My prior involvement with the victim?* I never laid eyes on her before. What are you saying?"

"I'm saying, how come she's asking for you by name?"

Six

They tell me I'm lucky, a miracle, a medical conundrum. I know I am not. The nurses bustle about exchanging glances, discussing me in hushed whispers. They wonder how I survived amidst the butchery, though they refrain from divulging the details. I do not need their indiscretion. I know all there is to know about butchery and the evil which stalks the unwary. They giggle to each other when they think me asleep, swapping thoughts on the man responsible for my salvation. I listen despite my own caution, my curiosity playing Puck against my better judgment. From their conversation, I gather he has fallen from grace, his unique talent unappreciated and viewed with suspicion by the narrow-minded. My fault entirely; just the first of many ways in which I will poison him, despite my best intentions.

I know he has not yet returned. I would have sensed his presence even through the blackness of drug-induced sleep. I am not upset at his absence. He will come eventually. We have connected and there is only one way this can end.

Confinement unsettles me. The clean white walls of my antiseptic prison dampen my senses. I feel a familiar anxiety ripple in my head. Although to the casual observer I remain calm, inside I fidget mercilessly. I yearn to be out, at one with the elements, and yet I restrain myself, as I am bound to do. The nurses have become silent. The white-coated doctor tuts and shakes his head at me.

"You must try and eat something," he says as he scans my chart.

I have no appetite. I turn up my nose at the bland offerings. My senses are dull and it concerns me that I am not quite as I was. I know they are losing patience. They believe me to be awkward. I am not. I am simply waiting.

They send in their interrogators, an inept succession shrouded in false concern. They do not care for me or the horrors I have endured. They care for their reputation, for the case that threatens to overwhelm resources and bring the gutter press down upon them. I stay silent in the face of their questions, their cajoling and implied threats. I stare blankly ahead when they amend their strategy, soften their approach, and send in a female detective. I sense her inner turmoil. She is striving to get ahead, to beat the men at their own game. I, too, have suffered as a pawn to the whims of man, and as such I have some empathy with her, but not enough to alter my chosen course. There is only one person who can help me and I am content to wait.

Eventually, the man with the apparent responsibility for investigating the horror that is Bedlam stands before me and asks the question I've been waiting for, the key that unlocks my voice and restarts the game.

"Is there anyone we can call who you'd like to be here with you?"

I fix him with eyes he has so far avoided, and my lips twitch with anticipation. I feel a familiar resurgence of energy fizzling deep inside. My fingertips tingle and the steady beat of my heart accelerates just enough so that my shallow veins respond with gratitude, creating a flutter which ripples delicately throughout my frame.

"Joe McNeil ..." I whisper gently, and my voice fills the space between us with soft melodious sound.

Seven

"So, what do you think?"

McNeil shrugged. He wasn't sure what he thought anymore. His mind was filled with images of a young woman who, by rights, should be dead, and yet was a picture of health. Well, he qualified that: not healthy exactly, but she was alive, and he was familiar with that halfway state, had been there himself for the last twelve months.

Alive – but only just.

Going through the motions, one foot in front of the other, inhale, exhale. He felt strangely disconnected, as if his anchor chain had snapped and left him adrift. He couldn't shake the feeling that something was seriously out of kilter. He badly needed a drink, just the one, to take the edge off. Shoving his hands deep in his pockets to hide the tremors, he slumped against the wall and studied her through the viewing window. Her eyes were closed, but he knew she wasn't sleeping ... and he wasn't sure how he knew.

"Did you hear what I said?" Dennis rose from the plastic chair and stretched out the kinks from his back. "What do you think?"

"What do you mean, what do I think? I don't think anything. She survived – end of story."

"Joey, come on. You saw the state she was in. We mistook her for dead. Now look at her."

Dennis was right. She'd made a miraculous recovery. Less than two days and, physically, all that was left to indicate she'd been through any kind of trauma were the harrowing black circles around her eyes.

"No, Dennis, Roger mistook her for dead."

"Yeah, well, that's debatable," muttered Dennis. "She looked dead to me."

McNeil shrugged. They'd been over this a number of times, in the flat, on the journey down, and again here, in the hospital corridor. He was done with explaining how he'd simply been in the right place at the right time and that he had no idea how the girl knew his name or indeed why she'd asked to speak to him. He knew Dennis wanted to believe him, but didn't, and he wondered why he was being viewed with suspicion.

Despite Dennis' initial reluctance to involve him further in the case, he'd begged a chance to tag along and prove his account, and Dennis had agreed, rather too readily. McNeil had a sense of being manipulated but, for once, didn't care. He didn't know the girl, had never known her, yet was sufficiently intrigued by the strange circumstances surrounding her and was therefore willing to be used, if only to satisfy his own curiosity. If Dennis thought he would catch him out, he would be disappointed.

"Okay, so we're here," he muttered, feigning disinterest. "We dodged the press, slipped under Mather's radar. What now? What do you want me to do?"

"Just play it by ear. Go in there and treat it as a standard interview."

"But it's not, is it? A standard interview, undertaken by a detective with an outstanding shrink appointment and suspicion hanging over his head – will it even count as a witness testimony? Let's face it, if I'm as fucked-up as you all seem to think, I shouldn't be here at all, let alone anywhere near her."

"She didn't accuse you of anything. She just asked for you. Nothing unusual in that ... or is there? You tell me."

McNeil gave a sour smile. "Well, you better be sure before I go in there, guv. I'd hate for you to have any doubts about my integrity."

"Let me worry about that, detective. I haven't completed my report on your antics at the crime scene yet. I might just bin it if you come up trumps."

"How do you know I'm not going in there to apply a little pressure? Maybe I wasn't at Minkey's propping up the bar the other night. Maybe I was playing trick or treat, Bedlam style."

Dennis sent him a warning glance. "Joey, don't push it. You know, even I have limits, and, right now, I'm wavering between giving you another chance and writing you off."

"You need me or I wouldn't be here, Dennis. Let's not kid ourselves."

Dennis frowned. "I need the old Joey. Is that who I have today?"

McNeil ignored him. He wasn't sure who he was anymore. He just knew his gut was chewed, he was spoiling for a fight, and, for once, he couldn't blame it on alcohol. He drew in a lungful of recycled, antiseptic-laced hospital air. None of this was Dennis' fault.

McNeil gestured toward the window and the girl beyond. "What did she actually say to you?"

"Not a lot, just your name."

He narrowed his eyes, studied her through the glass and got the feeling she was doing the same, though her eyes were still closed. He shrugged. "I did save her life."

"And you're positive that's all you did?"

"I'd say that was enough, wouldn't you? If someone saved my life, I reckon I'd want to say thank you."

"Maybe you're right. Maybe that's all she wants, but, while you're in there receiving her heartfelt gratitude, we need a statement. She's been avoiding our questions."

"Avoiding? Maybe she doesn't have any answers."

"Well, regardless, a description of the killer would be handy. And by that I don't mean a hooded fiend or a guy in a vampire costume. I've had a bellyful of Halloween sightings and crank calls. You'd think people would have better things to do than waste our bloody time when we have a major enquiry and fuck all resources."

McNeil smiled. "Hey, don't be so quick to rule out hooded fiends. You need to keep an open mind, Dennis."

"*An open mind?* I'll give you an open mind. There's a monster out there for sure, but he won't be wearing a cloak and a set of devil horns. He'll be some sick psycho who works nine-to-five, picks the kids up from school, and washes the car every Sunday." Dennis scowled bitterly. "The only way we'll nab the bastard is if someone comes forward with information or our little corpse bride starts talking."

"That's a bit harsh, Dennis. She's a victim. Where's your sympathy? She could be your daughter, for God's sake."

Dennis shrugged ambivalently. "I don't know, there's just something about her. The way she looks at you. She gave DC Anders a right turn."

McNeil shrugged. "Kate's a good copper."

"Exactly. See what you think when you go in. Maybe she'll drop her guard for you. If she does, we need to know if she saw anything at all. What happened to her? How did she come to be there? You know the drill."

"And you trust me not to mess it up?" McNeil couldn't forget the feel of Dennis' hands around his throat or the way he had spoken about Kit.

"Don't kid yourself. I'll be right here watching through the window. Don't mess up, Joey. I don't want a repeat of the other day. I see the first sign of any kind of meltdown and you're out of there for good, my report signed, sealed, and dropped straight into Mather's in-tray. Do you hear?

McNeil turned back to the window, leant his brow against the pane, and watched as his exhaled breath clouded the glass. His palms were suddenly clammy, his gut churned. Despite his curiosity, every instinct was telling him to walk away, to leave behind the investigation, the job, the life, and not look back.

"Why, Dennis?"

"Why what?"

"I know what you all think of me, that I'm one step away from the nuthouse. So, why are you risking your career by putting me in there?"

Dennis shrugged. "Because, despite your recent behaviour, you're a good man, and you used to be a good detective. I think you could be again, but you need to exorcise your demons."

McNeil reached out, slowly and deliberately scribing the word 'Kit' in the condensation with his finger. He thought of her warm embrace when he slept. "Maybe I'm happy to keep them," he murmured softly.

"Then you're a fool, Joey, and no one can help you."

Eight

Finally, inevitably, he comes to me. Relief and regret flood my entire being, vying for poll position as my brain challenges my contradictory instincts. This is wrong, I am wrong, and I know it. Regrettably, relief triumphs, and satisfaction settles in the pit of my stomach.

Confusion clouds his face as our eyes meet. I'm not surprised. I've been told that my eyes are an arresting sight. I am unable to agree or disagree. I do not choose to look upon myself. Nevertheless, he holds my gaze far longer than any man has previously dared. The fear that I expect from him is not evident, merely a curiosity equal to my own. I feel warmth inside, as hope wars with dread, and give in to temptation. I inhale gently and catch his musky scent, traces of soap, a whiff of alcohol and the mints he's used to cloak it, but nothing more. I will him to step closer so I might test myself further, but he merely cocks his head and smiles warily at me.

"Hi," he says finally, when further silence would have implied a rudeness that I sense he is trying to avoid. His voice is low and husky. Either his throat is sore or he imagines he will beguile me, as one might when talking gently to a skittish creature. He is mistaken, for, in this time and place, I am the beguiler.

"Hey, you're looking well. A good deal better than the last time I saw you," he continues. "The doctors must be pleased with your progress."

'Pleased' is the wrong word. I suspect the doctors are astounded at my progress, but I allow him to continue in this ruse to win me over. I settle back against the pillows and watch with some amusement as my lack of response begins to unsettle him. I sense his need to look away, to break eye contact so he might re-evaluate the situation without my scrutiny, but he resists, and I am drawn to him even more because of this.

"You've been very lucky ... under the circumstances. Things could have been very different." He leans back against the closed door, hands in pockets, an attempt at nonchalance while he gathers his poise. Dipping his head just a fraction allows him to study me through a veil of lowered lashes. I smile inside at his cunning.

Lucky? Perhaps. And yes, things could have been so very different if it hadn't been for him. And yet, I get the feeling that when he refers to me as fortunate, he doesn't actually mean the fact that he saved me, brought me back from the brink. He sees more than he actually understands, and, for the moment, that's a good thing. If he understood, he would not think me lucky at all. He would consider me well and truly damned.

"Do you remember anything at all?" He pulls away from the door, steps closer, and relief courses through me. He mistakes my soft gasp for fear, which couldn't be further from the truth. I do not fear him, merely what I might do to him.

"I'm sorry," he murmurs. "I should have introduced myself." He pulls his ID from his wallet, extends it toward me, and I dismiss it with the slightest dip of my gaze. I have no need to inspect credentials representing his authority, his permission to be here.

"Joe McNeil," he continues. "You asked to see me."

I did indeed, but for a moment I am content simply to savour his confusion. He pauses, waits for me to fill the gap, and, when I decline, he accepts the gauntlet and continues.

"I need to ask you a few questions ... establish your identity ... if you're up to it?" He pulls up a chair and sits, not too close, but near enough that if I chose I could reach out and touch him.

I recall the feel of his fingertips, his lips on mine, his breath filling my lungs, guiding me back from past to present. I yearn for a repeat. I resist the temptation. I am, if nothing else, adept at waiting.

"Hello, Joe McNeil." My own voice is hushed, little more than a whisper. It seems an age since I've spoken aloud. Lately, my conversations have, by necessity, become internal. One-sided, I know, but more than adequate for self-analysis and self-annihilation. I moisten my dry lips and lower my own lashes. I am, by far, the expert in cunning. "Please, ask what you wish."

"Perhaps we could start with a name?" A quick smile and he settles back in his seat as if he expects this to be a long conversation. I hope it is.

I study him unashamedly and wonder if he realises how much he reveals about himself. His hair is short and damp with the morning rain. His clothes are creased, his knuckles scuffed. He wears a tie reluctantly. He is not here out of a sense of duty. He is here because already I am in his head and he is unable to resist.

"A name?" he prompts.

I have been called many things in my time, name-calling as opposed to name-giving, but, long ago, I suspect I was cherished enough to have an identity bestowed upon me. I close my eyes and try to remember. There is nothing but blackness. It frustrates me to the point of irritation. I recognise the importance of my answer and, strangely, I do want to oblige. I have no wish to alienate Joe McNeil, the man who is the answer to my silent prayers.

"Call me Nell," I finally reply. The name is plucked from the dark recesses of my mind, though it feels right as it plays across my tongue.

He smiles again. This time I see a glimpse inside his head, beyond the initial sadness and regret that pierced my shell. I am intrigued by the conflicting emotions. I feel a ripple of guilt at what I intend for him. This man is more tortured than I, and I am intrigued by the notion. That in itself is a first. He kindles interest beyond the obvious physical attraction.

"Nell ... good. That's a good start."

My name sounds far finer when he says it. It comes out with a long held breath, as if he, too, is martyred to relief. I imagine it whispered against my ear, his warm breath caressing my skin. He reaches out across the space between us, his effort to contain the tremor in his outstretched hand quite commendable. My heart bangs in my chest. I am betrayed by butterflies of hope as they flutter frantically in the pit of my stomach, yet I resist his touch. I clench my hands tightly beneath the sheets and leave his hand to fall. It is too soon. I am not yet strong enough. Sadly, he may never be.

He shrugs off my rebuff, bemused but oblivious to my intent, blissful in his ignorance. "Last name?" he coaxes and I pull my attention back. He awaits my reply, feigning disinterest – badly. His curiosity, like that of the cat, will be his undoing.

"Just Nell," I reply.

A sudden frown knits his scarred brow as he studies me and wonders why I'm being obstructive. I'm not. I'm being *evasive*, for a very good reason – to protect us both. On this occasion, the truth, the whole truth, and nothing but the truth, would certainly bring about our downfall.

"Okay, Nell," he begins, "we need more than that. Can you give me your address? You must have a family. You've been here two days. We need to let them know you're safe."

Safe? I almost laugh out loud. He has so much yet to learn.

Family? Bitterness sears my tongue and I conceal the resulting wince. I have no family, not in the normal, nuclear sense. Maybe once, but no more. I was, until he interceded, simply alone. Now, together, whether he likes it or not, we are an 'us' in a chaotic world of 'them'.

My eyes narrow as I recall the silver blade. I wet my lips with the tip of my tongue as the memory struggles free. I take a rapid breath to clear my mind, and watch Joe's brow rise in confusion. I suspect he thinks me odd. He will think far worse of me by the time we are done.

He shrugs. "Okay, no family, but you must live somewhere." He sticks to the script, to his list of standard witness-victim-suspect questions. I wonder which one he believes me to be, and how long he will control his curiosity. I feel it bubbling beneath the surface of his pseudo-professionalism. I meet it mischievously. I welcome the challenge. It distracts me from the anxiety and need that he seems to propagate within me. I part my lips and inhale once more. Still nothing.

"Here, there, everywhere ..." I eventually reply, with a soft sigh and the slightest twitch of my lips. I have no wish to reveal my origins, my lair, the place I go to lick my wounds. He is mine and I have no desire to share him.

He leans toward me, clears his throat, business-like now despite the crooked tie and blackened eye, obviously irritated at my vague response. I have no doubt that he has interrogated many and that his current dishevelled countenance belies his experience. On this occasion, however, he is short of the mark, and clearly fails to realise that he has met his match. I need to calm his male pride, smooth his ruffled feathers, but resist the overwhelming urge to reach out and soothe him with my touch.

"You saved me," I whisper innocently. "I remember. Thank you."

He smiles tightly, his brows knit in confusion as my words tease the silken threads of his memory. I know the recollection of our first meeting burns as hot within him as it does within me. There is no way that it cannot. He may currently deny it, but he is as trapped as I.

"What else do you remember?" he murmurs.

And the net draws ever tighter.

I remember his scent, the feel of his lips, but now is neither the time nor the place to amuse myself with those recollections. "I remember very little," I reply, and it's true. He was my first real memory, and as such is imprinted like a chick hatched from an egg. I could tell him what occurred before, on the very edge of nowhere, and I could describe what awaits us in the dark corners of our imagination, but I sense a need to wait. He isn't quite ready for that.

"You were found beaten and naked alongside the bodies of two men. Perhaps you remember that?"

His words hit me like a blow to the face. My head screams with sudden memory, my heart jolts agonisingly with alarm. I feel a surge of absolute and utter dread. It cloaks me, it squeezes me, until I am forced to gasp for breath.

This game of cat and mouse is suddenly over, frivolous, lustful thoughts dashed instantly from my mind. All my accumulated hopes and fears crumble to ash in the face of reality.

Two?

There should only have been one – Jacob.

I turn to him, my composure now askew, concern and vulnerability seeping silently from my pores. I know he sees only one aspect of me, the side which appeals to his own delicate state of mind, my fragility, as opposed to my depravity, and I am both relieved and fearful for him.

"You know who did this, don't you?" he asks, and I watch the collapse of my carefully constructed persona as it mirrors in his eyes.

Of course I know the perpetrator of this crime, the director of this freak show, this end-of-the-pier excuse for theatre, for I am the one who unleashed the fiend. In my striving for freedom, for an end to the endless, I have let loose a madman.

A glance at the viewing window reveals Joe's superior, watching us, suspicion and frustration held at bay behind glass. I have played this game before and I am far cleverer than they imagine, these bumbling policemen with their obvious subterfuge. And yet, on this occasion, time is my enemy. I cannot still the fear that creeps silently at the mere thought of Jacob, igniting each cell as it journeys from head to heart.

"Why did you ask for me?" he continues, following my gaze, resisting the urge to lean toward me and reveal the urgency of his tone to our audience. And, in that small action, he compounds our deceit and allows the conception of our conspiracy.

My relief is palpable. We are one step closer, he and I. "You know why," I breathe softly.

"I do?"

I smile, and his pupils widen in response. My smile is legend. I do not bestow it often.

"We are in danger," I state simply. It is the truth, and, if he believes nothing else about me, he must believe that.

"*We?*"

"You are responsible for me. I am responsible for you. We are the same, you and I, burdened by our responsibilities."

His brows furrow in confusion. "What do you mean, *responsible?* I can't help you unless you tell me who did this."

"Jacob." There, I have voiced my deepest fear and the world has not collapsed around me. There is hope.

"Jacob?"

"He will find us, Joe McNeil. Make no mistake." I hold his gaze as he falters.

"And when he does?"

I rejoice silently. Belief is not far away. I see it in his eyes. I hear it in his choice of 'when' rather than 'if'. It must be encouraged closer.

I withdraw my arm slowly from beneath the sheet and extend my hand. "We must be ready."

He takes my hand, as I know he will, unable to resist. He is warmth to my chill, rough to my smooth, yin to my yang. I feel every depression in his skin as my fingertips skim his palm. I control the energy triggered by his touch. This is not about me. The pad of his thumb brushes my inner wrist distractedly, and, as his gaze follows the gentle caress, I hear his gasp, see his pupils dilate with recognition.

"Who are you?" he whispers hoarsely.

I smile my sweet seductive smile. My slender fingers entwine with his. "Don't you recognise me, Joe?"

The twin serpents, energised by my quickening pulse, squirm beneath his thumb and he yanks his hand away. Shocked, horrified – but ultimately mine.

Oh yes. He is definitely the one ...

Nine

"What happened?"

McNeil sat on the edge of the gurney and stared vacantly ahead, as if he'd been dragged from a deep sleep and hadn't quite caught up. His head pounded. He was sick to his stomach. He was aware of subdued voices, fragmented images, a firm hand on the back of his head, and the sting of a needle. He raised a hand to fend off the doctor and was promptly restrained.

"You had some kind of seizure, Joey. One minute you were talking to the witness, the next you were on the floor, convulsing. You hit your head on the way down. Sit still while they stitch you up."

"Look at me." The doctor shone a light in McNeil's eyes, checking his reactions. "Any flashing lights?"

McNeil scowled. "Only the one in your hand."

"Sorry. Any headache, nausea?"

"Some."

"Can you remember falling?"

"No."

"Can you remember anything before you fell?"

Dennis leaned in too close. McNeil edged away, and the doctor muttered and pulled him back.

He remembered everything with crystal clarity, right up to the point when he had taken her hand, but as he understood none of it, he kept his mouth firmly shut and shook his head. He had a sense of something else, just beyond his reach, something important that he'd missed. The feeling crept over him along with the nausea, cloaking him in a fine film of perspiration.

"Do you have any history of seizures, blackouts, or fainting?" The doctor drew blood from his arm, and he watched distractedly as it filled the syringe. His mind was elsewhere, trying to make sense of the jumble. Trouble was, she was in there too, taking up space. He inhaled, struggled to focus. It wasn't Kit – he was used to her, comfortable with her sharing his thoughts, keeping him company. The doctor waited, watching him closely.

"No ..." he stammered. "No history of falling over or falling down."

"Are you taking any medication, prescribed or otherwise?"

"No." He had been, in the beginning, when he had first lost Kit and had been scared to sleep in case he missed her call. But then he'd discovered her again in his dreams, and the little blue pills had been consigned to the bottom of a drawer.

"Could you have eaten something contaminated in the last forty-eight hours? You're sweating, running a temperature."

McNeil shook his head. He couldn't remember eating anything. Maybe that was the problem.

"Could he have picked something up from the girl?" suggested Dennis. "She was covered in all kinds of shit. You remember, Joey? You were spitting out slime."

McNeil didn't need reminding. Cold skin, pale lips, and striking violet eyes. He couldn't get the image of her out of his head. She was vying for space. He bit down hard on his bottom lip and used the pain to try and shut her out.

The doctor nodded. "It's possible, but unlikely. We've had a few incidences of food poisoning ..." He withdrew the syringe and stuck a plaster over the puncture site. "Or maybe you just had a heavy night drinking?" He focused on McNeil's discoloured left eye and raised a questioning brow. "Have you had a recent head injury, maybe a time when you couldn't remember what you'd done or where you'd been?"

Oh sure, thought McNeil. He'd had plenty of occasions when he couldn't recall his own last name, but they had nothing to do with a head injury and everything to do with the drink. He shrugged belligerently and ignored Dennis' 'I told you so' expression. He didn't need confirmation that he was a wreck. He just wanted them both to step back before he threw up all over them.

"We'll see what the blood results tell us," continued the doctor. "I advise you to see your own GP in a day or two, but, in the meantime, just take it easy. Drink plenty of fluids – non-alcoholic. If it's a bug, it'll take a couple of days to run its course. If you experience any more problems, your GP will organise further tests."

McNeil slid unsteadily from the gurney. The two men invaded his space, crowding him. Unwelcome panic rose inside, hot and frantic. In his head, a little warning voice chided him, not words, just a whispered breath, and he clamped down hard on it. "So, is that it? We done?"

The doctor nodded. "Stitches need to come out in seven days, till then be careful. No contact sports ..."

"Hear that, Dennis?" McNeil forced a smile. "Looks like I'm off the football team. Doctor's orders."

Dennis waited until the doctor was out of earshot. "Never mind the bloody football. I'm sure the lads have managed perfectly well without you and your tackle for the last twelve months. Let's not get side-tracked. What did she say?"

What she hadn't said was more significant. McNeil wasn't so spaced that he couldn't recall the way she had watched him, played with him, unnerved him. But he knew none of that would interest Dennis and would more than likely fuel concern over his current mental health. "Didn't you catch what the doctor said? I have a serious head injury. I can't remember things."

Dennis snorted, "Head injury? Alcohol poisoning, more like, and I'm sure you haven't forgotten that I was watching through the window. She spoke to you. I saw her."

McNeil pushed him aside. "I need to find the gents."

"You need to tell me what she said first."

"Before or after I throw up on your shoes?"

Dennis tossed him a scowl. "Bloody hell, Joey, the clock is ticking here. I've got a killer running around out there and two flea-bitten bodies in the morgue. That reporter from the 'Herald' is chomping at the bit for something to write, and you know as well as I do that if we don't give her something, she'll just make it up. I need to know what you know, and pretty sharpish. You haven't got time to succumb to the bloody vapours every time a girl holds your hand."

McNeil blinked slowly. The memory still tingled in his palm. He clenched his fist to suppress it. He wondered how much Dennis had actually seen. Maybe nothing, because there was nothing to see. Ghosts and shadows. It wouldn't be the first time his mind had played tricks on him. He needed to be left alone in a darkened room with his paranoia and 'what ifs', but he knew that wouldn't happen unless he gave Dennis something, anything.

"Horse meat," he offered with a half-smile.

"What?"

"It'll be that lasagne I had the other night that's done me in. I should sue them. It's supposed to be full of veterinary happy juice. No wonder I've got the trots. It was all over the news. Didn't you hear? Selling horsemeat as beef. It's a disgrace."

Dennis swung his head in disbelief. "You think this is a joking matter? I'll give you bloody horse meat. What did she say?"

"She said she was in danger."

"Well, bugger me, there's a surprise. Case closed, let's all go home. In danger from who? A bloody phantom who slits throats and hangs his victims up for later?"

"Some bloke called Jacob."

"Last name? Description?"

McNeil dipped his head and took a breath. "Dennis, I don't know. I didn't get that far. You ask her. She talks in riddles. Have they done a tox screen? If not, I think they should. You want my opinion? She's crazy. I'm not even sure she knows what she's saying."

"Crazy or not, she's our only witness, and we need more than that if we want to tie this up quickly. And believe me, Joey, we need a quick turnaround on this one."

"Yeah, well, not from me. I'm done. You heard the doc. I need to take it easy. My brain is fried, my guts are headed straight for the pan and then I'm gone, out of here and home to my bed. Do me a favour, Dennis. Don't call me. Send your report to Mather if you must, but don't call me."

"What about the investigation? Are you dropping the ball?"

"I never had the ball. I thought I was off the case, a liability."

"You're off when I tell you you're off."

McNeil shrugged. "Make your bloody mind up. Her name is Nell. She's running from a man called Jacob. That's all she told me. That's all I know."

That wasn't entirely true. He recalled everything she'd said. It replayed in his head jerkily like an ancient VCR on fast forward. Not just the words, but the lilting inflection, the look in her eyes, the expression on her face when she spoke. And then, suddenly, his mind hit freeze-frame on the twin-headed serpent tattooed on her wrist.

"Did she give a description? I mean, who is this man? An old boyfriend? A pimp? Come on, Joey, she must have said more than that."

McNeil paused, one hand on the men's room door. "You're right, she did. She said, 'thank you.'"

When he re-emerged from the bathroom, the hallway was empty. Dennis had given up and left, no doubt to chase up the rest of the team after finally accepting that McNeil was a step too close to the psyche couch than was beneficial to the case. He was relieved, not least because he was sick of Dennis breathing down his neck, but essentially because he agreed with his diagnosis. He couldn't help his obsession, took comfort from it, but was the first to admit that it was affecting his judgment. Even now, despite his inner voices screaming at him to walk away, he was drawn back. He needed to speak to the girl for his own reasons, and this time he didn't want any witnesses.

Ten

Her eyes were closed when he entered. A lunch tray lay untouched at her side. He drew his jacket closer, aware of how cool the room seemed, which was odd in a hospital that was otherwise stiflingly overheated. Perhaps she'd opened a window, or maybe it was just him and the virus he'd apparently fallen foul of.

He crossed quietly to the internal viewing window and closed the blind within the double-glazed panel. This visit was off the record, and he wanted to keep it that way.

He still felt wired. The dominoes lining up in his head were all set to tumble. He needed to get home where he felt secure, where he felt Kit's reassuring presence more strongly. And he would, as soon as he was certain about Nell.

When he turned back around, she was watching him, her violet eyes unblinking, and he wavered beneath her gaze, his resolve dissipating, his curiosity, like the virus, growing exponentially.

"How are you, Joe?" she breathed, lingering as she softly sounded out his name.

The hairs on the back of his neck prickled as if she had run her fingers across his skin. He contained the resulting shiver and stepped closer.

"I'm fine," he lied. This was madness. She was a witness, he was a policeman, all he had to do was clarify a few points and get things straight in his head. But, caught as he was, like a stunned rabbit in the glare of her gaze, all thoughts of his planned questions began to fade and muddle in his head.

"Are you quite sure about that? You don't look it." She shuffled up on the bed, tucked her legs up beneath the covers and rested her elbows on her knees. "What's wrong, Joe McNeil? You can tell me."

"I ... I'm not here to talk about me." He screwed his eyes shut, scrubbed at them with the heel of his hand and tried hard to think about why he was actually there, why he was standing next to her hospital bed going through the motions, pretending to do his job, when inside he was slowly dying. For a drink. For an end to the torment. For Kit.

When he reopened them, she was still watching him. "I told you, I'm fine," he said, for his own benefit as much as hers.

He stepped away and turned slowly on the spot, gathering his composure as he made a casual inventory of the stark room. All the while she watched him like a cat with a mouse, flexing her claws as she waited. He turned back and caught her raised brow. She didn't believe a word he said, and why should she? He'd been living a lie since the day Kit had gone. Lately, he'd even been fooling himself, tying himself up in ever-tightening knots of hopes and dreams, white lies and black lies ... lots of dirty black lies. It was little wonder that his sincerity and sanity was in doubt.

"Don't worry, Joe," she purred soothingly. "The effects will soon wear off."

His concentration, shaky at best, wavered further as he struggled to get past the hypnotic rhythm of her breathless sound to the actual words beneath. "The effects? You've lost me. What do you mean?"

"Of course," she continued with a soft sigh, "it requires a strong will. However, I'm sure you have one, Joe, or you wouldn't be here now."

Strong will? She couldn't be further from the truth. If she'd offered him a drink, he would have taken it. If she'd offered him a gun, he would have gladly put it to his own head.

She held his gaze, unblinking, and he had a real urge to rub his palm where they had touched, to erase any trace of her from his skin. Had she poisoned him, infected him? Was there a yellow flag outside the door that he'd overlooked? *Get a grip*, he murmured silently. She was playing games and he was allowing it.

"It's the same with any addiction: once in your head, under your skin, it's difficult to relinquish it, to withdraw and accept that it's over and time to move on ... don't you agree?"

She wasn't referring to alcohol, and they both knew it.

"My head and what might be in it has nothing to do with you," he muttered. "I ... I just ..." He cleared his throat, forced himself back on track. He needed information and that was all, nothing else. "You implied earlier that you were in danger, that you needed my help. That's why I'm here, the only reason I'm here. Do you want me to help you or not?"

She inclined her head briefly.

"Good, then you need to tell me what happened beneath the viaduct. Just take your time and start at the beginning."

She sighed gently and began to twist the corner of the sheet between finger and thumb. Her skin appeared almost translucent under the harsh hospital lighting, and, although he tried to concentrate and to stick to the questions, he found himself distracted by the pale blue veins.

"In the beginning ... now that is profound, but I'm afraid it would take far too long, and we simply don't have the time."

There were faint marks on her arms and in the soft depression at the crook of her neck, track marks maybe, which would certainly explain her dislocated behaviour. He dragged his eyes from her skin and his attention back to her face. In truth, he wasn't concerned about how she'd found herself face down in the mud. He was more interested in the man she claimed was still after her ... and him, and in the strange tattoo on her wrist.

"We have plenty of time. You're not going anywhere. What did you mean before, about Jacob, about being in danger?"

Draping the covers haphazardly around her shoulders, she slipped from the bed and padded to the window, trailing the sheet behind her. An angel wrapped in her downy wings or a demon in a shroud, McNeil couldn't decide. Nevertheless, he studied her, absurdly fascinated, as she placed her palms against the glass and gazed out at the world.

"I know what Jacob is, what he did, what he still does."

Her breath misted the glass as she spoke, the condensation expanding and receding like a living thing with every exhalation.

"And what did he do?"

She sighed, leaning forward to rest her forehead against the cool glass, humming gently to herself. "The unthinkable, the unforgivable." She added the words to a tune McNeil recognised as a nursery rhyme. It distracted him as he struggled to remember the name.

"Did he kill those men?"

She turned to him and raised one brow quizzically. "Perhaps."

"Did you see him do it?"

"We don't need to see to believe something is so, isn't that right, Joe? Ask those who flock to church every Sunday or face Mecca when called to prayer. We all have things which we hold dear, and we do so regardless of evidence to the contrary. An unbeliever will always look upon the devout as fools, simply because they lack the capacity to open their mind to possibilities. Jacob is evil. I believe it, therefore it is so." She left the window, stepping closer, her head angled as she studied him. "Do you hold someone close to your heart, detective? Do you cling to possibilities in the face of disbelief?"

Despite his best intentions, despite his absolute resolve not to bring Kit with him into the room, he could not prevent it. She was there always, in his head, and Nell smiled as if she knew it. He accepted defeat, submitted to the lure and took the bait. "What possibilities?"

"The possibility that you are right and they are wrong, and that someday soon the truth will be known." A slight twitch to her lips betrayed her amusement at the game. His heart sank, resolve hardening instantly. He had no desire to play, not with something as precious as hope.

"The truth," he continued bluntly. "A short word with endless possibilities. So let's start with that. What were you doing in Bedlam?"

"Running."

"Running from what, from whom?"

"Life, death, eternal torment. Take your pick."

Eternal torment, he knew all about that. He wore it daily like a horse hair shirt.

"How did you get there?"

"I jumped."

"Be serious. If you'd jumped, you'd be dead."

"Exactly."

The moment stretched between them, a vacuum that sucked out all reason. Nell blinked slowly, dusty lashes on pale skin. McNeil swallowed. He dropped his gaze, following the pale blue veins from her neck all the way to the pulse at her wrist. His palm burned and he clenched his fist to dispel the pain. He closed his eyes and recalled her cold lips as they'd been warmed by his. When he re-opened them, she was a step closer, her eyes narrowed, assessing, calculating. He took a breath and a matching step back. *Get a grip.*

"Tell me the truth about Jacob," he muttered. "Who is he?"

"A monster."

"That's not enough, Nell. I need a full name, an address, something that can help me find him."

"And is that what you intend to do – find him?"

"Of course. That's my job."

She shook her head. "Don't you understand? There's no need to go looking for him. *He* will find *you.*"

"No, I'm sorry, but I don't understand. I don't understand any of this, or you. Why would he be looking for me?"

"We don't have time for this, Joe. He will soon be here, and we must be gone before he arrives."

"I asked you a question. What has this to do with me?"

She fixed him with her violet eyes and shook her head impatiently. "We must hurry."

"*We?* There is no *we.* You are the victim of a crime. I'm investigating that crime. That's the only connection we have. Playing games, for whatever bizarre reason you feel is justified, won't help you."

"You think this is a game?"

"You tell me." He took a step toward her. "How do you know my name? Why did you ask for me?"

"I told you, you're responsible for all of this." She gestured vaguely with her hand. "Only you can put it right."

She spread her arms and glanced down at the hospital gown, as if recognising for the first time her precarious position in the here and now. His own gaze followed. Her feet were bare, her toes scarcely healed. Wherever she had come from, she had walked a long way. She inhaled gently, arched her back, and allowed the sheet to slip from her shoulders. He stooped to catch it. Her hand skimmed his and her hair brushed his cheek.

"Thank you, JoJo," she whispered.

McNeil jerked away, stepping backwards until the closed door prevented further retreat. Had she spoken out loud or was the voice in his head? He couldn't be sure. His heart pounded, perspiration prickled suddenly on his skin. There was only one person who had ever called him 'JoJo', and she had been gone for the last twelve months.

"What did you say?"

She approached him slowly, placing each foot carefully, as if she walked a tightrope. He watched, mesmerised, unable to resist, as she slid her hand beneath his jacket and placed her palm flat against his chest. He felt her coolness through the thin fabric of his shirt, inhaled her scent as it wrapped around him and his heart slowed its frantic response.

"Don't be scared, Joe," she whispered. "Trust me."

He felt himself falling, the edges of reality blurring as he struggled to regain his focus. Reaching out, he grabbed her slender shoulders and shoved her away, forcibly breaking the connection.

"Who are you?" he hissed.

"The best friend you've ever had."

"No!" He shook his head in denial. "I don't know you. You don't know me. This is either some kind of crazy game or I'm going mad, but, whichever it is, I won't do this anymore. I ... I'm leaving." He held her at bay with a raised hand, gut-churning panic rushing in to fill the space left behind as hope vacated.

"You can't walk away and leave me here, Joe."

"Just watch me."

He felt the imprint of her palm, despite its removal. The coolness still lingered, his skin continued to tingle. He turned and pulled open the door. "I can and I will. There's an officer posted at the nurse's station. You'll be quite safe. When you decide to give a proper statement, the twenty or so people who are currently flogging themselves to wrap up this investigation can get on with their job and put Jacob, or whoever is responsible, behind bars." He took a step into the corridor. "Of course, if you continue to play games then ... who knows what will happen?"

"If you leave, you'll never know the truth."

"The truth?" He hesitated with one hand on the door handle. *Please, Kit,* he begged silently, *help me.* But for once the voice in his head remained silent.

He inhaled slowly, headed off his panic attack and finally, when he had some measure of control, he raised his head and looked at her.

"The truth about what?"

"The truth about you."

Eleven

By the time he reached the lift, he was sweating. He knew he needed to get as far away from Nell as he could, but had no real idea why. Dennis had said that there was something strange about her, and, although McNeil agreed, he reckoned Dennis was merely sounding off, providing excuses to cloak his frustration. If Nell had tried it on with Dennis as she had with him, McNeil knew that Dennis would have had her transferred to a psyche ward or doubled the guard outside her room. She was crazy – there was no getting away from it. He wondered why she'd decided to lavish him with her psychosis.

He pressed for the ground floor and waited impatiently, pacing back and forth like a prize fighter limbering up for the starting bell. When it passed his floor and continued up, he cursed, slammed a flat hand at the brushed steel doors, and made for the stairwell instead. He descended the stairs two at a time, stumbling, heavy-footed, hanging onto the handrail to prevent going headfirst.

He paused in the lobby to get his bearings, remembered that he'd arrived in Dennis' car, and pulled out his phone to call a taxi. His heart pounded and he tried to slow it. Someone called at him to switch off his phone, drawing his attention to the many signs which indicated the same rule, and he muttered an apology and headed for the main door.

Head down, he was oblivious to the throng of people attempting to enter the building as he made to exit, until he was pushed to one side by the mêlée. Football fans and uniformed police jostled for position. The rival supporters shouted threats at each other across the expanse of the lobby, while harassed police tried to keep order.

Of course, it was Sunday – match day. McNeil recalled his time in uniform, standing in the cold, back to the pitch, scanning the crowds for known troublemakers. He had no desire to relive that segment of his career, so he kept his head down and forced a path through them. More than capable, and certainly willing, to deliver a well-aimed elbow as required, he was, however, substantially outnumbered, and, as the majority had come via the pub, he received a few blows himself before being jostled out of the throng and into the path of a well-dressed man. The man reached out and steadied him with a hand at his shoulder. McNeil pulled back, muttered an apology. The man stood a moment, blocking his way, his lips parted in a curious half-smile.

"Bad day?"

"You could say." McNeil attempted to sidestep him, but the man stepped the same way, and more liveried fans spilled into the lobby. He closed his eyes briefly to avert a wave of dizziness. When he reopened them, the man was still watching.

"Do you need help?"

Oh, sure, he needed help, but there was only one person who could give it, and she was long gone.

"No," he replied bluntly, and the man merely nodded, studying him with narrowed eyes as if he could see beneath the outward mess, the wrinkled suit, and the two day shadow, to the even bigger tangle below. McNeil felt his hackles rise, inordinately irritated not only by the man's scrutiny, but at the fact he still blocked his path.

He cocked his head insolently and stared straight at him. "Excuse me," he said, suddenly and inexplicably spoiling for a fight. The man merely smiled benignly in return and stepped aside, parting the red sea of supporters with a raised hand.

McNeil hurried past and forced his way through the revolving doors, relieved to finally get outside. He stood a moment, hands on his knees, head bowed, and breathed in all the exhaust-laced oxygen he could. He didn't understand what had just happened. The lobby had been oozing male testosterone and his fuse was all but lit, but he'd been ready to punch out a total stranger. He unclenched his fists and tried to relax.

He guessed, by the wary reaction of people stepping around him, that he looked a mess. He shook, sweat poured out of him, and blood from his head wound had dried on his shirt.

Concussion, withdrawal, or virus were all likely candidates for the way he felt, but he dismissed them with a scowl.

All he needed was Kit. All he could think about was Nell. She'd hexed him, jinxed him, done something, he was sure of it, though he had no idea what.

He cast a quick glance back the way he'd come. The lobby was still full, the man no longer visible. He tried to recall what he'd looked like, started to wonder if he'd actually been real when he couldn't remember a thing about him.

He dragged his fingers through his hair desperately. Maybe Dennis was right and he did need professional help. He thought of the card that still lay on his kitchen table, untouched. Defiance rather than common sense had left it face down on the melamine surface, but Kit's gentle scolding in his head had prevented him from tossing it in the bin. Maybe he would keep the appointment, if only to prove to himself that he wasn't going mad.

Collapsed in the back of the taxi, his thoughts strayed back to Nell and her demand to go with him. She'd assumed his agreement, and he almost had. For a fleeting moment, with her hand on his heart, it had seemed to him the right and only thing to do, to ignore procedure and protocol, take her from that room, and run far away, as if they were co-conspirators in a plot he knew nothing about. He felt misgiving creep over him, settling deep in his stomach, quite at home amongst the rest of the black things. She'd freaked him out, there was no denying it, and he'd fled when he should have stayed, but no way was he going back, not until he understood what was going on.

All the same, as the taxi pulled out of the hospital grounds and into the flow of traffic, he felt a shiver of something nasty slither in to accompany the doubt. If the PC on duty at the nurse's station did his job, there'd be nothing for McNeil to worry about. It was a big if, and McNeil wasn't entirely convinced, but, for now, it would have to do. The PC could babysit the witness and Dennis could find the killer. He had something far more important to do.

He pulled out his phone and brought up Minkey's number. It was first on his list of contacts, ahead of work and the local takeaway, which said something about the current state of his life.

"Minkey?"

"Joey."

McNeil scowled at the sharpness in Minkey's tone. He didn't have any energy left for contrition, but accepted he had ground to make up if he was to get what he wanted. It was time to make amends for Friday night.

"How's things?" he asked warily.

"You have the soddin' nerve to ask me that? Ask my insurers when they get through sorting out my claim."

"Your claim?"

"Don't play the bloody innocent, Joey. You're barred, for your own good as well as mine."

McNeil grimaced. "Hey, come on. I'm your best customer."

"Not any more. You wrecked the place on Friday night. I've got the man from the brewery down here right now, shaking his head and thinking I can't control the punters. As a purveyor of the finest alcoholic beverages, I never thought I'd say this, Joey, but you need to kill the booze, before it kills you."

"Finest beverages!" McNeil snorted. "You forget the blind eye I've been turning to all the dodgy crates you have stacked in the cellar? I bet the brewery ayatollah would be very interested in that."

"Piss off."

"Gladly."

"Hey, you're not the only bent copper I know. Ten a penny, you are."

"Bent?"

"Too right, bloody dented out of shape, you are."

"Do one, Minkey. I'm not in the mood today. I'm just sayin' people in glass houses ..." He sighed heavily. This wasn't getting him where he wanted to be. He steered the conversation back. "Anyway, on this occasion, I'm not after a drink or a fight. I'm turning over a new leaf, doctor's orders. I'm after information instead."

"Glass houses, eh?" Minkey wouldn't be steered. "Be careful you don't go and cut your own throat with that sharp wit of yours. Never mind barring you, I should be charging you for the damage."

"Was it that bad?"

"Bad enough, and here's me thinking a copper would have more self-restraint. You need to go back to school, Joey."

"Huh?"

"And learn to count to ten."

The taxi slowed amid more match day chaos. Fans, heading home, weaved their way between the traffic. The driver muttered under his breath, one eye on the clock as it ticked another pound. McNeil scowled. It would've been quicker and cheaper to have caught the bus.

"Hey, I'm doing that as we speak ... eight ... nine ... ten. So, information?"

"Information about what?"

"There was a bloke in the bar on Friday, not a regular, covered in tattoos. Any idea where I could find him?"

"The bruiser who laid you out cold?"

McNeil winced. He vaguely recalled some altercation that had erupted following a spilled drink. Maybe that was where the girl with the ample cleavage had come into it. He had an image of glistening breasts ... "Yeah, that's the one."

"I'd leave that alone if I were you, Joey. You were lucky to get out in one piece. Curtis is not one to mess about, and, if you want my opinion, copper or not, you pretty much got what you deserved."

McNeil wasn't sure what they'd been fighting over. He still had some way to go before he recovered the whole episode.

"Don't worry about me, Minkey. I just need to know where to find him."

"His cousin runs a tattoo parlour down the back of Minchem Road, somewhere past the Indian takeaway. You may have met him. Archie Pollack."

McNeil smiled. "Yeah, I know Archie. I thought he was inside?"

"He is. Curtis is looking after the business for him. Up from London, so I hear. As if we haven't got enough crazies of our own. Like I said, Joey, you should leave well alone. He's got a reputation."

"A reputation for what?"

"Not for me to say, but word is he's connected, and he's got some unsavoury mates."

"Worse than him?"

"Much worse."

"I should fit right in, then."

"Nah, Joey. I'm being serious. He's out of your league. With or without a badge, he's not going to take favourably to you knocking on his door. What do you want him for anyway?"

McNeil could hear the sound of the espresso machine in the background.

"Coffee?"

"Yeah, get used to that sound, Joey. That's all I'm prepared to serve you in the future. Stupid little shit, you'll end up getting yourself killed if you're not careful, and I'll bet none of your high and mighty copper mates would give a damn."

McNeil smiled. "Oh, I don't know. There's one in particular would just love to see me tagged and bagged."

"See, that's what I mean. Law unto themselves, bloody coppers."

"You forget I'm one of them."

"Yeah, but you don't behave like one. You're okay, Joey. You just need to sort yourself out."

McNeil shrugged. If enough people said it out loud, maybe it would happen. "I don't suppose you know how I got home the other night?"

Minkey laughed. "Last I saw, you were being hauled out from under by some old bird with a hell of a right hook. She nigh on took the back of Curtis' head off with one of my chairs. 'Course he was so tanked, he barely felt it. I thought they left together, but maybe she hoisted you over her shoulder and took you home herself." He paused shrewdly. "Who'd you wake up next to, Joey?"

McNeil ignored him. "Minchem Road. I'll drop by later and see if Curtis is home."

"Just don't go after dark."

"Why not?"

"Some funny buggers hang out down there. I'd hate to read about you in the obituary column. Not while you still owe me for damages."

"Don't worry, I'll take a torch."

There was a pause, filled only by the noise of the taxi indicating as it drew in alongside the kerb.

"Hey, Joey," continued Minkey. "Are you okay? You sound ... different. More messed up than usual, or maybe just sober?"

McNeil reached across and paid the driver. As he slammed the door and watched the vehicle pull away, he turned his attention back to Minkey.

"Having a bad one, Minkey, and just working my way through it. Sometimes it's hard. Today it's a killer."

"Yeah, well, hang in there, Joey, and, like I said, watch your back."

Twelve

It had to be there somewhere. He'd kept all her things carefully, just as she'd left them, waiting for her return, but now they were scattered all over the bedroom floor, clothes abandoned along with their hangers, shoes missing their pairs, thrown to one side as he upended every box and pulled out every drawer from bottom to top. He dropped to his knees, frustration getting the better of him. The need for a drink had him sweating. The need for the truth outweighed even that.

"Please, Kit, you have to help me here, sweetheart," he murmured. "I can't do this on my own. I can't work it out. I'm trying. Believe me, I'm trying."

He didn't expect a reply, but when even her soft voice in his head remained silent, he lashed out at the nightstand, smashing the flimsy wood and opening up the old wound across his knuckles. He swung his gaze dispiritedly from his bloody hand to the wrecked cupboard. Amidst the splintered wood was the box he'd been looking for.

He smiled sadly. The small pine box had seen better days. Chipped paint and a crooked hinge. The engraved flowers on the lid were worn to the point where they could barely be seen. He'd tried to surprise her with a new one, but she'd declined the gift with a soft smile and a gentle kiss that he could still feel, warm and fleeting, as if she'd brushed past and pressed a smile against his lips. A childhood gift crafted by an uncle, the box was as much a part of her past as the memories inside. It had meant so much to her, he couldn't believe that he'd forgotten its location. He was doing a lot of that lately – forgetting. So distraught at her loss, so intent on finding her, he was starting to lose sight of what they'd shared. Overcome with sudden self-doubt and weary resignation, he leaned back against the bed and opened the lid.

Once, when new, the little ballerina inside would have danced. Now, the mechanism was tired, the key lost, and the ballerina remained in the prone position. He knew how that felt. It was some time since he'd been fully wound and ready to go.

With some reluctance, he pulled out the contents, a mixture of cheap jewellery and keepsakes that meant a lot to Kit but very little to anyone else. A first concert ticket, a wrist band from a music festival, earrings in the shape of tiny stars, a button from her favourite coat, the first brownie badge she'd ever earned, and a small collection of photos – photo-booth snaps of them both acting the fool. He recalled the occasion vividly and smiled at the memory. On the back she'd written, 'Kit loves JoJo xx.'

Kit was the only one who'd called him that – until today. No one else would have dared. She had gotten under his skin and had a way of whispering it that made his heart quicken with anticipation.

He dug deeper in the box. He wasn't looking for memories, he was looking for the charm bracelet she always wore, the bracelet that had found its way back to him in an evidence bag, blood-stained and broken, the only thing left from that fateful evening.

Holding the fragile chain up to the light, he studied the broken links. It had been assumed the bracelet had snapped as a result of some kind of struggle, that someone had grabbed Kit by the wrist and the bracelet had come apart. McNeil held the two ends together, and it was immediately apparent that something was missing; it couldn't have spanned Kit's wrist in its current length. He counted the charms slowly: a silver heart for Valentine's Day, a miniature violin, a mortar board to celebrate her graduation, and a hedgehog. There were others, a total of nine. The tenth, the one he particularly wanted to find, was missing. It had not been found at the scene or returned in the evidence bag. McNeil suddenly realised how important it was to find out why.

He pulled himself up off the floor and slowly scanned the room. It was a mess, and had been before he'd decided to turn everything upside down searching. He was meant to be taking things easy, not making things worse. He pushed the headache and nausea to the back of his mind and glanced down at the broken bracelet in his hand. He'd been waiting twelve long months for a break, and yet it had been here all along. It was time to get a grip and let go of the paranoia.

It was time to find Kit.

It was a desolate spot, the place where Kit had stepped away from his life. An overgrown mineral track hugged the shoulder of a forgotten waterway. Both canal and train line had once been vital to commerce in the days when heavy industry fed and housed the populus. The tracks had long since gone to smelter. The water lay heavy and stagnant, thick with pollution and neglect. McNeil hadn't been back since the operation to dredge the water. He'd known they wouldn't find her, knew it as surely as if she had stood next to him and placed her hand in his, but, even so, he had been in torment as he'd awaited the diver's verdict. Dennis had dragged him away. Mather had pulled rank, insisted that he go home and leave it to the rest of the team. He couldn't be part of the investigation, he'd realised that, particularly as he'd been listed as a suspect from the outset. Protocol and procedure – necessary evils. But he hadn't gone home. He had stood in the exact spot where he stood now and looked on impotently as his world collapsed around him.,He stood in silence and relived it all.

Where had she gone? Why had she gone? Twelve months later and he was still asking the same questions.

The afternoon was drawing to an early close. The sky had that heavy feel, pressing down on everything below it. Perhaps the rain would turn to snow and disguise the ugly landscape beneath a pristine white blanket. McNeil sighed, not entirely convinced at the logic of deceit, however well-intentioned. The truth would always out, eventually. The light was fading, due more to the season than the hour, shorter days the drawback to all winter investigations. Although it made his search more difficult, it was somehow fitting. This fleeting time, between day and night, was how he visualised Kit, trapped somehow between one place and another, just waiting for a new dawn. First, though, he had the night to get through, and it seemed he had been struggling in the dark for far too long.

He couldn't understand what had brought Kit down to this desolate place, and yet this was where her car was found. The investigating team had theorised and decided she must have picked up her killer, given a lift to the person who would ultimately take her life. McNeil didn't buy that. Kit wouldn't have picked up a stranger, and she wasn't dead. She was just waiting somewhere to be found.

The team had tried to link her disappearance to others spanning several years. In some cases, a body had been found, in others the families had been left in limbo, their daughter, mother, wife, or lover lost forever. McNeil didn't buy that either. In his mind, he couldn't accept that Kit was just one in a list of many. She was far too precious for that. He had subsequently discounted every theory put forward as each one resulted in the same conclusion. Kit was dead. And that couldn't be right, because he knew deep inside that she wasn't.

He closed his eyes and visualised the scene. The car nosed into the scrub that edged the track. Passenger door open, engine still running when first discovered. That's what hurt the most, that they had been so close to saving her. There was blood, traces not pools, on the ground adjacent to the open door and on the nearside wheel arch. Her bracelet had been found, in the long grass, after an extensive search of the scene. He turned his attention now to that area.

The grass, in winter dormancy, lay long and flattened against the earth. In poor light, and without tools or indeed a discernible plan, he had little chance of finding anything. He didn't accept the investigating team's conclusions, and he didn't trust their SOCOs, and essentially that was the cause of his bust-up with Mary Cameron. He just couldn't believe she'd done her job properly. If she had, she would have found something that would have resulted in Kit's recovery. If he were being honest, he'd been looking to blame someone and Mary had fitted the role, but if the missing charm had not been located during the search, then it was elsewhere, perhaps taken by Kit's abductor. Nevertheless, he dropped to his haunches amongst the weeds and ineffectually teased aside the damp and lifeless mass with his fingers.

He was overcome with sudden melancholy, unsurprised when thoughts of Kit brought a strange tightness to his chest. He massaged the numbness with a trembling hand, but, instead of Kit's sweet face bringing comfort, an image of Nell slid broodingly into his head, violet eyes instead of blue. He stilled his hand in the same spot where she had laid her palm. His fingers spread wide as hers had done, and he felt her coolness against his skin. *Get a grip*, he muttered as he yanked his hand away. He dragged in a breath, exhaled slowly, and felt the pressure ease. Stuffing his hands in his pockets, he turned back to assess the scene.

"I will find you," he whispered, and he felt Kit's smile, gentle against his cheek.

Thirteen

As always he is near – Jacob, my nemesis. He watches and waits with delicious anticipation for me to perform, to dance to his tune and ultimately fall. That is his greatest pleasure, to witness the act of failure, the dread, the up-swelling of hope which transforms quickly to remorse, defeat, and, finally, fear. He feeds greedily upon it, and to date I have been his star performer. I am nothing if not consistent. It seems that I have fallen repeatedly, though the memories fade, each time replaced and overwritten by a nightmare more terrible than the one before. Each time it is he who has reached out his chill hand and empty heart, and pulled me back. This time, fate has diverted the natural order, the play of the game, and I have taken a step, albeit unwittingly, and connected with one who is poised to fall far further than I have ever known.

I await Jacob's response with equal measures of trepidation and exhilaration. My fear is spiced with the thrill of holding the wild card in an insidious game of truth or dare. I am not a truthful person, it goes against my very nature to reveal my inner core, but I do thrive on risk, the insatiable rollercoaster of life and death. In this venture, success, as always, is stacked in Jacob's favour, but there is a chink in his plan, and that chink is Joe McNeil.

I am certain Jacob observed our first meeting from the darkness he inhabits, if not in person, then he will have learned of our allegiance via his minions, those who seek his pleasure and fear his wrath. He will know how we touched, Joe and I, beneath the viaduct's giant, iron canopy, adrift amongst the flotsam and jetsam that is Bedlam, our lips finding each other, sealing our fate, connecting us for the challenge to come.

A kiss of life, love, or death?

The intent immaterial, the outcome catastrophic, for together, Joe and I have ignited the touch paper, the deadly fuse which, if allowed to burn, will set alight a pyre that not even Jacob, in his arrogance, can escape. To remain the victor, he must snub out the flame. We must therefore guard it jealously.

I know Jacob. I know the myriad of twisted logic that inhabits his foul mind, and, because of that, I know he will underestimate my saviour, my fallen knight in tarnished armour, my talisman. It takes no stretch of the imagination to assume the depth of Jacob's amusement as I strip the layers of protection, one agonising level at a time, from a man who is already flayed by loss and despair. He will assume Joe's retreat is indicative of fear, but he is mistaken. A lesser man would indeed have stepped away long before Joe, but Joe has a need which I can fill, whether he wishes it or not. It may seem to some unnecessarily cruel, but he must be laid bare before he may see his future fully. I have learnt everything I know about cruelty from Jacob – emotional torture, and more besides. And it is the more that Jacob should now fear.

I allow a secret smile to play across my lips as I consider the depths of Jacob's complacency. He laughs prematurely. I play the long game, have been doing so for what seems an eternity. Each time I have fallen, I have risen anew and better equipped. I have no doubt that Joe McNeil will come to understand the importance of his role, eventually. He must, or I will surely cease to exist, and he is set for oblivion. Until then, we must engage in the cat and mouse games which Jacob lives to play.

My ears, attuned to his sound above all others, hear his soft footfall long before he arrives. He is prowling, as he is wont to do. I close my eyes and inhale softly, preparing for what is to come. I imagine the smile which hides the snarl, and the sweet talk which sugars his bitter bite. He will charm those in his path and discard those in his wake. A tsunami of evil approaches, and I am powerless. I take another shallow breath and call silently to Joe. I sense his confusion and his pain. Sadly, both are necessary, and I gather them greedily to my breast.

He does not understand.
Ultimately, he will.
He seeks his lost love as I seek him.
Eventually, he must choose.

Fourteen

The door to the tattoo shop was heavily reinforced with a metal shutter welded in place. The grill was daubed in graffiti, some obscene, most unintelligible, and all contributing to the rundown image of the shop and surrounding buildings. McNeil sat awhile in his car and watched from across the street as clients came and went, the heavy bell above the door announcing their presence. The armaments seemed a little excessive for a few pots of ink and an electric needle.

After half-an-hour of plummeting temperatures in a car with a broken heater, he decided it was time to stretch his legs and pay Curtis a visit. He'd have preferred to surprise him, catch him on the back foot, and maybe deliver a swift retaliation for the black eye he was still nursing, but a glance at the sky dissuaded him from delaying any longer. It would soon be dark, and he had no desire to spend any longer than necessary in this part of town. As Minkey had rightly pointed out, this was not a desirable location. Second only to Bedlam, these streets were a policeman's worst nightmare. A warren of interconnecting alleys and derelict buildings, the area was home to a subculture who considered the law only in the context of how to stay beyond it rather than within it.

He'd never worked this part of town, but the McNeil of old would have relished the challenge to break down some iron clad doors and close a few cases in the process. He'd been successful in many similar raids before transferring to his current post, a golden boy, earmarked for fast track promotion. As Dennis had been at pains to point out, he'd been a good detective, but lately he'd been less interested in breaking cases and far too keen on breaking heads in his search for Kit. Today, he felt his own head was split in two. It pounded mercilessly, steadily worsening since his visit to the canal. There was a storm brewing and, little by little, he was being drawn into the eye.

The shop interior was poorly lit, and it took a moment of squinting on McNeil's part before his eyes adjusted and he could fully appreciate the amount of fantastical artwork on display. It was everywhere: walls, ceiling, backs of doors. Everything that could be decorated was, some of it beautiful, some the stuff of nightmares, like stepping into the pages of an X-rated graphic novel and having someone slam the book closed behind you. It certainly wasn't the place for a mind infused with paranoia. His pounding temple agreed. He let the door go reluctantly, and allowed the bell to announce his arrival.

Two youths lounged insolently on a ripped leather sofa. Bedecked with piercings, earlobes heavy with adornments, they followed his progress to the desk with glassy eyes. The air was heavy and sweet. A layer of smoke hung just beneath the ceiling. There was more than body art on sale here. Opposite, a young girl sat nervously chewing the ends of her hair, her make-up thick, her wrists criss-crossed with scars of distress and disharmony. He caught her eye, and a swift glance at the door was sufficient for her to forgo her place in the queue and leave.

"Well, looky here. You back for more?" Curtis drew back the beaded curtain that restricted access to the rear of the studio and leaned heavily against the door frame. His bulk filled the space, his face and arms further advertisement of his services. He was bigger and uglier than McNeil recalled, and he carried a jagged wound across the bridge of his nose. Trade-off for the black eye. McNeil felt a little less aggrieved.

"I need some information."

"And?"

"And I was hoping you'd supply it."

"Hope is for losers."

"Losers? You're the one who assaulted a police officer."

"An off-his-face-with-booze police officer."

McNeil shrugged. "Assault is assault."

Curtis snorted. "Prove it. You think anyone in Minkey's is going to stand up for a copper?"

"I don't need proof. My word against yours, mate, and I'm the respectable one. I could arrest you, close down Archie's business, basically make your life as shitty as mine, or you could just tell me what I need to know."

"Yeah, I s'pose you could try, but then the press might get wind of drunken coppers picking fights. I read the papers, maybe you should too, mate. If you did, you'd know the law-abiding, tax-paying public is getting sick of policemen and public servants who don't know how to behave." He angled in closer. McNeil focused on the abundance of stubble erupting through a cross hatch of indigo ink as Curtis' jaw worked and the words kept coming. "Apparently, last year they even had a detective under suspicion of murder ... now, what was his name?"

McNeil looked to the smoky ceiling and sniffed loudly. "You want to play that game, it's your choice."

Curtis followed his gaze with narrowed eyes, his mouth turning down in an ugly grimace. He turned to the youths. "Do one. We're closed."

They lumbered to their feet, scowling. "We're waiting for a ..."

"I said, do one. Come back in an hour. I'm doin' some business here."

The youths took their time shuffling to the door, lethargy rather than insolence slowing their retreat. McNeil waited patiently; Curtis less so. The spider inscribed across his left cheek flexed its web as he tightened his jaw in response to their dawdling.

"Bloody kids!" he muttered as he slammed the door shut and dropped the latch behind them. "So, what is it you need to know that's so important you'd risk a false arrest, detective?"

"I'm looking for a tattoo."

Curtis angled his broad face and smiled slyly. "Really?"

"Really."

"Okay," continued Curtis. "I'll run with that, but you're on the clock. I have a business to run. What kind of tattoo would you like, Detective McNeil?"

"You know my name?"

Curtis' laughter bubbled out of him like his lungs were drowning in crap. "I make it my business to know everything about tossers who think they can break my nose and walk away.

Everyone in Bedlam knows your name, and all about you. You should be more careful, detective. Should've kept a tighter hold on your lady, shouldn't you?" He stepped closer and the humour darkened. "What would you like? A heart tattooed on your chest with 'Joe loves Kit'?"

McNeil stiffened, his stomach tightened, and a sudden rush of rage flooded him. He couldn't afford to lose control, not here. The whole point of coming was to try and understand what had happened at the hospital, to attempt to put another piece in the bizarre jigsaw that currently occupied his mind. His head was full of images which he believed were connected, but didn't know why. He recalled Minkey's words, took a breath, and started counting.

"Or maybe that should be 'Joe *loved* Kit'. Gotta get the tense right. I'm a stickler for literacy. You wouldn't think it, I know." He leaned in close, and McNeil stood his ground and kept counting. He was up to seven and his fists were already clenched so tight that the tremors were up to his elbows. "Just for the record," continued Curtis, "I know nothing about your girlfriend's disappearance, if that's what this visit is all about, but, hey, if you want my opinion, it's little wonder she up and left. You have an attitude problem, pal, and next time you decide to get antsy and start a fight, you'd better make damn sure you've got some back-up, because I'm telling you now, copper or not, you're headed for serious trouble."

McNeil got to ten and stayed silent. It was all coming back. He'd gone to Minkey's looking for John Bales, the water bailiff who had discovered Kit's car all those months before. He'd hoped if he applied a little persuasive pressure, he might recall something, anything, that could throw light on Kit's last movements. But the guy failed to show, frustration got the better of him, and he'd sought solace as always in the bottom of a glass. Maybe Curtis had every right to be pissed, but he'd made a mistake in goading him about Kit.

"Don't."

One word of warning, quietly spoken, but the look that accompanied it was sufficient for Curtis to re-evaluate McNeil's tolerance level. There was a moment of charged silence as each man tried to second guess the other and, when the testosterone mist finally dissipated, McNeil fixed his eyes on the elaborate python wound around Curtis' thick neck.

"Let's get back to tattoos, snakes, serpents, that kind of shit?"

"What about them?"

"Are they popular? Have you done many?"

"One or two." He flexed his neck muscles and the python came alive. It was a trick but, even so, it took a few seconds before McNeil's concussed brain caught up with it, and he failed to hide the confusion that flashed across his face. Curtis curled his lips in a knowing smile. "What's up, detective? Under the weather? Desperate for a hair of the dog? Or something a little stronger?"

He leaned his meaty forearms on the counter and flexed his bulldog-illustrated biceps. The resulting canine grimace was accompanied by Curtis' wet laughter. McNeil caught an updraft of perspiration and muscle lubricant. The guy worked out and, by the smell of him, he'd been busy in the back shop. McNeil ignored the jibe and stepped away to avoid the stink.

"Do you keep a record of your snake designs?"

"Sure. I have an A4 glossy brochure of all my favourite designs. I send it out monthly to all my clients. You want me to add you to my mailing list?" He shook his head. "What do you think? Do I look like I keep fuckin' records?"

"So, say someone walks in off the street and says 'my mate had a dragon tattooed on his arse and I want the same design', how do you know which one he means?"

"On the walls." Curtis gestured to the designs before tapping at his head. "And in here. You don't see what you want, then you draw me a picture."

McNeil scanned the walls again. Some of the designs seemed familiar. Maybe he'd seen them before on suspects or bodies. But the twin-headed serpent was nowhere to be seen. He took a shallow breath, in through the nose out through the mouth. It was a coping strategy. Already, the place was getting to him, the walls pressing in, the images distorting despite his averted gaze. He thought of the blue pills at home in a drawer, then he checked his pockets and pulled out his notebook and pencil.

"It's a two-headed snake." He attempted to replicate what he'd glimpsed on Nell's wrist. He gripped the pencil tightly to prevent the tremor which came out of nowhere. "Kind of like that, entwined, one black snake and one white."

He passed the sketch to Curtis and stepped back. His hand tingled and he flexed it slowly. He ignored the cold that seeped through his chest wall.

"Never seen it before," grunted Curtis, his words at odds with his expression. "And your time is up. I have clients waiting and a living to earn. So, unless you want me to put that baby on your hide right now, I'm going to have to ask you to leave."

He pushed past McNeil in an attempt to force him out of the shop door, leaving the private rear room exposed. McNeil sidestepped Curtis' bulk, swept aside the bead curtain and found himself in a treatment room. The walls here were covered in yet more graphic art. Some strangely compelling, others disturbing. All those that possessed eyes seemed to have them trained on him, the images warped, teeth bared, talons flexed. He felt a wave of nausea and steadied himself with a hand on the treatment couch.

"I said it's time to go. Come back with a warrant and maybe we can talk." Curtis' snarl dragged him back.

"The two-headed snake, have you seen it before?"

"I just told you, no."

"I'd think about it if I were you. You want me to check your operating licence, your outstanding warrants, or maybe just bring a dog in here and see what he can sniff out? Because I can and I will do all of those things unless you tell me what you know about the serpent."

"I already told. I don't know anything. I'm an artist, not a fuckin' zoologist. You still pissed or just plain stupid?"

"Not pissed, just persistent. You see, Curtis, every time you lie to me, the snake round your neck squirms like it's just swallowed a rat. Now that's what I'd call a design fault on someone who has honesty issues."

Curtis scowled. "Look, it's not one of mine or Archie's."

"Go on."

"All I know is what everyone else does, including you. It's a symbol. Black and white – good and evil ..."

"Yin and yang ..." muttered McNeil.

"Yeah. I get kids, gang members, coming in here getting tats which show their allegiance. You know the kind of thing."

McNeil nodded.

"Well, the two-headed serpent is kind of like that, only it's not kids. More like a members' club. Like I said, it's not one of mine. It's just what I've heard."

"So where will I find out more?"

Curtis shrugged. "Why do you need to know more? You want to join?"

"It's part of an on-going investigation."

"Police investigations aren't my problem."

"I can make it your problem."

"Big man, huh?" Curtis sneered.

"You want to find out how big I am?" McNeil pulled out his phone. "One call and the ball starts rolling. All that red tape, it's a bugger to unravel. Might have to close you down for ... who knows ... weeks, months even."

"Okay, okay. You so short of mates that you wanna play dib-dib-dib with a new gang, that's up to you. There's a kid who comes in here. Runs a few errands. He hangs out at a squat in Bedlam. He might be there, he might not. He might be able to help you, but don't hold your breath. If he comes in, I'll tell him you're looking for him."

"Does he have a name, this errand boy?"

"I call him 'Weed'."

"Weed?"

"He's a green-haired runt who smokes like an old man."

"Fair enough." McNeil scribbled down his number on a scrap torn from the notebook. "Ask him to give me a call."

"Sure," replied Curtis, and McNeil knew by the look on his face that he had no intention of speaking to anyone.

"Maybe I'll just wander down there and see for myself."

"It'll be dark soon."

"So?"

"Just sayin'"

"Just saying what?"

Curtis gave a sly grin. "That's when the bad things come out to play."

Fifteen

It was dark when he got back to the flat. Sleet followed him up the path, slamming relentlessly against his hunched shoulders. He pulled up his collar and quickened his step. So much for keeping his stitches dry; his hair was soaked, flattened against his scalp, and he was chilled to the bone. Running entirely on fumes, his internal red light had flashed its warning somewhere between the canal and the tattoo shop. He'd ignored the signs and was now facing the consequences. Supposing the two-headed serpent had reared up and sunk its fangs in his flesh, he wouldn't have noticed. It had been a hell of a day. He just hoped he wasn't set for an equally hellish night.

The interior was just as he had left it, cold and empty, Kit's possessions strewn everywhere, providing the only spots of colour in an otherwise monochrome space. He paused in the doorway. The room was infused with her scent. Ordinarily, he would have inhaled greedily and taken comfort from it, but the exhaustion which had plagued him since the episode with Nell subverted any emotional interaction. He stepped over her clothes, didn't have the will to gather them up and to hold them close in place of her. He couldn't take anymore today.

He stripped off his wet clothes and stood a moment, shivering, while he considered whether his body was about to shut down for want of food or alcohol. For once, neither seemed adequate. He reached for the pills he'd resisted for so long, and climbed into bed. Tonight he needed sleep, and he was going to make damn sure he got it.

Sometime in the early hours, in that limbo time before dawn, when day creatures are tucked in their burrows and night creatures seek them out, the temperature in the flat dropped even further, and McNeil stirred.

He grumbled in his sleep and reached out to retrieve the covers, tugging harder when he met with resistance. Typical Kit, she always did hog the duvet.

"Hey, sweetheart, you have to share. I'm freezing my bits off here."

The covers suddenly gave and he felt her warmth as she sidled close and slid her arms around him. Soft, smooth, scented skin – how could he resist? She stretched languidly against him, her naked breasts against his back, fingers playing gently at his belly. He responded, slowly at first, but as longing pulled him from slumber and her hand slid lower, he turned to face her and sought her sweet mouth.

"I've missed you ..." he murmured, his words lost as she deepened the kiss. Her fragrant hair swept his face and he closed his eyes and breathed in her essence. Slowly and irresistibly, he was drawn toward a climax he had yearned for throughout months of despair. She pushed him back against the pillow, gently, and rose above him, her hands braced against his shoulders. Her silken skin caressed him like an exquisite cloth, every movement a pleasurable torture. The interminable searching, the endless wait, it was finally over, and all was swept away as her pace quickened, his body reacted, and he gripped her in a final desperate thrust. "Promise me you won't leave again ..." he breathed heavily against her ear as he held her tight, laid across him, warm and replete. She raised her head and placed her finger against his lips.

"Hush ..." she whispered, her voice pure honey, a balm to a battered soul. She smiled her sweet smile and in the soft pre-dawn light the room was bathed in a violet glow.

He woke to an empty bed and the certain knowledge that his nightmare was far from over.

Sixteen

The doctor's office wasn't what he was expecting. Doctor – who was he kidding? – the psychiatrist, the shrink, the guy who was all set to take one look at him and announce him disturbed, crazy, whatever, wasn't situated in the usual Department medical offices. He'd been there before, when he'd first lost Kit, after they'd decided he wasn't complicit in her disappearance but before they'd lifted his suspension and returned him to duty. Then, it had been a formality, where he'd sensed apology and sympathy in the doctor's manner, as if sitting there, behind his desk, he'd known exactly what lay ahead for McNeil, and he was giving him an easy ride in preparation.

He checked the address on the card and the time on his watch, and debated on the value of going in at all. There were other places he had to be, the hospital for one. He'd intended going round there first thing, catching Nell unawares, when he was firing on all cylinders and before she had a chance to perfect her mysterious and spooky act. And that's all it was, he was sure of it, a game she was playing to while away the time to draw attention away from the fact that maybe she knew more than she should about the murder of the vagrants. But he'd overslept, woken to grim reality, and, if truth be told, he wasn't in any fit state for another one of Nell's performances. The only thing he was sure about was that the pills were a mistake. Last night had been far too real.

The doctor had his suite of offices in a rambling Victorian building set on the outskirts of town, a once-fashionable area gone to seed that was gradually being rejuvenated with money from those with an interest in making more of it. McNeil didn't care who made money if it meant the rundown suburbs were tamed. The area had been sopping up criminal flotsam and jetsam from Bedlam like a sponge, so it was good to see the big old houses turned back from squats and DSS bedsits, even if it did condemn and condense the less affluent in Bedlam's inner ghetto. At least it was easier to police.

Gilmour House had a Grade II listed exterior and an infamous past that McNeil only knew of because it had once been owned by a man who, like good King Henry, changed wives as regularly as his socks. A religious zealot, he had murdered four of them before the good people of Bedlam discovered his nefarious fancies. Of course, that was when Bedlam had good people, which was long before McNeil's time. He'd read about the case in police college, and had studied the sepia photo of the grim-faced, handlebar-moustached murderer with macabre fascination. The wives had been poisoned and buried before they were fully dead. The man had gone to the gallows after a grave digger heard devilish moans seeping out of the latest burial plot. By the time the good wives of Benjamin Rath were exhumed, the lids of their coffins were scarred, their finger nails broken and bloody, and they had long since breathed their last.

By curious coincidence, Benjamin Rath had also held a degree in psychiatry from a time when the profession trod a fine line between genius and lunacy, and lobotomies were the panacea of all mental ills. The irony wasn't lost on McNeil, given the house's current occupant and his own questionable sanity.

Because of the listing, the exterior of the house had remained as in Rath's time, sash windows and old red brick untouched by the developers, but inside was a modernist capsule designed to make a statement. To McNeil, in his fragile state, the harsh lighting and minimalist décor merely jarred. It might well be Feng Shui and filtered, but he dismissed it with an irritable shake of his head. He was only doing this for Dennis, and the sooner it was over, the better.

There was no one at reception and no one waiting to be seen, just an underlying smell of new carpet and fresh paint. He stood a moment, waiting, listening for any sound that might indicate the imminent arrival of the receptionist, before giving in to temptation and moving round to the other side of the desk. In the absence of an appointment book, he moved the computer mouse, but all he got for his trouble was a screen saver and a request for a password. He checked his watch impatiently and wandered to the wall-mounted leaflet rack. There were a multitude of additional therapies on offer, all designed to combat the twenty-first century plagues of emotional trauma, relationship issues, and addiction, no doubt for a hefty price. He wondered who was picking up the tab for his visit. He doubted the Department would have the funds to splash out on such a gold standard facility.

He pulled out one leaflet at random, of the happy-clappy discover-your-inner-self genre, basically a help group where people sat around and made everyone else miserable with their own misery. He had enough of his own without dipping into the collective.

"Good morning. You must be Detective McNeil."

McNeil turned, a similar greeting on his lips, but it stalled when he recognised the well-dressed man from the day before who had offered assistance in the hospital lobby. He narrowed his eyes, assessed this coincidence for a moment, and then shrugged it off. He was a doctor; doctors hung around in hospitals. He extended his hand and nodded his salutation.

"I think we already met."

"Yes. I believe you wanted to punch me."

McNeil winced. "You could tell just by looking at me?"

"It was rather obvious."

"Sorry. Bad day."

"We all have bad days."

"Not like mine."

The doctor smiled benignly and, although undoubtedly well-intentioned, McNeil found his manner patronising. He didn't like it, which wasn't the best start to their meeting.

"May I call you Joe?"

McNeil shrugged. The good doctor could call him any damn thing he liked. Five minutes in the building and he was ready to leave. He wanted to tell him he'd changed his mind and the appointment was a mistake, but he held his tongue. He called to Kit, but she was keeping silent, too. He was on his own.

"Joe, my name is Dr Richardson. If you'd like to follow me, we can find somewhere a little more convivial for our chat."

Chat? Chatting was for friends with time on their hands and nothing better to do than discuss the weather, the football, or the state of the economy if they were really bored. It was the wrong term entirely for a discussion with a man who was being paid to listen. Nevertheless, McNeil followed as they left the stark lobby and stepped back in time to the Victorian remains of the building. There was an immediate change in ambience and lighting, the florescent brightness of the reception superseded by illumination so subdued that it took McNeil a moment to ensure that he was placing his feet in the right place as they climbed a broad staircase.

"You trying to save on the electric?" he muttered as he gripped the rail.

"My apologies. We're still in the midst of re-development and there seems to be a problem with the wiring in this part of the building. No matter how many times the electrician undertakes a repair, it insists on reverting to type – a factory default, no doubt, that ensures we expend the maximum funds in return for diminishing service. I assure you the consulting room is adequately lit for our purposes."

At the top of the stairs, the landing branched both ways. Up here, instead of new carpet, there was a pervading smell of old plaster. Richardson led him to the left and a stout oak door which stood slightly ajar. McNeil hung back, distracted by the sound of running feet at the end of the other corridor. With the memory of Benjamin Rath fresh in his mind, he tensed, turning to glance over his shoulder as Richardson continued to mutter about the wiring.

"Nothing is ever black and white, is it?"

McNeil swung back around, frowning, but before he could put words to his thoughts, children's laughter filled the hall and drew his attention away from Richardson's retreating back. Two little girls scampered down the stairs behind him, playing chase and pulling pigtails. McNeil let out a breath. *Get a grip.*

"So," began Richardson, as he ushered McNeil into the room and gestured for him to take a seat, "what brings you here today?"

McNeil raised a brow. Richardson knew exactly why he was there; his file was laid out on the desk in front of him. So much for the friendly chat. He realised this was going to be one of those conversations which, in reality, was simply a long list of questions directed at him. He was a detective, he knew how these things worked, and if he'd a mind for being awkward, he could play along.

"You tell me."

"Well, what do you hope to gain from our meeting?"

"I have no idea."

"In that case, I'll start. I would hope that together we might, through discussion and reflection, help you to overcome the problems you're experiencing, and come to terms with your situation."

"Problems?"

Richardson settled back in his chair and studied McNeil for a moment before retrieving the glasses which had slid to the end of his nose. "There have been concerns raised about your current obsession, your inconsistent grasp on reality and ... your lack of adherence to departmental regulations."

"Oh, those problems."

"Have you come straight from work, Joe?"

McNeil smiled sourly. No, he'd come straight from heaven and landed in hell, courtesy of a couple of pills and the sweetest sex he'd ever had. Trouble was, it was all in his head and he didn't think Richardson would want to hear about that, even if there was an appropriate leaflet in the lobby. Or maybe he'd want to hear every heart-stopping, blood-pumping, detail, but McNeil wasn't inclined to share.

"No," he answered instead. "I always look like shite. I don't sleep very well."

Richardson's gaze hovered for a moment on McNeil's blackened eye before he smiled indulgently. "Well, that's certainly something I can help you with." He reached for a prescription pad and scrawled something illegible upon it. "Normally I'd ask you to take this to reception as you leave and Selina would dispense it for you, but, sadly, Selina has a domestic emergency today, babysitting I believe. So if you'll excuse me a moment, I'll make it up for you myself."

"There were kids playing on the landing," offered McNeil.

Richardson rose from his seat. "You saw them?"

"Yeah, two little girls. They were headed down the stairs."

Richardson frowned. "You must be mistaken. Selina is home with her children."

McNeil shrugged. "Well, somebody's kids are running around in a poorly lit building – you might want to sort that out before Health and Safety come knocking."

"I agree, Joe. It definitely needs sorting out. Give me a moment and I'll do just that."

Left alone in the consulting room, McNeil's gaze naturally fell on the file left tantalisingly within reach on the desk. Did he really want to know what they all thought of him? No, probably not. Had it been left out deliberately to test his reaction? Definitely. McNeil smiled. When it came to mind games, Dr. Richardson had obviously forgotten he was an experienced interrogator and knew every trick in the book.

He left his seat and began to prowl the room. He soon became aware of something that did appeal to his detective nose and innate curiosity. He allowed his hand to run down the mahogany filing cabinet, an unobtrusive tug revealing that Dr. Richardson unlocked his cabinet in the morning and probably didn't lock up till he went home at night. Why that should be of interest, he wasn't sure.

He slid open the top drawer. It was loosely filled with manila files. After a cautious look to the door, McNeil thumbed through them. Disappointingly, there were no names to identify the clients, simply numbers. He was about to pull out the first one, investigate further and satisfy his idle curiosity, when he heard the creaking boards on the landing announce Richardson's return.

"No little girls, Joe." He resumed his seat, smiled indulgently, and placed a small brown bottle on the desk in front of him. "They seem to have disappeared." He pushed the bottle towards McNeil. "You're obviously overtired and not quite yourself. I'm sure these will help enormously. Take one morning and night. They'll help you relax and see things a little more clearly."

McNeil was sure they wouldn't. Richardson may well be correct about his diagnosis, but not the remedy. There was only one cure for what ailed him, and her name was Kit. "To be honest, I'd rather sort things out myself."

"But you're not sorting things out, are you? Which is why you're here today. Tell me, Joe, how much do you drink in an average week?"

McNeil scowled. "When I finally get an average week, I'll let you know."

Richardson smiled pleasantly, but McNeil wasn't fooled.

"Let's talk about your childhood, Joe."

"Let's not."

"Were you a happy child, Joe? Do you have good memories?"

"I don't remember. I was just a kid. It was a long time ago."

Richardson persevered. "I understand you were brought up by an aunt after the death of your parents."

McNeil frowned. "Where are you getting this from?"

"From your record, Joe."

"What's my record got to do with you?" He felt himself bristle at Richardson's intrusion. He had no intention of discussing his childhood, happy or not, but like the helpless recipient of a subliminal message, the prompt had been set, and the jumble in his head was suddenly pushed to one side by an image of a small boy in a faded Star Wars T-shirt. The boy sat cross legged on a doorstep, his back to a closed door. One eye had been closed by a fist, one brow split open by another. His bottom lip trembled. His hands were clasped tightly over his ears. Blood oozed between his fingers.

Richardson sighed. "You know, Joe, I'm just trying to help you."

McNeil's hand strayed to the scar that dissected his right eyebrow. He took a slow breath. "Sorry, but no, you're not. You're sitting there, dabbling with my psyche, deciding my future at the behest of my boss, and neither of you give a shit about it anyway. But, hey, don't worry, you'll still get your fee. Let's just get this over with and then we can both get on with life."

"Okay, if that's the way you feel, we'll leave the subject of what happened to your parents if you're uncomfortable discussing it, and we'll cut straight to the reason why your boss thought it pertinent that you meet with me. Tell me, Joe, why do you believe that Kit is still alive when all evidence points to the contrary?"

"Kit?"

"It's all in your record, Joe."

"You mean you've been discussing me behind my back?"

"That makes you sound a little paranoid, Joe, which rather proves my point. I haven't discussed you with anyone. I do, however, know all about what happened to you, and I've observed your behaviour. I'm curious as to why you maintain your belief concerning Kit, even though you risk your job and friendships because of it."

"Because I know she's alive."

"How do you know?"

"Because I feel it in here." He placed a palm against his chest, withdrawing it swiftly when the action reminded him of Nell rather than Kit.

"Have you seen her?"

He swallowed awkwardly, distracted, and trying hard not to be. "No ... not while I'm awake." That sounded weird even to his own ears, but it was out and he couldn't take it back. He cursed at his own ineptitude, and the doctor looked at him a little harder.

"Have you spoken with her?"

"Yes ... no ... not exactly ..."

"What does that mean?"

Fuck. He didn't want to have this discussion with a man whose job was to dig into the pain of others. He felt exposed, vulnerable, and he was wasting time which could have been better spent, but, despite that, he had an overwhelming need to say out loud what he felt deep inside. "It means I hear her in my head. I feel her next to me at night. I sense her presence when I need her, and, before you send out for the strait jacket, I'm not crazy ... I ..."

"You miss her, Joe. It's understandable and perfectly normal. I don't think you're crazy, but I do think you need to take a step back and evaluate what you've just told me."

"*Evaluate?* What is this, some test where a high score means I'm sane and a low one a fuckin' head case? This is my life we're talking about. Do you think I want to live like this? I can tell you I don't. I don't want Kit in my head. I want her here in my arms. I want people to believe what I'm saying and help me find her."

"Is she here now?"

"*What?*"

"Kit – do you hear her now?"

McNeil shook his head. He felt his heart rate climbing, the steady thud getting louder. "You don't get it. You're not listening to what I'm saying. She's not a ghost. She isn't stuck on a fuckin' cloud somewhere."

"I am listening, Joe, with great interest. But do you realise how confusing your reality is to those who don't share it? You insist Kit is still alive, yet, by your own admission, she behaves like a spirit, haunting your mind and your dreams."

"My reality?" Perspiration prickled his brow and he dashed it away with the back of his hand. "Look, if I had an answer, an explanation, then I wouldn't be here. All I know is: she's alive somewhere, and I need to find her."

"Do you believe in ghosts, Joe?"

"What?"

"The paranormal. Do you believe in life after death, in things that go bump in the night?"

"I believe in life and death, and nothing in between."

"And yet you yourself are evidence to the contrary."

"I don't follow you ..."

"The girl you revived."

"What about her?"

"Don't you read the newspapers, Joe? You're headline news this morning. The resurrection man, the policeman who revives the dead. They're calling it a miracle."

"She wasn't dead."

"Are you sure?"

"What is this? Of course she wasn't dead. I mean, her heart had stopped ... I think ... but she wasn't dead, not like they all thought. You're a doctor, you know how these things work. People can't be brought back. If they could, we'd all be at it, and the world would be overrun with people who should be six feet under. If she really was dead, she'd still be fucking dead, wouldn't she?"

"I know that, Joe. What I'm asking is what do you *believe?*"

McNeil clenched his hands tightly in his lap in an attempt to quell the tremors. *Inhale, exhale.* He tried to do it surreptitiously but failed. "If I believed I could bring someone back from the dead, I could think of a few others I'd rather spend my time on. I'd be out there, on the road, with my touring medicine show hawking batwings and eye of newt to desperate souls who know no better, and making a fortune in the process."

"That sounds a little heartless, Joe, and I'm sure you're not. Do you regret your actions?"

"I'm just sick of having to defend them."

"I'm sure the girl is grateful to you."

"Forget her. She's not important."

"Do you wish it had been Kit?"

McNeil shook his head in disbelief. "How many fucking' times do I have to say this? Kit is not *dead.*"

Richardson shrugged. "And, as you've just made quite clear, Joe, neither was the girl. Tell me about the last time you saw her."

"Nell?"

"Ah, you know her name. Good. So not a total waste of your time after all, and I'm sure she agrees. The girl is alive because of you, whether you accept that or not. My faith in you is restored, Joe. You are not the uncaring monster you pretend to be. But no, I meant Kit. Tell me about the last time you saw Kit."

"Why?"

"I'd just like to understand how you parted. Was there anything said or unsaid? A misunderstanding perhaps? Sometimes it's difficult to move on where there's an element of regret or guilt."

"Are you asking if we argued, if we parted on bad terms, am I wracked with guilt and blaming myself? Because, believe me, I blame myself daily for not being there when she needed me. But no, I didn't drive her away and the only regret I have is that I've kept her waiting this long, and I'm still nowhere near finding out what happened, or where she might be."

"Perhaps she doesn't want to be found. Have you considered that? Maybe it's time to move on, to accept that part of your life is over, and seek out a new relationship. You're a young man, Joe. You have a life ahead of you that is currently restrained by the past. I'm afraid there comes a point where you have to let go."

McNeil reared up angrily and flung back his chair. If this was meant to be therapy, it wasn't working. He was more wound up now than when he came in.

"Session over, doctor. Send your bill to DCI Mather."

"I'm sorry if I touched upon a raw nerve, Joe, but this is just the beginning, the felling of the first tree in a forest of doubt. It will hurt. The truth always does. You have to appreciate that things are seldom as straight forward as we imagine."

McNeil's head was suddenly bursting with whispered voices all competing for attention. He backed to the door, trying to look contained and in control, while inside his panic was rising. "While you're busy making kindling out of hope, what about Kit?"

Richardson angled his head thoughtfully. "You need to go back to the very beginning, Joe, either here with me, in a safe environment, or out there, with no protection. You choose."

"Protection from what?"

"The truth, Joe. Life is seldom black and white. To co-exist, we must learn to live within the grey."

Seventeen

His phone vibrated angrily as he left the doctor's office. He ignored it, as he had throughout the consultation. Whoever was calling could wait. He had other stuff to think about. Richardson might well be a sanctimonious prick, but he was correct about one thing: he'd spent too long looking in dark corners for Kit, and it was time to switch on the light. He'd neglected the importance of what had precipitated her disappearance. He needed to go back to square one.

Maybe she'd gone to the canal for a specific reason, though he couldn't imagine what that might have been, or perhaps the investigating team were correct and she had picked up someone who had forced her to drive there but, either way, the location was significant to both scenarios. It was time he caught a look at the police files.

He started the car, cursing at the feeble excuse for a heater. Sleet covered the windshield. It was early for snow, but the weathermen had warned it was on the way. He shivered, unsure whether his chills were due to the cold, his encounter with Richardson, or just his general demeanour. He felt he was going round in circles. He reached in his jacket pocket to shut off his phone, and pulled out Richardson's prescription instead. He couldn't recall picking it up off the desk. The bottle sat snugly in his palm, distracting him in an 'eat-me / drink-me' kind of way. It wasn't that far off the mark. He felt like he'd been stuck down a rabbit hole for the last twelve months. His hand began to tremble, and the more he tried to quell it, the worse the tremors became, until the pills inside the bottle rattled enticingly against the glass. He couldn't go on much longer, pretending nothing was wrong. He called softly to Kit, but his mind was too full of what-ifs for him to hear her clearly, if she was there at all.

He let out a sigh, unscrewed the cap and shook out one capsule. What the hell, in for a penny ...

By the time he got to the station, he was feeling chilled, and it had nothing to do with the weather. Supposing he'd cracked open the capsule and snorted the contents, the drugs couldn't have got into his blood stream any quicker. He climbed unsteadily from the car and stood a moment with a hand on the door. The first flakes of real snow began to fall. He turned his face to the sky and focused on the snow tunnelling towards him. There was something refreshing about the way it scoured his cheeks. He closed his eyes. *Inhale, exhale.* When he was back in control, he ducked his head and hurried across the car park.

Dennis intercepted him halfway to the building. "Where the bloody hell have you been? I've called you more times this morning than I called the wife when we were courting. Do you never answer your phone?"

McNeil shrugged. "I was busy."

"Yeah? Doing what?"

"You know what. You made the appointment. I've been to see the shrink."

Dennis raised his brows in surprise, as if McNeil's non-attendance had been a given. "What did he say?"

"Not a lot."

"What did *you* say?"

"Even less."

"Are you seeing him again?"

"Not if I can help it."

Dennis shook his head with frustration. "Joey, I know I keep repeating myself, but, this time, I really mean it. I'm about done with you."

"Dennis, you told me to go and I went. The guy was ... well, he was a shrink, what more can I say? Would you be happy telling a stranger all your innermost thoughts and dirty secrets?"

"Dirty secrets?"

"I'm generalising, Dennis."

"Forget secrets, dirty or otherwise. We don't have time for that now. Smarten yourself up. Mather wants to see you. He's not a happy man."

"When is he ever?"

"This is serious, Joey. Have you seen the papers this morning?"

"I don't read the papers. Too much bad news gives me indigestion."

Dennis snorted. "Indigestion? I'm surprised your digestive system isn't pickled with the amount of booze you've put away lately."

McNeil ignored him. "Journalists are just out to grab the next big story. It's not news, it's creative writing."

"Yeah, well, just make sure you haven't been talking to them. Mather is practically apoplectic. That bird, Clarissa What's-her-face from the 'Herald', is having a field day."

McNeil tried to edge away. Having been forewarned of the likely content of the local broadsheet, he had no desire to be held to task by Dennis or Mather. He had more pressing things to do, and as none of them were strictly within the rules, he didn't need Dennis breathing down his neck while he bent them. He hadn't been allowed a role in the enquiry into Kit's disappearance, and he didn't have clearance to look at the files, but he needed to know what the investigating team had pulled together, what additional evidence had led them to surmise that she was dead and at what point they'd decided to give up.

"I'll catch up with Mather later."

Dennis grabbed him by the sleeve. "No, you won't. He sent me to find you, 'to bring you in' were his actual words. A word in your ear, Joey. Tread carefully. He's gunning for you."

"Why?"

"Isn't that obvious?"

"Not to me."

"Well, Joey, that says it all."

Mather's office was on the top floor, as befitting his inflated opinion of himself. He'd acquired it by default after some wheeling and dealing. He was partial to the view. It looked south, away from Bedlam, green fields and distant rolling hills, the Promised Land, the rural idyll that Mather aspired to on retirement.

The windowsill was filled with plants that helped sustain the dream while he wished his life away. He nurtured them like children, which was more than could be said for his own brood who had leapt from the nest at the first opportunity, taking most of the branch with them. It had left the man with a bitter taste in his mouth, which he regularly spat out at those who didn't meet his exacting standards.

The squad was relieved by his choice of location, as it meant he, his geraniums, and his bile, were distanced from them, and, as a result, they were left in comparative peace until a case worthy of his involvement reared its head. McNeil wasn't bothered either way, since he held no particular affection for the team or Mather. The only downside that he could see was that the office was a long way from the car park when a swift exit was called for. He considered that today might just be one of those occasions.

Both men paused outside the door, dentist surgery dread adding reluctance to their step. Dennis gave McNeil a final once over. "How's your head?"

"Still on my shoulders."

"Well, let's try and keep it that way. I stuck my neck out for you, so don't let me down in there. Mather thinks you're a loose cannon. I'm beginning to agree with him, but don't make me come out and say it. I'll cover your back as long as I can but, if there's anything at all that you haven't told me, now's the time to spit it out."

McNeil shook his head. "I'm just doing my job. How about you?"

Dennis reached out and straightened his tie. "Shit. Have you been fighting again?"

"No."

"You've got blood all over your collar."

"I must have cut myself shaving."

Dennis peered closer. "You either have a shaky hand or you need glasses. You almost nicked your jugular."

McNeil shoved his shaky hands in his pockets. "*Almost?* Lucky me," he added with a slow smile. The meds were kicking in and he felt just fine.

"Bloody hell, you can't help yourself, can you? I'm just trying to help you, Joey."

"Yeah, you're not the first person to say that to me today. All of a sudden everyone wants to help me. I wonder why."

"If you need to wonder about it, Joey, then I'm insulted, and you have a problem," muttered Dennis as he knocked at the door. "Just don't get down wind of him. Mather can smell trouble a mile off."

DCI Mather was seated at his desk, phone in hand, when they entered the room. A short man, he had only just made the grade before height restrictions were crucial to recruitment. He made up for his lack of stature with an expanding girth, which was currently squeezed between the arms of his executive leather chair, the rewards of high rank, or, more likely, the spoils from the latest police auction. Either way, he had the plushest office in the station. He slammed the handset down and scowled at them both.

"DI Todd, DS McNeil, glad you could make it. I said nine-thirty, but what's an hour here or there when a major investigation is grinding to a halt? Bedlam must rest easy at night knowing you two clowns are policing its streets."

McNeil shot an apologetic glance at Dennis. It was unfortunate that he was the innocent caught in the spread of Mather's scattergun wrath. Dennis tightened his jaw and said nothing. McNeil awaited permission to sit, while Dennis edged back out of the line of fire and took up sentry post against the door, as if he feared McNeil might try to slip out of it.

"What the hell is going on, McNeil?"

"I have no idea, sir." He shifted his weight from one leg to the other. He had a fuzzy feeling in his head, and he rolled his neck and blinked to restore concentration. It was difficult. Mather had the heating turned up, and all he could think about was loosening his tie and sinking a cold one.

Mather narrowed his eyes and studied him a little closer. "I'm sorry if I'm keeping you awake, detective. Perhaps if you spent less time in the local hostelries, you'd be a little fresher in the mornings."

"Sir."

"Have you been talking to the press?"

"About what?"

"The school jumble sale, the cancellation of the number nineteen bus – what in God's name do you think? About the case!"

"No, sir."

"Then what the bloody hell is all this shite?" Mather picked up a newspaper and flung it across his desk.

McNeil didn't get the chance to read the headlines before Mather snatched it back and launched into an abridged version. "That bloody woman from the 'Herald' has got her teeth into this. Page one no less." Mather started reading.

Miracles do happen. Bedlam Detective brings woman back to life

Mystery surrounds the unconfirmed event which occurred at the scene of a double murder. A police spokesman refused to comment on the possibility of a serial killer at large or to confirm the identities of the victims.

I can reveal, however, that the detective responsible for the timely intervention, which saved the unnamed young woman's life, was previously investigated over the disappearance of his long-term girlfriend. Detective McNeil was recently photographed after a bar room brawl.

Saint or sinner? Let us know what you think?

"*Miracles? Bar room brawls?* What the fuck is going on here, McNeil? You're a professional. You're meant to behave like one. Look at the bloody photo, for Christ's sake. You look like you belong on the Jeremy Kyle Show."

McNeil didn't know how they'd got it, or why, but it wasn't his best shot. He angled his head to take in the detail while Mather brandished it like a weapon. Taken after his run in with Curtis, he was being manhandled out of Minkey's by two men he didn't recognise. He was hammered, his face was battered, his clothes a mess. He was a disgrace to himself and the force, and there was no getting around it. He shrugged his apology, unclear whether an explanation was ultimately what Mather wanted or whether a simple bollocking would suffice.

"Sit down," barked Mather, "before you fall down, and explain to me why I shouldn't just rip up your warrant card and send you down to the Job Centre. Come on, we haven't got all day. What have you got to say for yourself?"

McNeil slid into the seat, his take on the whole matter slightly skewed. The fuzziness was now a warm glow. He was beginning to think more kindly about Dr Richardson.

"It's not as bad as it looks, sir. For a start, the girl wasn't actually dead, so not really a miracle, more a stroke of luck – for her, not me. Next time I see someone gasping their last, I'll just keep on walking and stay out of trouble. And the photo, well, that was all just a misunderstanding."

"The girl? Are you saying Roger screwed up? That all of this is his fault?"

McNeil shot a glance at Dennis. He was focused on the geraniums, but the scowl said it all.

"Not exactly, no."

"Not exactly. That just about sums you up, McNeil. Not exactly this, not exactly that." He screwed up the paper and flung it in the waste basket. "Forget the bloody girl. I couldn't give a snowman's carrot about the girl. Of course she wasn't dead. Only an idiot would believe all this talk of miracles. So, Roger had a bad day, the first in forty years. I think we can give him that one for free. What I'm bothered about, DS McNeil, what has me hot under the collar and spitting blood, are photos of my bloody coppers getting rat-arsed. Misunderstanding! Do you think I came down in the last shower? You were bloody hammered, and it's not a one-off, is it? Don't think because I'm up here among the civilized people that I don't hear what's going on. I hear everything, McNeil, and what I hear about you is giving me great cause for concern. It doesn't do the department's reputation any good, and, believe me, McNeil, it doesn't do you any favours either. This is just the kind of thing that keeps journalists in a job. The article goes on at length about police standards, your disgraceful behaviour, and your girlfriend's murder. It suggests that we mishandled the case, that you believe we mishandled the case ..."

"She's not dead," McNeil ignored the warning look thrown his way by Dennis, "and you've all written her off. If that's not mishandling, then I don't know what is."

Mather glared at Dennis. "I thought you had him under control."

"I do. He is. Things are just a little tense at the moment. It's the anniversary of Kit's ... disappearance. It's a bad time for him and this recent case hasn't helped. He's been seeing a doctor, haven't you, DS McNeil?"

McNeil smiled, which he guessed wasn't the required response; he could tell by Dennis' incredulous look and Mather's indignant snort.

"From what I hear, that's not all you've been seeing ... bloody ghosts and ghouls. You're a copper, for God's sake. Forget the fairies at the bottom of the garden and the monsters under your bed, and pull yourself together." The meds, designed to relax, merely compounded his disgrace as the smile slid into a smirk in response to Mather's outburst. "You see what I mean? He thinks this is a damn joke. Have you been drinking, detective?"

"No, sir," he slurred.

Mather squeezed back in his seat and McNeil watched distractedly as his complexion morphed through various fiery shades before gradually returning to a more usual florid. He reckoned Mather was employing some discreet inhaling and exhaling therapy of his own, and, while he did, an uncomfortable silence filled the office. The man hadn't got to his position without developing a knack for wriggling out of tight situations. McNeil waited while Mather plotted.

"Damage limitation, that's what's needed here," he finally announced, jabbing a finger at McNeil. "You, detective, are going to smarten up and prepare for a press release, an interview with Ms Hell-hath-no-fury herself. In it, you'll recite words prepared for you by someone whose brain is not addled by heaven-knows-what and who understands the precarious relationship we enjoy with the tabloid vultures. This will ensure that every person who picks up the next copy of that bloody newspaper believes you to be a paragon of modern policing. I will not have sinners on my watch, DS McNeil. Do you hear what I'm saying?"

"Loud and clear ... sir."

"Good. Get on to that, DI Todd. I expect a draft document on my desk by close of business."

Dennis stepped forward. "Me? You want me to write it?"

"He's your boy, Dennis. Man up and take some responsibility. He messes in the nest, you clear it up. Maybe that'll encourage you to keep a closer eye on him."

Dennis shot a murderous look at McNeil.

"Oh, and while you're here, how is the case going, DI Todd?"

"Slowly, sir."

Mather scowled. "That's not what I want to hear. Do we know how they died?"

"Their throats were slit. Something small and sharp. Possibly a scalpel or cut-throat razor." Dennis' shot a quick glance at McNeil and his blood-stained collar. "There were other wounds, stab wounds. And, of course, the wounds to the throat were exacerbated by the meat hooks."

McNeil's lips twitched. "Meat hooks will do that," he murmured.

Mather glared at McNeil. "And do we know how they got up there? What have forensics said?"

"Not a lot, sir. I'm still awaiting their report," replied Dennis. "The meat hooks were suspended from ropes which were secured beneath the parapet. There was no sign of any ladder. We have no idea how the bodies were lifted."

"They weren't lifted. They were dropped," McNeil interjected.

"Huh?"

McNeil shrugged. "Seems pretty obvious to me. They were dropped from above. You know, like concrete from a flyover, Pooh sticks from a bridge." He closed his eyes as a sudden image flashed in his head. The men, drunk, half-dazed, the flash of a silver blade and then the sickening crunch of pointed metal as it severed larynx and embedded in spine. "Their heads were almost ripped off. What else could cause that kind of damage but the force of the drop?"

"But why?" asked Dennis.

"For kicks. To smash a car. To race sticks. To see what happens."

"All that, just for kicks?"

"Yeah, to see what happens when you launch two dead guys two hundred feet with a hook through their necks. Kind of bungee with extra 'eeee'."

Dennis nodded slowly, thinking it through. "The rope was fixed beneath the parapet. Why not just tie it off on the top of the bridge?"

"Maybe they prepared the ropes in advance and didn't want them seen."

"*They?*"

"One man couldn't have subdued both victims, hauled up the ropes, and then manhandled the bodies over the parapet."

"What are you saying?"

McNeil shrugged. He didn't really know what he was saying or where the words were coming from. He hadn't given the victims any thought at all before he'd stepped into Mather's office. He'd been too obsessed with Nell and Kit.

"I'm saying it looked staged."

"So, in your opinion, totally unconnected to the girl. A coincidence?" cut in Mather.

"Maybe. I don't know." He rubbed at his eyes. The heat in the room was dehydrating. He needed a drink, and, at this point, even water would have done. Richardson had said the meds would help him see things more clearly. McNeil didn't think that included crime scene exclusives. "I'm just thinking out loud."

Mather swung his gaze from one man to the other. "And the girl, has she given a statement?"

"She's still confused," said Dennis. "DS McNeil did obtain some vital information as to her attacker's identity, and we're following up on those leads."

"Jacob ... she said his name was Jacob," muttered McNeil, his mind still on the image of the corpses swinging gently back and forth in the breeze. He imagined the wind strengthening, dashing the bodies like inanimate pendulums against the viaduct supports, boots ringing out dully against the iron work. The macabre beat aped his escalating heart rate. He'd heard that sound before. Boots against wood, jerking, kicking, pounding, and then deathly silence.

He swallowed in an attempt to generate some saliva. He longed to loosen his tie, but instead ran a finger inside his shirt collar to relieve the constriction. When he pulled his hand away, his fingers were spotted with fresh blood. He shot a quick glance at Dennis and shoved his hand in his pocket.

"Jacob? Who's Jacob, the bloody milkman?"

McNeil refocused on Mather. "No, sir. Jacob, the man she was running from."

"Had a good conversation with her, did you?"

"Bits and pieces. As DI Todd explained, she was a little confused."

Mather swung his gaze back to McNeil and narrowed his eyes. "Not the only one, by all accounts, eh?"

"I'm not sure I know what you mean, sir."

"Exactly. A word of advice, detective. Do not take me for a fool. If you're up to something, I will find out. If, as I suspect, you're simply not up to the job, then that will soon become apparent. But, while you're still here drawing a salary, I want you out there working for your money. I want you sober and civil, and, most of all, I want results. One wrong step, one more incident that finds its way into print and causes my blood pressure to peak, and I will have your badge. Do you hear what I'm saying?"

McNeil shrugged.

"That is not an answer, detective."

McNeil pulled himself out of the chair and straightened up. "Yes, sir, I understand fully. Keep my mouth shut and do as I'm told."

Mather extended a stubby finger, punctuating each sentence with a furious jab. "DI Todd, the responsibility for this officer remains entirely with you. Do not make me regret this. Now, get him out of here before I do something that risks my pension."

Eighteen

"Thanks for that, Joey."

"Sorry."

"Are you?" hissed Dennis, as he shouldered McNeil into the lift. "You don't bloody look it. In fact, if I didn't know any better, I'd think you were half-cut."

McNeil smiled stupidly and spread his arms wide. "Not guilty, Dennis. I haven't touched a drop. Just drunk on life, I guess."

"Well, it's time you sobered up. I want you down at the hospital and, this time, I want a proper statement. When you've done that, get yourself straight back here. No stops, no fights, and no excuses."

"What about you? I thought you were meant to be holding my leash."

"Me? I'm going to be writing your speech, bailing you out when I should be catching killers. If there's any sense in that, let me know, because I'm buggered if I can see it."

"Hey, make sure it's a good one."

"You know, Joey, sometimes I wonder why I bother with you, or how you manage to wriggle out of tight spots with Mather, but then you come up with a cracker and it reminds me that inside that screwed-up mind of yours, there's a good detective just fighting to get out."

"A cracker?"

"Launching Popeye and Jaimsey from the top. I like it. It's worth further investigation. As you say, pretty obvious when you think about it. I'll check with the lab and set the boys onto it while you go and visit at the hospital." He patted McNeil's shoulder, the closest he'd get to showing real affection. "Hang in there, Joey."

McNeil smiled wearily. "I'm hanging, Dennis."

They parted ways on the first floor. McNeil ducked his head and avoided conversation on the way down to the squad room, which wasn't difficult, as most people chose to give him a wide berth. The threat of guilt by association was a sure-fire way of sorting the men from the boys, the runners from the also-rans. So far, only Dennis had stood up to the plate, albeit reluctantly. Nevertheless, he caught a few curious glances, which proved that the grape vine was thriving and his bollocking by Mather was common knowledge. No doubt they were all wondering how he'd kept his job. He wondered about that, too. He'd expected a suspension at the very least; was hoping for it, if truth be told. Perhaps Mather was just letting out a little more rope in the hopes he would trip over it. The way he was feeling, he had no qualms about slipping his head in the noose.

He ducked into the men's room, splashed water on his face, and slaked his thirst. Glancing at the mirror above the basin, he understood why colleagues were avoiding him. His face was grey with fatigue. His eye, no longer swollen, had settled to an interesting palette, which bizarrely would have complemented his non-designer stubble if he'd been trying for the zombie look. But at least the bleeding had stopped, and, in McNeil's confused reality, that was something to be thankful for. He just didn't have the energy left to wonder about it.

The office was almost empty and he managed to reach his desk without incident or further interrogation. Most of the team was out chasing up leads and taking statements. It was what he should be doing, what he'd promised Dennis he would do when he'd played his repentant card outside Mather's office.

He was sorry that he'd caused trouble for Dennis – that bit was true – but the part where he'd promised to concentrate on the job and forget about Kit was a lie, and Dennis had known it. All the same, he'd given him the benefit of the doubt and accepted his excuse that he needed to spruce up a little before he attempted round two with Nell. The fact that it was actually round three, and he was dreading it, was neither here nor there.

Whether he was willing to admit it or not, he was obsessed by two young women, Kit and Nell, neither of whom were dead, and, while he'd been banging heads trying to prove it, the rest of the team had been busy doing the day job, knocking on doors, calling in favours, and collecting the evidence which was currently displayed on a six by eight whiteboard. A collection of crime scene photos took centre stage. McNeil wasn't sure which was more disturbing, the apocalyptic devastation beneath the viaduct or the view from the parapet looking down. All sense of perspective had been distorted by the angle of the lens, and the closer he looked at it, the more intense the illusion became.

The bottomless pit, pushing him over, pulling him in.

He recalled Nell's words: *could she really have stepped out into the abyss and survived?* He almost believed it. Nothing about her made any sense. He let his eyes stray to the photos taken before he'd arrived at the scene, before it was realised that she was not a body, not a corpse, but a surviving victim.

The photos were ugly, disrespectful close-ups of bloodied and battered flesh. All the same, he was drawn to them with morbid fascination in the same way that he was drawn to her. He angled his head to see her more clearly. Hesitantly, he reached out to trace the outlines with his finger. "Who are you?" he murmured. He studied her face, pale, mud-splattered, and blood-stained. Dead – but not quite.

Was that how he would find Kit?

For the first time since her loss, since the day she had disappeared from his life, he experienced a gut-wrenching moment of doubt. It welled up inside, a thousand tormentors fighting to be heard, chiding him, baiting him and sneering at his impotence.

Was he too late?

As he stared, his focus blurred and the image distorted. The track marks on her arms became isolated stations on an underground map of indigo veins, the slight wounds on her neck now vicious tears in smooth alabaster flesh. Blood pulsed from every wound, as if a beast had gorged upon her. The horror stunned him. He shook his head, squinting in an attempt to clear his vision, but, just as in the tattoo shop, the images played with his mind and mocked at his uncertainty, until it was no longer Nell who lay stretched out, broken and discarded in the mud, but his beloved Kit. Her outstretched hand beckoned him, the tattooed serpents leapt out from her wrist and twisted in his direction, tongues darting, eyes gleaming.

"Damn you," he hissed. "Damn you to hell, whoever you are."

He yanked his hand away, ripping the photo from the board as he staggered back. Colliding with a chair which clattered to the floor, he allowed the image to slip from his grasp. At the far end of the room, the few remaining occupants looked up from their computers and exchanged concerned looks.

Get a grip, he muttered, *get a fucking grip*. He stooped and picked up the photo. His palm burned and his chest tightened. Instead of re-attaching the image to the board, he slipped it into his breast pocket and sucked in a frantic breath.

Inhale, exhale.

He'd overstayed his welcome, the meds were wearing off, and anxiety was seeping back in. He needed to locate what he'd actually come for and get out, before Mather decided to wind in the rope and leave him to dangle just like Popeye and Jaimsey.

His computer access to Kit's file was blocked. He knew that already. He'd tried before. There was only one alternative, and that was to look at the paper files in storage. Armed with the crime reference numbers, he made his way to Records.

Charlotte, the civilian record keeper, looked up as he entered the room. She was young and attractive, and McNeil wasn't so messed up that he hadn't noticed. He just wasn't in the market.

"Hi, Joey. I haven't seen you in a while. You look a little rough. Are you okay?" Her voice was soft, her concern genuine. She reached out to comfort him as if he was recently bereaved, and he stepped away. She meant well, but he didn't want it, not from her. It was one thing keeping up a front with people who didn't care, but he knew how easy it would be to be felled by a kind word. And he couldn't afford to fall until he found Kit.

He dragged out a smile for her instead. "I'm fine, Charlotte, just had a rough couple of days."

"You're not kidding. You've got a hell of a shiner there. I've got nail varnish in exactly the same shade."

His lips twitched in genuine amusement. "They say purple is the new black." Maybe she wasn't aware of the stories about him that were circulating the station, or perhaps she didn't care.

Either way, he got the feeling that, like Dennis, she was a runner, and he was glad of it.

"What can I do for you, Joey?" she asked.

He didn't have clearance for the records he wanted, and, although Charlotte was an angel with more than a soft spot for him, she was also a stickler for procedure, more through fear of the consequences than any love for rules and regulations, and there was no way she'd accept his need to look at anything related to Kit.

"I need to look at the evidence collected from the Bedlam crime scene."

"Oh my goodness, that's a terrible case. I don't know how you boys cope with stuff like that. It'd give me nightmares."

McNeil nodded. He knew all about nightmares. "There are some sick individuals out there, that's for sure."

"I heard what you did." She gave him one of her smiles and he wondered if she really was as coy as she made out, or whether she was actually making a play and he was just too stupid to see it. "Lucky you turned up," she continued. "That poor girl! Can you imagine everyone thinking you're dead when really you're not?"

McNeil forced a return smile and swallowed the irony. "The sooner we get the man who did it, the sooner the girl can get her life back." He made a show of checking his watch, anxious to get a move on before Dennis realised he wasn't where he was meant to be.

"Sorry, Joey, I'm just about to lock up and nip out for a break. Can you come back in thirty minutes?"

"It'll only take me five minutes. Dennis is waiting."

Charlotte hesitated. "I'm not even sure we have that stuff down here. It should all be up in the incident room."

"Mather sent me down here. There's something missing, probably got mixed up. He's fit to burst an artery up there in his ivory tower." He leaned in a little closer, all the better to sugar-coat his white lies. "I told him how efficient you were, how you knew where everything was, that I'd be back before he could water his plants. I kind of need to keep in his good books."

"Well, I could go for coffee later ... You could join me."

"No, you go and have your break. I'll keep an eye on things here." He smiled, used a little of the charm that hadn't been out of the tin for so long, he wasn't even sure it still worked.

"I'm not supposed to leave the office unmanned. You know that." She was wavering and he squeezed a little harder.

"It won't be. I'll be here. I'll close the door behind me and no one will be any the wiser. It'll be our little secret."

"I'd still need to check you into the log."

"Okay, let's do that now, and then you can shoot off for that coffee." He reeled off the Bedlam crime number and signed his name alongside the entry she made in the log.

"Is there anything else I can do for you?" she asked "Anything at all?" She sounded hopeful, and he didn't want to be responsible for raising or dashing her hopes.

"No, Charlotte, that's fine. I'll let DCI Mather know how helpful you've been."

***

If the thickness of the file was an indicator of the lengths to which the investigating team had gone, then Kit's file didn't say much about the effort expended to find her. McNeil shook his head in dismay. It seemed he was the only one who had taken her disappearance seriously. He flicked through it quickly, scanning the various statements. He slowed when he came to the one provided by John Bales, the man who had failed to show up to their pre-arranged meeting. He wanted to know why, and, to find out, he needed the man's address.

He pulled out the statement. Attached to it by a paperclip was a photo of Bales. McNeil paused. It wasn't a holiday snap. It was the standard photo taken by a booking officer. Bales looked shifty, and, as was now obvious, Bales also had a record. Perhaps even more pertinent, McNeil had seen the man quite recently. Well, to be precise, a black and white image of the man, on the front page of the 'Herald'. He was one of the two men who had hauled him out of Minkey's. If Bales had been in the bar all night, why hadn't he made his presence known? McNeil checked his watch. He didn't have time to check the computer for Bales' past history. Charlotte would be back soon.

He crossed to the door, cracked it open and checked that the corridor outside was still empty. While he waited for the photocopier to do its stuff with Bales' statement, McNeil turned to the rest of Kit's file, and he was drawn reluctantly to the statement provided by Kit's father, the Reverend George Robinson Foulkes. The Reverend had strongly disapproved of his daughter's relationship. McNeil had always known it, despite Kit's protestations to the contrary. The statement removed any lingering doubt. Having already lost one daughter tragically in childhood, Foulks believed his remaining daughter had wasted her life, and ultimately lost her life, because of him. Although it fell short of actually accusing him of being party to her disappearance, the implication was there. To Reverend Foulkes, there had only been one person responsible for the loss of his daughter. McNeil's gut twisted.

Perhaps the Reverend wasn't so far off the mark.

Nineteen

He felt calmer once he'd escaped the confines of the station. Perhaps the snow was helping. All that white, pure stuff, covering up the mess beneath. It wouldn't do much for the crime scene, although by now, all the evidence that was needed had been collected or photographed, and all that remained was tattered police tape flapping in the breeze.

McNeil parked at the far end of the viaduct and stepped over the tape. Some genius on the council had come up with the idea of designating the disused monolith as a nature trail, one of those meandering footpaths from somewhere to nowhere. Trouble was, nature had taken exception to the decision and clawed its way back. The track was overgrown. Beneath the snow lay rusted metal and broken glass. The wind blew straight at him from across the valley, harsh and unrelenting. There was a decent view if you looked straight ahead. Looking down wasn't recommended, unless you had a head for heights and were considered mentally sound.

As McNeil had struck out on both counts, he viewed from a distance, assessing the spot where Nell, according to her account, had stepped out. The forensics had shown no evidence of her ever being there, no fibres, footprints, or DNA, and it seemed ridiculous in the extreme that she could have survived such a fall. Nevertheless, he focused on the iron railing where he imagined she had stood, toes over the edge, arms spread wide.

He could see her.

Pale flesh illuminated by moonlight, hair swept to one side by the breeze, head tipped gently as if enjoying a caress. He exhaled slowly, afraid to shatter the illusion, aware of the tension in her muscles as she attempted to retain her pose. He reluctantly stepped closer, treading carefully, each step in the virgin snow drawing him closer to the edge. And then he was next to her. Not daring to look or to touch, he felt her presence in the same way he felt Kit, living, breathing, a mere hair's breadth away. He laid his hands on the rail, felt the snow melt beneath his fingers and peered down.

Below, there was nothing but space, a terrible void filled with tunnelling snow drawing him down to Bedlam's open maw. He gripped the railing tightly, fearful that he might succumb to the lure and take that step himself. There was a strange finality about the place, as if it were the end of something and the beginning was elsewhere, with a leap of faith required to connect the two. He glanced at the iron strut to his right, where her hand should be gripping tightly, yet, instead, she balanced like a gymnast on the high beam, arms outstretched. His eyes were inexplicably drawn upwards, tempted by her nearness and her need. Naked flesh. Violet eyes. Silver knife ... and then nothing but swirling snow and the imaginings of a worn out mind.

Had she really jumped? He doubted it, but he knew others had in the past, and the air was thick with memory and regret. He felt it all around him, closing in, wrapping him up in a blanket of freezing fog. He exhaled and watched as his breath swirled for a moment before dissipating in the frigid atmosphere.

He reached for the strut, closed his hand firmly around the icy metal, and hauled himself up, standing where she had stood, wavering as she had done, resisting the urge to step further. He took an icy breath and looked down, not at what lay two hundred feet below him – he avoided that determinedly. The lure was great, and he lacked the willpower necessary to resist. Instead, he focused on the ledge beneath the walkway and the rusted beams where the ropes had been fastened. Two one-hundred-and-eighty-foot coils of nylon cable now lay in the evidence room at the station, while suppliers were contacted and purchasers were identified and crossed off the list. McNeil knew from the crime scene photos exactly where the rope had been knotted, where the killer had crouched as he'd secured one end of the macabre puppetry. He leaned out further as he angled for a better look. There was no snow on the ledge, protected as it was from the biting wind by a skirt of Victorian embellishment. Closing his eyes briefly, he tried to re-visualise

Nell's image, her pale hand outstretched, the silver knife held between frozen fingers.

There was blood on the blade. One solitary red bead hung from the tip. McNeil watched, mesmerised, as it released its tenuous hold and dropped through frozen air. He held his breath, scared that the slightest exhalation would disturb the image and subvert its natural course. As the blood splashed soundlessly against the frozen metal, the knife followed, bouncing against the iron work, falling to rest in a niche created between two grotesque iron gargoyles. The creatures curled their hideous lips at him.

He felt Nell's smile against his cheek. Not a caress, but a jibe, as she taunted him onwards.

He ignored the drop and the panic which was building exponentially, and lowered himself over the railing. He crouched, knees bent, one hand gripping tightly to one of the many horizontal tension rods that laced the substructure. The rusted metal bit into his skin, and he absorbed the pain, sucking desperate breaths through gritted teeth, willing his heart to slow down. His fear wasn't of falling, but of letting go. He tightened his hold. When he was steady, he reached out further, twisting his body out over the void, fumbling blindly amongst a hundred years or more of bird shit and debris. As his hand finally closed around the smooth blade, he let out the breath he'd been holding, and relief flooded through him.

He hauled himself back. Adrenalin alone carried him over the railing and deposited him in a heap in the snow. He forced his clenched hand to relax, to give up its treasure, and, when his fingers unfurled, the blade lay sharp and gleaming. A trace of fresh blood etched a fine line across his palm. He raised his hand and sucked the wound clean.

He couldn't explain it, didn't even try, but knew that he was one step closer to working it out.

The snow intensified until it was difficult to see the ends of the viaduct. He narrowed his eyes, squinting against the visual disturbance, and, as he turned his gaze toward where he had left his car, he saw someone standing there, watching him.

Holding the knife carefully between finger and thumb, he pulled himself up, uncertain whether it was a figure or merely a trick of the light, a shadow caused by refracting snow and beleaguered sunlight, or someone with an interest in what he was doing. His first instinct to approach was tempered by hesitation, unsure if his mind was simply summoning more ghosts to haunt him.

"Kit?" he whispered.

She was there, waiting for him, head bent against the driving snow. He saw her clearly. Not in his mind's eye, but out there, in the here and now, dusted with snow. One hand on the car, the other raised, outstretched, as she beckoned him. He heard her call to him, not the whispered breaths in his head that he'd learned to live with, but clear and strong, as if she stood alongside him, and, when she lifted her head, the smile she sent his way was sweet and beautiful and real.

His heart lurched and he began to run. Slipping and stumbling in the fresh snow, his co-ordination, his balance all awry. He dragged in a desperate lungful of cold air barbed with icy shards, and tried to shout, to call her name again to ensure there was no mistake, that she knew he had seen her, that she was safe, but the words froze in his throat. She lifted her face to the snow, a curtain of frosted hair slipping stiffly to reveal her face once more. Despite the distance, he could see her features clearly, too clearly. Translucent skin dusted white with snow, lips blue with the cold. The microscopic detail jarred his consciousness, acerbically searing his sweet remembered image. He closed his eyes briefly to reset the picture, recklessly ignoring the doubt that mingled with reason and diluted hope. He didn't care: she was back and that was all his mind could register.

When he reopened his eyes, the space she had occupied was empty. The voice, no longer sweet, crowded his head, mocking him with soft laughter as it wrapped around him, tangling his thoughts, infusing him with despair. He dropped to his knees, anger and frustration warring with his own weakness.

"What do you want?" he yelled into the emptiness. "What are you trying to tell me?"

There was no answer, no noise but for the disorientating acoustics. The wind squealed at him, an impudent child chasing between the iron struts and railings, throwing snow around as it taunted him.

He rose unsteadily and dusted the snow from his clothes with shaking hands. Ghosts and ghouls. Mather was right. He needed a drink, something to set him up for round three with Nell. He settled reluctantly for another one of the good doctor's pills.

Grateful to be out of the biting wind, he slid into the car and popped open the glove compartment, rifling blindly amongst the mess until he pulled out an evidence bag. He dropped in the blade and sealed it up. His own prints could easily be eliminated, and, if he were lucky, there might be traces left on the smooth surface for forensics to play with. It would gain him some badly needed brownie points, though he wondered how he'd explain to Dennis how he'd known where the knife would be.

He started the engine, and the car puttered and stalled before flickering half-heartedly back to life. Desperate now to be away from this place of dislocated memories, he slammed a hand on the steering wheel with frustration. The engine whined, the tyres slid, and the car fishtailed before gaining purchase. Outside, on the passenger door, etched carefully within a thin coating of drifted snow, one word stood out alone and unread.

JoJo x.

Twenty

It's a fact I've pondered often, this need for man to win the game, to be the victor in all things. Jacob is no different in this respect, though he would baulk at the idea of being categorised with the pack. He considers that he is a breed apart, superior in all things. It seems, however, that he has met a worthy opponent in Joe McNeil. His performance today proves that with certainty. He has overcome the immediate challenge in perhaps unorthodox fashion, and I await Jacob's response with trepidation and a certain relish.

It will be swift and it will be bloody.

His first move is subtle, as he dons his many guises and beguiles the staff. When I wake, he is at my bedside. He fills the room with his presence, sucking out the oxygen and replacing it with pure evil. I slow my breathing. I can outlast this party trick.

"Dearest Nell." His voice strokes my skin and I armour myself discreetly. "What shall I do with you, my dear?"

He prowls the room in idle retrospection, trailing his hand across cold tile and colder glass, sampling the starched sheets between finger and thumb, but it is simply a ruse. While he casts a disinterested gaze to the bland furnishings and limited technology, his mind is working, calculating, processing, and, when finally he pulls up a chair and sits, I know that already his retribution is decided.

"Is this how you show your gratitude?" he asks.

I hold my tongue, avert my gaze, and avoid the confrontation for as long as is reasonable. I cannot afford to let fear overpower me. And I do fear him, as only one who has similarly suffered could know.

He laughs, that low rumble that only I can hear, and I realise now that he intends something heinous. I can only guess at his intention.

"Where is your protector, Nell, your knight who will vanquish the beast on your behalf? I do not see him." He leans forward, clasps long tapered fingers together and taps them thoughtfully on his chin. "I fear you may yet be betrayed. Your noble knight holds the colours of another. You have a rival for his affections, and he is fierce in her protection. It will take considerable pressure to corrupt his chosen course. And therein lies the problem, dear Nell. For, as you know, my want is greater than yours, and I must have him ... at any cost."

I lift my head and meet his eye. He is a vessel filled with hate, and it takes all my considerable willpower to hold his gaze.

"Have you eaten, my dear?" he asks. "You look so pale."

He reaches across and grasps my chin so hard that my lip is crushed against my teeth and I taste blood on my tongue. My eyes roll back in my head. I stifle a moan.

He smirks. "There, there, my dear. Fear not, Jacob is here." He loosens his iron grip, angling my face this way and that as he studies my composure and seeks to undo it. I long to wrench myself from his grasp, but, as his hold softens, my body betrays me and I lean into his caress.

"I will not listen," I hiss, but my feeble words merely fuel his assault and he trails his fingers softly across my skin, down my neck, lingering in the shallow depression of my collar bone and the valley of my breasts. When I struggle to suppress my gasp at his touch, he follows a trail to my wrist and the serpents welcome him. He tightens his grip until white hot pain shoots up my arm and the serpents sink their fangs into my flesh.

"You believe you are strong, but you are not. You believe you are clever, and I grant you that. You are devious and growing more cunning by the day, but you will never outwit me. No one can."

"Joe McNeil is like no other. He will see through your tricks and false words."

"Is that a challenge? Do you offer him up freely?"

"He is not mine to offer."

"Not yet. But you wish it so, do you not? Do you savour his scent and long for his touch? Do you lust after him in place of me?"

I pull back my hand, but only because he allows it. His gaze travels my thinly clothed body. He could remove my gown in an instant. He could have me remove it just as easily. He could in fact do anything he chooses, and, through necessity and self-preservation, I would agree, but instead, he merely smiles indulgently, and my belly churns with even greater dread. I know that smile. It is the precursor to another game.

"I have done everything you asked," I reply mutinously, and indeed I have already bowed to his demands numerous times. In my head, I excuse my actions, but somewhere deep inside there is a small secret place where I covet remorse and regret. I am reprehensible, a stain on humanity, yet he is the grand director of this elaborate spectacle and must ultimately take the bow ... or the fall.

"*Everything?* I think not, Nell. There is still work to be done. Do not imagine that I will forgo the prize I seek."

"You are wrong. He is not who you believe him to be."

He puffs himself up indignantly. I risk his wrath by contradicting his order, his vision of how things will resolve. I must temper my rebellion lest I provoke him beyond control.

"No, Nell. You are the one who does not understand. You have confused the hunted with the hunter. He is prey and cannot save you, no matter how much you may desire it."

Joe McNeil is the only one who can save me. I know it, and Jacob knows it, which is exactly why he poses such a threat, and why Jacob seeks to discredit my hope.

"You have chosen a protector with many flaws, dear Nell. I fear that he will be easy to subvert. He has weaknesses, addictions. Why, even now, he leans upon countless crutches to see him through the day. He is obsessed with one lost girl. Do you imagine he has room in his life for two?"

"I did not choose him," I mutter.

"Then who do you think sent him to you?"

I stay silent as his smile taunts me.

"Do as I ask and I will uphold my end of our bargain. Fail me, and there will be dire consequences."

He reaches into his jacket and pulls out a scalpel. It glints as he plays it between his fingers, back and forth, as if he were practising some elaborate piano exercise.

"Very well," he says finally. "I am ready for the next step. Are you?"

Twenty-One

There was a mini battalion of journalists and press photographers encamped around the hospital entrance when McNeil arrived. They hadn't been present when he'd left the previous day, and he wondered what had happened overnight to yank their chain. He hoped it was coincidence and unconnected to his fall from grace.

His hopes were quickly dashed when they zeroed in on him with fervour akin to wolves scenting fresh blood. Mindful of his warning from Mather, he raised a hand to block any photos and doggedly pushed his way through the throng.

"Detective McNeil, would you care to comment on the latest developments?"

Latest developments? He ducked his head and kept going, increasingly aware that the doctor's little helpers were busily doing their thing, and, as a result, he might well say something he shouldn't. His head buzzed in a good way and, although he now felt able to take on the world, a little voice in his head cautioned against it. It wasn't Kit, and it wasn't Nell. His head was so crowded now, he'd given up trying to make sense of it.

"How do you feel, knowing you saved a monster?"

McNeil turned and the photographer caught the look of confusion on his face, a perfect portrait shot that would no doubt grace the morning dailies. If the lens were powerful enough, it might also have caught the dilated pupils and the slight flush rising beneath the grey pallor. McNeil blinked against the flash and stumbled backwards, his fall prevented by yet another photographer whose camera slipped from his grasp and clattered to the ground.

"Shit, did you see that? Bloody copper pushed me," shouted the man, and several others leapt in to capture the event for posterity, clicking wildly, jostling for position.

McNeil cursed. Whatever he said or did was going to be misconstrued and misreported. It seemed the freedom of the press allowed for a certain licence where the truth was concerned. He extricated himself and swung around to face his accuser, fists clenched, muscles bunched. He could feel his heart rate climbing, hear the blood pulsing loudly in his ears, but when he recognised eager expectation on the man's face, he hauled himself back and raised his hands in apology instead.

"I have no comment to make," he said carefully, enunciating every word. "If you require information on any case, then I suggest you contact the press office."

He pushed forward, reaching the sanctuary of the lobby as a woman's voice called after him.

"Don't you want to give us your side of the story, detective? The public has a right to know if the police department isn't doing its job."

He paused at the revolving door, missing his opportunity to step forward into the next vacant rotation. Glancing back, he spotted Clarissa Temple standing to one side of the pack. He knew why Mather kept her at arm's length. She was a Thatcheresque clone, a strong, ballsy woman who went for the throat and wouldn't let go. She had history with Mather, and McNeil wasn't sure what the guv had done to warrant such single-minded determination, but the woman was out to ruin him by whatever means possible. McNeil knew he was merely cannon fodder in a battle that had raged between them both for years, but it didn't lessen the immediate threat.

Clarissa eyed him now, assessing, calculating her strategy, choosing her weapons, and McNeil ignored the obvious risk and smiled. She cocked her head, puzzled, interested, obviously expecting him to rise to her bait, and he had, just not in the way she had expected. Clarissa and her poison pen could keep, but if the department wasn't prepared to take him seriously about Kit's disappearance, then McNeil wasn't averse to colluding with the enemy. In fact, any enemy of Mather's might well prove to be a friend to him.

He raised a single brow in covert acceptance and she dipped her head in reply, taking advantage of a surge within the pack to thrust a business card in his hand. He closed his fingers around it, the sharp edges digging into the fresh cut left by the blade.

His palm tingled and his attention was immediately drawn back to Nell. What had happened to create such a furore?

He took the stairs as an alternative to the lift. The possibility of finding himself locked in a small space with an insistent reporter or an overbearing nurse had him sweating. He couldn't guarantee his own behaviour anymore, and it scared him.

The stairwell, by comparison, was spacious, cool, and empty. There was a lingering, clinical smell that teased his nostrils in a bad way, like a sneeze that wouldn't come or a memory that remained just out of reach. It taunted him. He stood a moment with one hand on the banister, gathered his wits, calmed his nerves, and allowed his eyes to drift shut. He called silently for Kit, and was rewarded by her soft laughter and warm breath against his cheek. He re-opened them reluctantly, more than happy to linger in her company a while longer and delay his return to the real world.

The real world had other ideas.

Instead of taking his first step up toward the third floor, McNeil's attention was inexplicably drawn down to the double doors leading to the basement. Lights flickered beyond the twin porthole windows, and he narrowed his eyes in confusion as the doors swung slowly open to reveal the corridor beyond.

The smell hit him first, and he reeled back as ammonia, disinfectant, and decay caught the back of his throat. He retched reflexively. Then came the noise, rhythmic pounding that grew louder by the second, angry fists on a locked door, heavy boots on a wooden floor, desperate heads on unrelenting walls. The sound swelled like water trapped beneath the ground, systematically testing the limits of its captivity, seeking an escape. The corridor was green with algae, chipped tiles camouflaged as nature sought to reclaim them. Weeds forced their way through cracks in the floor, spreading out, virus-like, shoots becoming trees before his very eyes, until the chaos threatened to erupt from within and breech the safety of the stairwell.

A small boy crept out from the darkness and stood in the doorway, watching him. Ivy crept silently up one leg. Green mould stained his T-shirt. One hand was clamped so firmly over his mouth that his cheeks were pinched, the other hung awkwardly by his side, the small wrist swollen, fingers bent out of shape.

McNeil flexed his own scarred knuckles, tightening his grip on the metal handrail as fear and horror combined in his gut. He stumbled back, caught the stair behind with his heel, and sat down with a sudden bump. He jammed his eyes shut, dropped his head between his knees, and drew a desperate breath. *Get a grip!* He wanted to shout it out loud, but the words were stillborn.

When he opened his eyes, the doors were closed, silence cloaked the stairwell, and the boy had gone.

By the time he got to the ward, he knew by the extra police presence that something serious had occurred, and he guessed that whatever it was would be coming back to bite him. He couldn't afford to let his guard down, to reveal his vulnerability. His heart raced, his chest was tight. He was ready to crack, could feel it building, and only the fuzziness in his head was preventing it. It cushioned the impact, smoothing out the rough edges and sharp corners of his nightmare. *Inhale, exhale.* He practised it as he walked.

Dennis was waiting outside Nell's room. Scene of Crime officers were already in situ. Yellow and black tape zigzagged the corridor. McNeil's chest tightened another notch. He wondered if it was possible to die of acute anxiety and paranoia, and whether it would be such a bad thing if he did. He felt a cool palm against his chest, slowing his heart rate, focusing his mind. The fact that it was Nell, not Kit, stopped him in his tracks. He'd made a terrible mistake. He shouldn't have left her.

"Where the hell have you been?"

McNeil swallowed and took a few seconds to compose himself. "Nowhere. I came straight down here, just like you said."

"Via the pub?"

"Give credit where it's due, Dennis. I'm on doctor's orders. I haven't touched a drop since Friday."

"Really?" Dennis studied him a little closer and McNeil shifted uncomfortably.

"Yes, really."

"So where have you been?"

"I had stuff to do."

"*Stuff?* I gave you strict instructions to get straight down here. Where the bloody hell have you been for the last six hours?"

Six hours? McNeil faltered. He'd spent no more than thirty minutes at the station, and he'd come straight to the hospital from the viaduct. He hadn't spent five hours up there, he knew he hadn't. His mind fogged with confusion.

"Why, what's happened?" he asked. He caught the sly look on Mary Cameron's face as she pushed past in her white cover-all, camera in hand, and braced himself for the reply.

"We've lost the witness."

"Dead?"

"Missing."

McNeil exhaled. "You mean, discharged? Checked out?"

"No. She was assessed by psychiatry after exhibiting behaviours overnight that suggested self-harm. She was about to be moved to a secure unit when she attacked an orderly. She used a scalpel. Slit his throat. Left him for dead." Dennis gave McNeil a sidelong glance. "Looks like we had our killer all along."

"When did all this happen?"

"Four hours ago. Who knows, you might have been able to prevent it if you'd actually done as you were told and got here on time."

"Or I might have got my own throat slit. That would have solved a few problems for you."

"Don't think I didn't consider that already."

McNeil crossed to the viewing window and watched as the SOCOs did their work. Apart from the arterial spray that peppered the white walls and bed, the room seemed disturbingly unaffected by the event. What little furniture there was remained exactly where McNeil remembered. There was no sign of a struggle.

"Where's the victim?"

"ICU. He was in here maybe ten minutes. When the rest of the staff arrived, this is what they found." Dennis gestured with a broad hand.

"And the girl?"

"Long gone."

"And we're sure it was her?"

"What do you mean?"

McNeil frowned. "This doesn't feel right, any of it. Why would she attack him? Where'd she get the weapon?"

"You said yourself she was crazy. We have the victim and the weapon she used against him. There's no mistake. She's out there and she's dangerous."

"*Out there*? You think she left the hospital?"

"It's possible, but if she has, she won't get far. Unless she lifted something as she ran, all she has on is a hospital gown. I expect you noticed it's snowing out there. We're checking the CCTV. We haven't spotted her yet."

"Are you seriously expecting me to believe that she could overpower anyone? You recall how small she is, how beat-up she was. What's the victim saying?"

"Not a lot. Like I said, he's in ICU."

"So, basically, circumstantial evidence?"

Dennis stepped close. "For the moment, yes. But that's what we're rolling with. We're two, possibly three, bodies down now, and she's the prime suspect."

McNeil shook his head incredulously. "Has anybody considered that Nell might have been the intended victim here, taken by the guy who attacked her in the first place? This looks more like Jacob's handiwork. Think about it. He comes to get her and the orderly gets in his way." He gestured with an open hand to the blood-spattered room. "This doesn't make sense. Nell was scared, crazy maybe, spooky definitely, but essentially scared, scared that the man who attacked her was going to come back and finish the job."

"There was an officer at the nurse's station. Nobody came in here other than doctors and nurses."

"Yeah? So where was he when all this happened?"

"Someone got stuck in the lift. He went to offer assistance." Dennis grimaced. "I know ... you don't need to say it."

McNeil inhaled slowly. He couldn't work it out in his head. The chemical buzz that had seemed so fine when he'd arrived and held him together earlier was now slowing his thought process, winding him down, readying his body for desperately needed sleep. He tried to concentrate. The room was covered in someone's blood, there was no denying that.

"Okay," he relented, "maybe she lashed out in self-defence, misread the situation, mistook the orderly for someone else, I don't know – but a killer? There's no way she could have manhandled two men twice her size over the parapet. I've just been up there. I would have had trouble doing it."

"You've been up there?"

"Yes, I just told you."

"Why?"

"Why? Because it's a crime scene and I'm working the case, and I needed to know whether my theory held water. Fuck, Dennis, why shouldn't I be up there? It's my bloody job. I thought you'd be pleased I was being so conscientious for a change."

"I told you to get straight down here and get a statement from a witness, a statement you failed to get previously because you were either drunk or hung-over or bloody stupid. What I didn't do is tell you to go do your own thing. We work as a team, Joey. Do you understand what that means?"

McNeil scowled. A surge of heat shot through him. He reached out and placed a steadying hand against the wall. *Had the doctor said one or two capsules twice a day?* He couldn't remember. His throat was dry and he cast about, trying to locate the hallway water fountain.

"What's wrong with you now?" Dennis narrowed his eyes and McNeil ducked his own.

"Nothing is wrong with me. Did you forget I have ten stitches in the back of my head? Sorry if that makes me act a little stupid, Dennis. I'm meant to be on sick leave, remember?"

"All the more reason to bugger off home out of my sight. Go home, Joey."

"But ..."

"But nothing. You just can't help messing up, and I can't take the risk of carrying you anymore. Christ, look at you. You actually look worse than you did this morning, if that's possible. I asked you to do one thing. I asked you to get down here and take a statement. One bloody thing and you couldn't do it. Could you?"

"I'm here, aren't I?"

"Yeah, too bloody late. Were you listening this morning when Mather made me responsible for all your crap? Was that just a line you were spinning when you said you'd get your act together? I don't know you anymore, Joey. Go home and stay home. Maybe I can salvage something from this mess, but don't bank on it. I'll call you later when I've had a chance to speak to Mather."

McNeil shook his head. "You're wrong about me, Dennis."

"I hope I am, I really do, but you don't help yourself, and you certainly don't help *me*. You should have been here, Joey. If you had been, maybe we wouldn't be looking at another crime scene."

McNeil shrugged. "Fine, I'll go, but you're making a mistake, Dennis. Don't say I didn't warn you."

"Warn me? What the bloody hell does that mean?"

"It means whatever you want it to mean." He stepped away, anxious to put some space between them before he dealt a fatal blow to their friendship. He turned back when he remembered the evidence bag in his pocket. His hand tightened around the plastic and he hesitated. Would he be compounding Nell's guilt by handing it over? And what did it matter if he did? It was his job, after all. All the same, he felt reluctance deep inside. She was guilty of something, he just didn't know what, and hanging onto evidence, no matter how it was obtained, was wrong.

"Hey, Dennis, about that team work you were talking about – catch!"

Dennis fumbled the catch, and the blade clattered to the floor in its protective sleeve. He stooped and picked it up between finger and thumb.

"What's this?"

"The murder weapon, just in case you decide to fall back on real evidence."

"Whoa ..." Dennis reached out and caught McNeil's sleeve. "Where did you get this?"

"The viaduct, when I was up there doing my own thing."

"SOCOs went all over there."

McNeil's lip curled slyly. He couldn't resist it. Mary Cameron was heading for a fall. "Yeah, well, they missed it."

"Where'd you find it?"

"On a ledge under the parapet, not far from where the ropes were tied."

"You climbed down there?"

"I suppose I must have," McNeil replied vaguely. He wasn't totally sure how he'd overcome his fear of heights and got down there on his own. It was all a bit hazy, now he had time to think about it.

"And you didn't think to call it in, get it lifted in accordance with procedure? You know procedure ... that thing you're meant to follow so when we get a case to court it doesn't blow up in our face."

McNeil pulled out of Dennis' grip and took a step back. "Get someone to check the crime scene photos. The blade was there all along. Don't blame me if someone wasn't doing their job." He turned and headed back down the corridor. If Dennis wanted him gone, that was fine.

"Joey ..."

"What?"

"How did you know it was there?"

McNeil threw a bitter smile over his shoulder.

"Intuition."

Twenty-Two

When he got to the flat, a delivery van was nosed into his parking spot, its tailgate halfway across the centre line. He leaned on the steering wheel and rested his chin on his forearm, watching wearily as the rhythmic flash of the hazard lights held up the traffic in the narrow street.

"Come on, get a move on," he muttered. His eyelids drooped. Five more minutes and he'd be crashed out on his bed, and the rest of the world could go to hell.

The men were manhandling a mattress, taking their time, messing about as they struggled between parked cars and bags left out for the refuse lorry. McNeil's patience was already frayed by fatigue when someone pulled up behind him and leaned on the horn.

He started counting, just like Minkey had advised, but when he got to ten and the van hadn't moved and the guy was still beeping, he turned around, ready to suggest politely that he might like to shut the fuck up.

The words got stuck somewhere between his mouth and the pit of his stomach.

Curled up on the back seat, barely visible beneath his discarded overcoat, was Nell. Violet eyes stared straight at him.

"I told you not to leave me," she scolded softly.

"And I told you I was done with your mind games, done with you."

"You'll never be done with me. That's not how it works."

McNeil tried to swallow. His throat was parched, his chest tight. Sudden perspiration pricked his brow. He closed his eyes briefly. He wanted everything and everyone to go away and leave him alone – all the crap, the mistakes, and the unanswered questions. He wanted to rewind twelve months and start again with Kit, as if nothing had happened. He wondered what he'd done in his life that was so bad that he deserved so much heartache.

The guy behind drew him back reluctantly with his manic tooting, and, on glancing to the front, he realised the idiots with the mattress had finished their delivery and the van had moved off. He swung into the parking space, switched off the engine, and sat for a moment with his hands on the wheel, inhaling slowly, discreetly. *Get a grip*, he chanted silently, but it did little to settle his unease.

Lifting his gaze, he watched Nell through the rear-view mirror. It seemed safer, somehow, to view her indirectly. Unlike the mythical Medusa, he didn't fear being turned to stone; his fear involved something far more primal.

"There's an arrest warrant out for you. I should call it in."

"But you won't."

"What makes you so sure?"

She gave the slightest of shrugs in response.

"Why shouldn't I call it in?" he pressed.

"It would be unwise."

"Is that a threat?"

"A warning."

"For whom?"

"For both of us."

"Explain ..."

She wriggled her arms into his coat and pulled it tightly around her thin frame. It wrapped around her twice. "Not here."

McNeil checked the street. Now the commotion with the delivery was over, the road was quiet. Evening was settling in. The street lights punctuated the darkness with a hazy glow.

Snow deadened the ancillary sounds and shrunk the world to the confines of the car. There were no passers-by to observe his actions, or stop and stare in wonder and horror as he escorted a blood-covered girl into his flat. But, if he took her in, he'd have taken a step toward a line he wasn't quite ready to cross.

"I'm a police officer. I'm bound by the law. I have to do what's right. I don't have a choice."

He pulled out his phone, found Dennis' number, and paused. She watched him, unblinking, waiting, and, as she did, his need to know the truth caused his resolve to waver.

"You always have a choice," she continued softly. "It's entirely up to you whether you make the right one. I can only guide you."

The whispered voices in his head urged him and cautioned him, in equal measure, until he felt like a rope stretched taut in a tug of war. He had no idea which team would win or whether he'd be torn apart in the process of the game. As far as Dennis was concerned, he was a write-off. As far as Kit was concerned, he was a failure. He supposed there was nothing further left to lose.

"Okay," he said finally. "Five minutes. You get five minutes to tell me what's going on, and, if it's a pile of crap, I'll take you in myself."

She inclined her head in agreement, exhaled softly, and relief filled the confines of the car like a heady perfume.

He checked the street both ways as he held the car door open for her, and, when satisfied that there were no witnesses, he ushered her across the pavement and up the path. Her feet were bare. She left small impressions in the snow and his eyes were inexplicably drawn to the tracks.

Something shifted in his mind.

Something dark.

A small boy stood at the gate, one hand on the post, one foot raised and tucked behind the other, one shoe dangling from his clenched fist. The laces entwined tightly between grubby fingers. He had no coat despite the snow. His cheeks were stained with tears, his T-shirt stained with blood. The shoe swung gently back and forth, hitting the post with a rhythmic thud.

McNeil stared at him, as solemn grey eyes stared back, and then the child's gaze shifted and McNeil was once again aware of Nell at his side. She smiled, reached out her hand, and McNeil stepped away, uncertain. When he looked back at the gate, the boy had gone. Virgin snow remained.

He ushered her up the communal stairs, a hand almost, but not quite, at the small of her back, reluctant to touch her, fearful of his own reaction. His heart thudded wildly. Wary anticipation at what was to come quickened his step. He fumbled his keys, and, when they slipped from his fingers and fell to the floor, she crouched and retrieved them.

"Thanks," he said stiffly, as she dropped them into his open palm.

He closed the door behind them and leaned back against it, watching as Nell stood in the centre of the room, turning slowly on the spot, pirouetting on the balls of her feet as her eyes flicked back and forth, cataloguing the mess of his life. Kit's clothes were still strewn about. The nightstand lay where he had abandoned it the day before, smashed and useless. He felt suddenly vulnerable, afraid that this external chaos revealed too much by mirroring the struggle going on in his head. He was losing control, and he knew it.

His overcoat slipped from her thin frame, and, without its protection, the blood staining her hospital gown was revealed. McNeil was shocked at the amount. He wondered how the owner had survived such a blood-letting, if indeed he would. And then he wondered if any of it was actually hers.

"Are you hurt?" he asked gently. This was not the time for a brutal interrogation, yet the urge to demand, rather than cajole, the truth out of her hovered close. He held it at bay with an unsteady hand.

"Not in the physical sense," she murmured. A shiver shook her entire body.

He watched it ripple like a live thing beneath her skin and exit with a shudder.

"Are you cold?" McNeil slipped out of his own jacket and draped it over the back of a chair. The flat was freezing, yet perspiration still clung to him, cold and unwelcome.

"Not especially," she replied.

"You look it."

"Appearances can be deceptive."

McNeil nodded. Wasn't that the truth? "Look, the heating is temperamental, the gas fire needs persuading, but the shower is hot. Go and clean up, and I'll make you something to eat. You look like you could do with it."

She raised a brow and stepped toward him, that funny little deliberate step that drew his eye and attention, one foot placed exactly in front of the other as if a fraction either way would pitch her into some bottomless pit. He thought of the crime scene, the slippery access boards, the endless mud ... and the look in her eyes when they first locked with his.

"I thought I only had five minutes," she said, drawing his attention back to her with a jolt.

"I won't start counting until you're done." In his head, all of a sudden, a child's voice breathless and high-pitched. 'Ready or not, here I come.' He flinched, felt his stomach helter-skelter to the floor, and reached out to steady himself.

"Promise," she breathed, stepping closer.

Avoiding the pit himself, he took a cautious step back and shook his head. "My promises don't count for much these days. I make them and break them."

She inclined her head as if she knew exactly what he meant, then, in one fluid movement, pulled the gown over her head, let it slip to a heap at her feet, and stood naked before him.

He stood for a long moment, his eyes locked with hers, fighting the urge to let his gaze wander. He had no interest in her, not in that way, and yet desire struggled up from the depths of his darker self. He ignored it and held her gaze determinedly.

"The bathroom is through there." He gestured vaguely, and still she stood, watching him, testing his resolve. He knew it and sought out Kit in his head, his defence, his voice of reason in an increasingly twisted world. But he was met by silence. His dismay at Kit's absence was tempered by relief that the additional voices were silent too. It was up to him now, but he was slowly going mad. He had to be. "I'll leave you to it," he said wearily, and turned and headed into the kitchen.

When he could hear running water, and was satisfied that she no longer posed a threat to his equilibrium, he pushed her gown into a plastic bag, a nod to Dennis and procedure, though allowing her to clean up definitely wasn't following protocol. He shrugged to himself. He didn't believe she'd killed anyone, no matter what Dennis thought. But that didn't mean she wasn't capable of it.

He heated some soup and laid a bowl out ready for her on the kitchen table. He couldn't stomach anything himself. He had an unwelcome sensation in the pit of his stomach, like he'd gone out and left the gas on and his whole world was about to explode. 'Butterflies' wasn't the correct description. It implied an eager anticipation, and there was nothing eager about the blackness that curled inside him. It was more than dread, and it was building exponentially. He dropped his head in his hands. He needed sleep more than anything, the chance to re-charge. Things would seem clearer in the morning. He ran his fingers through his hair, avoiding the stitches. He'd almost forgotten about his blackout. Maybe he should see his GP, or go back to the shrink, before the voices and images decided to step out of his head and take up residence in the real world.

He looked up when she padded into the room, at her hair loosely wrapped in a towel, her arms folded protectively across her chest. Her feet, as usual, were bare, as if that was their natural state. His heart jolted. His breath caught in his throat. It could have been Kit standing before him wrapped snugly in her dressing gown, a knowing look on her face, invitation in her eyes, a secret smile curving her lips.

"What are you doing in that?" he hissed when violet eyes regarded his with cruel amusement.

Nell ran one hand gently down the other arm, caressing the soft fleece. "You didn't want me naked."

"I don't want you in her clothes, either."

"Then what do you want, Joe? It seems to me you're undecided on a number of things." She slipped into the seat opposite him, tucked her feet up under her, and picked up her spoon, sampling the soup delicately, as if she was unused to the concept.

He watched distractedly as she ate, and tried to pull in all the fragmented thoughts that were swirling in his head. What did he want? *Focus*, he murmured silently. He wanted to know who Nell was, what she was, and how she was connected to Jacob. He wanted to know who had killed the vagrants, what had happened at the hospital, and whose blood had been spilled. He wanted to know what was happening to him, whether he really was crazy, and why he was of interest to a man he'd never met, but, most of all, and more than all of that put together, he wanted to find Kit. And he suddenly realised that he was prepared to do absolutely anything to make that a reality.

"What happened at the hospital?"

"You left me. I warned you what would happen if you did."

"Why did you attack the orderly?" he asked.

"Do you believe that I did?"

"Your gown is covered in blood and it's not yours. It's not difficult to draw a conclusion from that."

"So, you believe it?" she sighed. "You accept the word of those who did not witness the event."

"What other option do I have?"

"There are many. You just have to be open to them." She raised a brow in challenge.

"We have the blood, the weapon, and victim's evidence, if he survives."

"We?"

"The team, the police, my colleagues." Even as he said it, McNeil accepted that Dennis was right – he was no longer a team player – certainly not since Kit, but, in truth, he wondered if he ever had been.

"And, of course, you trust their judgment," Nell taunted him slyly.

"On this occasion." Who was he kidding? He didn't trust anyone but himself, and even that relationship was proving to be unstable.

"Sounds like you've already made your mind up."

McNeil faltered. "What are you saying?"

"A closed mind is a dangerous thing. You of all people should know that. This is all a game of strategy, and we are both pawns within it. You should pray that you learn the rules before it's too late."

"No more games, Nell. I'm too old for them, and far too tired to play."

Nell cocked her head and swept his features, lingering on his scarred brow. He felt her scrutiny as it brushed his skin. "You always liked to play, Joe," she sighed softly. "What happened to you?"

"I said no games."

She shook her head dismissively.

"Take me through it from the beginning. Who attacked the orderly?"

"That's not the beginning."

"It is as far as I'm concerned. Who attacked the orderly?" he repeated.

"Who do you think?"

"Jacob?"

"You're a quick learner. There is hope for you yet."

"If that's the truth, then you'd better pray the orderly survives and backs up your account. Bedlam is crawling with police officers who think you went on a killing spree."

Nell smiled slyly. "Oh, there's no doubt that he'll survive." She replaced the spoon in the empty bowl carefully. "You should eat something," she murmured. "You need to keep your strength up."

"For what?"

"For what lies ahead. I told you Jacob is coming. I can help you ..."

"But ...?"

"But only if you help me."

"I can't help you until you tell me what this is all about. I won't help you unless you tell me the truth."

"What do you want to know?"

"I want to know what happened to Kit."

She held his gaze, face scoured of expression. "You'd be better knowing what happened to me."

"Better?"

"Safer."

McNeil's stomach tightened. She was right. If there was a threat, if he really were in danger from this unknown nemesis, then her knowledge was his greatest defence. But he wasn't here for her, or even for himself – he was here for Kit.

"All in good time. Tell me about Kit first."

"Kit? You assume I know anything."

"Don't play games. Of course you do."

Her lips twitched. "Ignorance has its benefits."

He scowled his response. "I need to know."

"Good or bad?"

"Everything. Good and bad."

"Do you promise to help me?"

"Help you do what?"

"Escape."

"Justice or Jacob?"

"Both."

He took a breath. Kit would never get justice if it was left to Mather and Dennis, but if he aligned himself with Nell, he knew his career would be over. This was it, the invisible line that separated him from the woman he loved. He crossed it at his own peril and in full knowledge of the consequences. "I promise," he said, as he steadied his nerve and stepped over the line.

Nell shook her head slowly. "You just admitted that you break promises."

"Not the important ones."

"I'm glad you understand the importance of this one. Shall we seal our agreement?" She reached for his hand across the table and he obliged. Turning it palm-up, she traced the thin wound made by the blade with her finger. The cut followed his life-line and ended abruptly just short of the end. "We are connected in more ways than you can imagine," she sighed, then she dipped her head and pressed her lips gently in his palm.

There was pain, white hot pain, that tracked its way up his arm and straight to his heart. He sucked in a desperate breath and resisted the impulse to yank his hand free. She closed his fingers tightly around the kiss, lifted her head, and studied him.

His eyes glazed over. Blurred images fought like colours on a palette, vivid and acerbic. Garbled voices cajoled and taunted in his ear. Sharp teeth nipped at his throat. His chest tightened until he believed his lungs would crush beneath the pressure and his heart would burst through sheer panic. *Inhale, exhale.* Suddenly overcome with hopeless fatigue, he struggled to find his way back, to focus, to hold her gaze.

"What do you know?" he whispered hoarsely.

"You need to sleep. We'll talk later."

"No," he insisted, "tell me now. What do you know?"

"I know Kit is alive. I know you will never see her again."

Twenty-Three

And now, finally, Joe McNeil is within my grasp, though it brings no pleasure to witness his pain, merely shame that I have stooped so low for my own despicable benefit. He stands before me, head bowed, shoulders slumped, depleted of hope, flayed raw and wounded beyond repair, and in him I see a sad reflection of myself, and I cower at my own propensity for evil. I am indeed a product of Jacob's warped mind, a disciple worthy of his highest honour, and, in my selfish greed, I have played directly into his hands. I imagine his mirth at how the game progresses, and I despair at my inability to turn the tables and influence the outcome. It is a fine balance.

I focus now on Joe, and concern slithers unbidden into my mind. I wonder if I have made a terrible mistake. His tide of frustration and anger has ebbed through sheer fatigue and hopelessness. His eyes are moist with unshed tears. His heart is broken. I feel the weight of it in my hands. The rhythm is sluggish, without hope there is no reason for it to beat, and I, of all creatures, should understand this. I have allowed the baring of his soul. Now I must heal him, and, when it is done and he is whole again, he will be mine alone, and he will vanquish the beast and all will be well. It has to be.

I reach out and, this time, he does not avoid my touch. Instead he leans in, seeking comfort, and my fingers skim his brow as he did mine what seems like an eternity ago. His skin is warm, unshaven and rough beneath my caress. I trace the contours of his face, the scars that give title to the chapters of his chequered life, and tease his lips softly with the pad of my thumb. He watches me, powerless, tense, and expectant, as I in turn inhale and devour his scent.

"No," he whispers hoarsely.

"Yes." I smile at his intake of breath, his inner voice that rages beneath the surface, demanding his attention. He is about to betray his love, and he knows it.

I step close and slide my hand to the back of his neck, drawing him down to meet me. My lips brush his tentatively, and I am instantly overwhelmed by the power that ignites as I taste him. My heart pounds, my skin tingles, my ears are filled with the heady thrum as blood pulses throughout my arid frame.

"No," he murmurs, as his lips respond to mine.

I swallow his denial and press closer.

He is wavering; his need is great, but loyalty holds him tightly. I feel his strength, the tension in his muscles as he holds back. His resistance is ultimately futile, it merely draws me on, and I move closer still until all that is between us is fabric, and all that keeps us apart are his memories of Kit. I must ensure that he has no room left in his mind for her. The page must be emptied, the slate wiped clean.

"This is wrong." His hands move against me despite his proclamation.

His exploration of my skin proves that it may well be wrong, but is pleasurable nonetheless. I take advantage of his weakness, and his need for comfort and oblivion, and deepen my kiss. My breath is within him, my energy seeking out his wounds, just as he did for me as I lay broken and spent in the wasteland that is Bedlam.

Still, I sense his reluctance.

Can he not see that this is how it is meant to be? Together, we are a force capable of taking on the world, of defeating a hundred Jacobs. And yet, I feel resistance in the dark corners of his mind, in the secret compartments of his heart. She will not give him up. Kit holds him with silken threads, and each one must be severed. She must release him. My need is far greater than hers. I have given up everything else. I will not give up my last chance. I will not give up Joe.

"Trust me," I whisper softly against his ear. I trail my tongue down his jaw line, graze my teeth against his neck, nipping, tasting, and rest my palm against his chest. And, just as he brought me back with a hand on my heart, I do the same for him, and I feel it thud to life, strong and vibrant.

His response is immediate and shocking.

"Is this what you want?" he snarls.

He slams me back against the wall. My head hits the plaster and my jaw rattles with the force. He leans in, head cocked arrogantly to one side as his expression transforms from abject misery to one of sly calculation. I know that look, and, although I fear it, I am drawn to it and excited by it in equal measure. He lifts me roughly by the waist and I straddle his hips, locking my legs around him, feeling his need, sharing my heat. I whimper as he moves against me, pressing close, breath hot and ragged on my skin.

Soon, very soon, he will be mine, and the realisation excites me further. He is everything I hoped for. I do not need to heal him. He has strength enough for both of us, and far more than Jacob ever imagined.

"I said, is this all you want? Sex?" he crushes his lips against mine, forcing his tongue into my mouth, and I taste blood, his and mine, as it mingles on my tongue.

I desire much more than sex, but, for the moment, I am at the mercy of my senses. I am willing to forgo the ultimate in exchange for the immediate. My need for him is so great, I am willing to risk almost anything to have him.

"Tell me, Nell, tell me what you want." He pushes up against me, his hands at my breasts, his hips grinding against me. "Or shall I just keep you hanging here?"

He stops then, hauls on the ropes, slams a foot on the brake, and awaits my response. His breathing is ragged, his heart pounds against mine. Exquisite torture, and I am almost gone.

"*Please,* Joe." I rest my brow slick with sweat against his shoulder, and siphon strength from muscles that quiver with restraint.

"*Please?*" he mocks with a bitter curl of his lip, and then he releases his grip, steps away, and allows me to fall to the floor.

"What are you doing?" I gasp.

"What am I doing?" He shakes his head as if I am the fool, instead of him.

How can he resist? How can he step back from the edge? It is Bedlam re-incarnate, my recurring nightmare amplified to the point of madness, only this time, he refuses to step out into the void with me, and I cannot succeed alone.

He leans over me. "Now you know how it feels to be used and taunted, to be promised something you crave, and have it pulled away at the last minute."

I already know how that feels. I have lived it for longer than I can remember, and now I have visited it upon him. Jacob's insidious influence has corrupted me beyond redemption. I hang my head.

"I would never betray Kit," he continues vehemently. "Never. I'll do anything, absolutely anything, to get her back, and, if that means selling my soul to the devil, I will, but I won't betray her, not here in my heart." He rests a trembling hand against his chest and sucks in a calming breath. "You can play your games and peddle your wares, and, if push comes to shove, I might even trade you to get what I want, but the difference between us, Nell, is that I am motivated by love, and you ... God only knows what's going on in that evil little mind of yours. You can't help me, you never could. You've just used me to play your warped little games."

I stare at him from my position of disgrace, the corner of the room where he has dumped me, where I belong, where I will always belong. To be used and abused is my role in life, and it has taken his brutal honesty to bring clarity to my disordered mind. He has turned the game, loaded the dice, and I finally realise the extent of the task ahead if I am to succeed.

My fury at my defeat and humiliation, my dismay at my own transparency, is tempered as I witness his determination. He stands before me, outrage alone lending him strength. I know, beneath, he is the same tortured man as before, the rule breaker, the thorn in the establishment's side, the unarmed gladiator, ready to take on the lion in the face of defeat. A surge of hope sears my soul. I was correct in my first assessment. He is the one, the only one, and it is now imperative that I ensure his continued co-operation.

I have erred greatly.

My mistake? To believe evil stronger than good, and hate more powerful than love.

I am resourceful. I can make anew from shattered hopes.

I raise my arm, extend my hand and watch his anger dissipate as the serpents steal his attention and curiosity blurs his resolve.

He takes my hand and pulls me gently to my feet. This time his eyes are steady. There is no pain, no anger, just an acceptance of the new order.

"Kit is alive, you said so yourself. I believe you, though I've no evidence to suggest that I should." He smiles ruefully, as if confused and ashamed by his own behaviour, and uncertain how to proceed. "I need your help to find her, Nell. In return, I'll do everything in my power to protect you from Jacob. I don't want anything from you but the truth. Do you understand?"

I focus on my hand held protectively in his, and I swallow this new hurt, this torture that is worse than any of Jacob's despicable imaginings. Joe believes I use my body simply to ensnare, that I am a wanton harlot who will pay whatever currency is demanded to further my cause, and indeed he is not wrong. My life to date has been a shameless litany of just such things, but when first I laid eyes upon him in that desolate spot beneath hells canopy, I knew with a certainty bred in my bones that he was different, *the one*. And now I realise that the only way to make him mine forever is to give him his heart's desire, and, alas, while Kit lives, that will never be mine.

His love for her has sealed her fate.

I sigh my dismay and incline my head in agreement. "I understand."

He squeezes my hand gently. Relief fills the space between us and cushions my sadness. I have never felt as bereft, and, as if he senses this, as if we are now joined in spirit, he pulls me to him and cradles me in a gentle embrace. I lay my head against his chest, lulled by the beat of his heart, and he rests his chin lightly on the crown of my head. We stand for a moment in mutual comfort before he disentangles himself and steps away.

"Now," he says firmly, "you need to tell me the truth."

And I wonder how he will survive the telling.

Twenty Four

He'd always believed Kit was alive, despite the lack of support from those around him, so he wasn't entirely sure why confirmation of the fact, by a girl who clearly had issues of her own, meant so much to him. A rational person might suppose that she was merely telling him what she assumed he wanted to hear, in the same way she had offered her body in some desperate attempt to win his approval. But McNeil had vetoed rational when Kit had disappeared into thin air.

Although it pained him to admit it, he'd been more than tempted by Nell's advances, and it had taken some resolve not to act upon it. He had been faithful to Kit for an entire year, but he was human, and now the memory of how Nell had made him feel was in his head, it simmered gently, taunting and teasing. As if in punishment, guilt and self-loathing also marinated in his gut. He was glad Kit had not been witness to his betrayal, but there was something about Nell, something that connected them from the moment he'd laid hands on her. He couldn't explain it. Perhaps she could.

"What do you know about Kit?" he asked.

He avoided looking directly at her, curled as she was in the corner of the sofa, hair brushed, Kit's dressing gown replaced by one of his washed-out football shirts. Instead, he paced the flat, picking up the scattered clothes, stacking dishes in the sink, keeping his distance – anything to avoid having to sit near her.

"I know she is lost and you seek her."

He turned on the tap, ran hot water into the sink, and began to wash dishes that had lain for a week. He was pushing through the barrier of fatigue and the fog of medication. Both were trying to shut him down. He had to keep busy to stay awake long enough to hear her story. He sensed he was in for a long night of reading between the lines. Nell spoke in riddles. He took the shrink's advice and downed another pill. Maybe the instant buzz he'd get would help to clear his vision.

"You could have got that from the newspapers," he called through the open door.

"She was quite beautiful," murmured Nell.

McNeil allowed the mug he was holding to slip from his hands. It landed in the water with a splash and he turned with a frown. "*Was?*"

He stepped back to the lounge, leaned against the doorframe and waited. He wanted to see as well as hear her reply, though he doubted it would make much difference. Despite his years of interrogating suspects, he still had no idea whether she was telling the truth or not.

Nell shrugged. "She is less so now."

"You've actually seen her?"

"Of course."

"When?" He held his breath, felt hope kindle, and willed it into a flame.

"Time is inconsequential," she murmured.

"This week? Last week? If you've seen her, you must remember when."

She shook her head vaguely. "This life, the last life, the next life ... I really can't recall."

"Okay, forget that," he continued impatiently. "Where is she? Where did you see her?"

"In a place of waiting."

McNeil pinched the bridge of his nose firmly between finger and thumb. A sudden pain shot through his head and he sucked in a breath. *Cherry blossom, skipping ropes, feet jumping up and down, hitting the ground with a rhythmic thud.* "Waiting for me?" he gasped.

Nell smiled sadly. "You'd like to think that, wouldn't you, but no. She does not wait for someone, she waits for *something* to happen. She has quite given up on you, Joe. You would do well to choose another." She patted the sofa, an invitation for him sit alongside her.

McNeil scowled and shook the pain, the bizarre image, and her invitation away. Theirs would be an uneasy alliance. "What do you mean, *waiting for something to happen?*"

Nell frowned. "It's hard to explain."

"Try."

"I'm trying. To understand the end, you must go back to the beginning ... always back to the beginning." Her voice drifted wistfully.

McNeil stepped closer and dragged in a calming breath. "Look, we don't have time for this. If she's being held somewhere, if she's in danger, then you need to help me find her. Can you show me where she is? If we go now in the car, could you direct me?"

"It's not as simple as that ..."

"Nell, it is. It can be that simple. Just show me where she is. *Please*, Nell. I won't involve you. I won't betray you. I'll protect you, whatever happens."

"You say that, but you have no idea what will happen, what has *already* happened."

"Then tell me!" He raked his fingers through his hair with frustration. They were going around in circles. He wanted to shake her. He wanted to put his hands around her throat and squeeze the truth out of her. Instead, he squatted before her and took her hand in his. He ignored the silent sense of foreboding that seeped skin to skin.

"I ... I cheated," she whispered. "I broke a promise and told a lie, and it can't be undone ... no matter how much you might want it."

"Nell," – he squeezed her hand reassuringly – "it doesn't matter what you've done. You can put it right. It's never too late."

Nell pulled her hand from his grasp and shook her head sadly. "But what about what you did ...?"

"What *did* I do?"

The buzz of his phone interrupted her response, and McNeil cursed as he checked the display. *Dennis*. He hesitated, unwilling to lose momentum with Nell and equally reluctant to get into another argument with Dennis. He caught Nell's eye, held a cautionary finger to his lips, pushed himself to his feet, and took the call.

"Yeah?"

"Where are you, Joey?"

"Home. Where do you think?"

"Alone?"

McNeil turned away from Nell. "No, I have a flat full of strippers here. We're having a party. What do you think?"

"Don't try and be clever, Joey. I'm too bloody knackered for that."

"Tell me about it. It's late, you got me out of bed. What do you want, Dennis?"

"Something's come up on the case. I need to discuss it with you."

"So, discuss."

"No, I mean face-to-face. There are some things you need to know, things that don't add up. I'll be around in ten minutes. Stay awake till then."

McNeil shot a quick glance at Nell. "Look, mate, now's not a good time. I'll catch you first thing at the station."

Dennis grunted. "Ten minutes, Joey. This is important."

McNeil switched off the phone and stuffed it back in his pocket. He considered his options. He needed to hear Nell out. He was so close. He could either do it in the car, on the run, or he could bide his time and bluff it out with Dennis. He was tempted by the first. But common sense prevailed.

"DI Todd is on his way. He can't find you here."

She nodded her agreement and rose from her seat. "I'll go."

"No, you won't. We're not finished."

"Does that mean you believe me?"

"I want to."

"That's good." She smiled at him. Her hair curtained her face as she dipped her head, and she brushed it back with a sigh, as if exhaustion was ready to claim her, too.

"Stay in the bedroom. Sleep if you want. Just don't make a sound. If he finds you here, it's not just your head in the noose." He held open the door and she brushed gently past. He felt a surge of hopeless regret as Kit's scent wafted out of the room, to be replaced by Nell's.

Distant banging on the door to the street intruded on his melancholy. He ignored it as he watched her pull back the quilt and slip silently into Kit's side of the bed, her hair spread out in the space next to his, her cheek resting gently on the pillow.

"Why do we have to do this?" he asked wearily. "Why can't you just tell me where she is?"

Nell raised her head and looked directly at him. "You don't need me to tell you. You know where she is, Joe. You've known all along."

Twenty-Five

"You need to get a decent intercom or a ground floor flat," grunted Dennis. "I've been laying siege to your door knocker for a full five minutes."

McNeil stepped back as Dennis shouldered his way in. His bloodhound nose twitched and his eyes narrowed as he assessed the space suspiciously.

"Yeah, I expect the whole building heard you. I look forward to the notes of complaint." McNeil risked a quick glance at the bedroom door. It was firmly closed. "So much for ten minutes, Dennis. You were already parked up outside when you rang, weren't you?"

Dennis ignored him. "You've tidied up." He sniffed noisily. "Cleaned as well, or have you taken to wearing perfume?"

"Air freshener, Dennis. It covers a multitude of sins."

Dennis raised a sceptical brow.

"I thought I'd better show willing," McNeil continued, "before the landlord got on my case."

"And the heating's finally working."

So it was. McNeil shrugged his confusion. He hadn't noticed. It had been ice cold when he and Nell had arrived, and they'd both generated a little heat of their own since then.

"Sit down, Dennis." He gestured to the sofa. "I'd offer you a drink, but I'm on the wagon and it's late, and, like I said earlier, this isn't a good time."

"You seem on edge, Joey. Did I interrupt something?"

"No. I'm knackered, Dennis, same as you."

Dennis swung his gaze around the room again. He paused at the bedroom door and McNeil held his breath. There was no sound. Dennis leaned back and stretched his arm along the back of the sofa, using the movement to iron the cricks from his neck and peer through the open door into the kitchen. "Don't tell me you've been cooking as well."

The feint aroma of mushroom soup lingered. McNeil's own attention was also drawn to the kitchen. He couldn't recall where he'd left the evidence bag containing Nell's gown. "I do eat, Dennis. I am human."

"Contrary to popular belief."

"What's that mean?"

"Nothing. Just the lads fooling around."

"Go on."

"They reckon you're a little too obsessed with the undead, with things that go bump in the night. That you've got a bloody notion in your head that this whole business is connected to Kit. Must admit, you turning up with a blood-stained collar didn't help."

"And how did they know that? I didn't speak to anyone at the station except for you and Mather and ..."

"And who?"

McNeil cursed silently, reluctant to mention Charlotte. He had no legitimate reason for his visit to records.

"Maybe it is all connected," he suggested quietly.

"And maybe half of Bedlam's police force is out chasing vampires and you've been recruited by the Count himself." Dennis guffawed his derision. "Joey, let it go. You bring it on yourself."

"Hey, you're the one who suggested there was something weird about her. I said all along that she wasn't dead. All I did, down there beneath the viaduct, was point out the obvious."

"You're absolutely right. I was wrong, I admit it, and I'm sorry if I inadvertently stuffed up your head."

"You didn't. I'm not as stupid as you all seem to think. I know the difference between the living and the dead."

"Do you?"

"For fuck's sake, Dennis, stop messing about. What's this all about? You said it was important, to do with the case. You got me out of bed. Are you going to tell me what's going on or would you rather just play 'let's kick a guy while he's down'? Because I'm telling you, Dennis, there'll come a point where I start to kick back."

"Whoa, settle down. No need to be so touchy. You've got to admit, though, the whole business with the girl was bloody weird. You spotting that she was alive when the medics didn't. Bet that doesn't happen very often, eh?"

"What are you saying?"

"Nothing. Nothing at all."

"Right. Well, get to the point, Dennis."

Dennis settled himself and stretched out his legs. He didn't look like he was going anywhere soon, and McNeil could feel edginess threatening his performance. He wasn't sure how long he could keep up the façade, when all he wanted to do was show Dennis the door and get back to Nell. Dennis was fishing, for some reason. The sooner they got down to it, the better.

"It's been a rough couple of days. How do you feel now, Joey?"

"Okay. Why?"

"You don't look it."

McNeil could feel the now familiar buzz generated by the meds. It filtered through him like warm anaesthetic, smoothing off the edges. He rolled his neck and shrugged dismissively. "Like I said, I'm knackered, and you're keeping me up."

"There's nothing you want to tell me?"

"Like what?" McNeil kept his eyes firmly on Dennis and resisted the urge to check the bedroom door again. He thought he heard a noise, was sure it was his imagination, but all the same remained distracted and tried hard not to show it.

Dennis sighed. "I don't know. Anything that might explain your recent behaviour."

McNeil shook his head. "No."

"Because, if there was anything, anything at all, you'd be as well to speak up now, you know. I can't help if you don't let me in on the secret."

"There is no secret."

"Nothing that's troubling you?"

"Just you, Dennis."

Dennis narrowed his eyes and McNeil stared straight back.

"Okay," he said eventually, "if you're sure."

"I'm sure."

"We got some results back."

"Yeah?"

"Drug screens on the girl."

McNeil dropped into a chair. Now he was interested, and relieved that the focus had shifted away from him. All the same, Dennis wasn't stupid, and McNeil knew he was definitely suspicious.

"She was so full of chemicals, they reckon it'll take her days, possibly weeks, to fully detox. She'll be unstable, dangerous even, until she does. She's not to be trusted under any circumstances. We need to get her back as soon as we can, for her own benefit as well as the general public's." Dennis cocked his head and studied McNeil. "You can't help me with that, can you?"

McNeil shook his head.

"No, I didn't think so," muttered Dennis. "Most were hallucinatory, injected, if the track marks are to be believed, and I guess that would help explain her behaviour."

McNeil shrugged. "You're not telling me anything I didn't already suspect. I told you to do a drug screen."

"Yes, you did, Joey." Dennis considered him a little longer and McNeil began to perspire. He swallowed to lubricate his drying throat. "Another good call. Mather might just owe you an apology."

"I won't hold my breath."

"Best not. The balance isn't tipped in your favour at the moment. Anyway, most of the drugs were run-of-the-mill – uppers, downers, in-betweeners – you get the picture, but one was harder to identify, a little-known plant extract."

"Most drugs are derived from plants."

Dennis arched a brow. "And you'd know all about that?"

"I'm a detective. I know as much as you."

"Yes, well. The boffins had to dig deep to find a reference. They do love a mystery. They said that in the right quantity, this little bugger could kill. In slightly less than the right quantity, it could mimic death."

"So, what are you saying? Someone wanted her dead and made a mistake, or someone just wanted her to look dead?"

Dennis shifted so he could study McNeil comfortably without craning his neck. "You tell me."

"Huh?"

"Despite all the medics at the crime scene, you were the only one who spotted she was alive. How did you know?"

"How did I know?" McNeil raised his brow in disbelief. "She opened her fuckin' eyes. It was a bit of a clue. I'm a detective. I'm good with clues."

"Jim Alderson, the guy from the lab, told me a great long story about how a derivative of this particular drug was used in the past as a method to spirit convicts out of prison. A bloody risky business, of course. Who knows how many scaffold dodgers failed to wake up again after sipping the concoction? Unless someone in collusion on the outside got to the poor bugger in time, they ended up six feet under in an unmarked grave."

"Benjamin Rath ..." muttered McNeil.

Dennis cocked his head. "Yes, he used the very same thing on his victims. Jim had all the details. Bloody funny business, that. Where did you hear about him?"

"Police college."

"You must have a good memory."

"I was thinking about him this morning."

"Right. I was thinking about tiling the bathroom this morning, but it takes all sorts, I suppose?"

"Don't worry, Dennis. I don't while away my time obsessing over body-snatchers and serial killers."

"I'm glad to hear it. Just popped into your head, did it?"

"Not exactly. I was at the spot where he supposedly murdered his wives. Dr Richardson has his office at Gilmour House." McNeil smiled slyly, a consequence of the meds and his recollection. "No shit, Dennis, that place has an atmosphere. Send the lads down there and they won't be taking the piss out of me anymore. They'll be too busy looking over their shoulder. I'm surprised the outraged of Bedlam didn't turn up with flaming torches and raze it to the ground when they discovered what Rath had been up to."

Dennis frowned. "Dr Richardson?"

"The shrink. Christ, Dennis, keep up, you're worse than me. Go home and get some sleep or Mather's going to be on your case as well as mine."

Dennis leaned forward and loosened his tie. He was obviously there for the long haul. "The shrink's name is Freidman. Leonard Freidman. Just like it said on the card I gave you. By the way, he called this afternoon to let me know you'd DNA'd this morning's appointment."

"I didn't see Freidman. I saw Richardson."

Dennis sighed. "If you didn't want to go, you just had to tell me. There was no need to fabricate a fictitious meeting."

"What the hell do you mean, *fictitious*? I did go. Maybe the Freidman guy was busy. Maybe Richardson stepped in. I don't know. All I do know is that he screwed with my head and I might just have to go back to get unscrewed."

Dennis scowled. "Joey, Freidman doesn't operate out of Gilmour House. You've been to the Department's medical offices before. You were there last year."

"I just figured they'd moved, or Mather had upped the stakes. Fuck, Dennis, you gave me the card. I went to the address written on it."

"Where's the card?"

McNeil stood, retrieved his jacket from the back of the chair, and rifled in the pocket. In his haste to prove his account, he pulled out the entire contents. The folded photocopy of the water bailiff's statement, the crime scene photo of Nell, and the business cards all fluttered to the floor. He placed his foot on the statement, scooped up the photo and left Dennis to pick up the cards. Dennis clumsily fumbled them up off the carpet, shuffled them right way up, and paused to study the uppermost one.

"What are you up to, Joey?" He held up the card that had been pushed in McNeil's hand by Clarissa Temple. He shook his head in obvious disbelief at McNeil's recklessness, and handed it back.

McNeil shrugged carelessly. "Hedging my bets," he murmured.

"Heading for a fall, more like. Don't go there, Joey. I'm telling you as a friend, and one who knows. It's not worth the risk."

"If you were a friend, you'd know after a year of chasing dead ends and shouting in deaf ears, I'm about ready to risk anything."

"That's what worries me, Joey, and sitting here now, I can tell you I'm seriously worried about you. That's why I'm here, because I'm your friend and I can see what you obviously can't."

McNeil smiled sourly. "And what's that, Dennis?"

Dennis opened his mouth to respond, but paused as his attention was drawn to the details on the second card. "This isn't the card I gave you, Joey. I've never heard of Richardson."

McNeil wasn't listening. His entire attention had slipped to the crime scene photo in his hand. He felt a stabbing pain in his head and winced to clear it.

"What's wrong?" asked Dennis.

"Nothing," mumbled McNeil as he folded the photo and slipped it in his pocket.

"Are you sure? You've gone a funny bloody colour."

"For fuck's sake, Dennis, how many times do I have to say it? I'm okay."

"Fine," snapped Dennis. "The card I gave you, where is it?"

"What?"

"Joey, bloody concentrate will you."

McNeil rose from his seat, crossed to the window, and leaned his head against the glass. It was snowing again. He wondered when it had started, whether Nell's footprints had been sufficiently covered when Dennis arrived. He wondered what Dennis really wanted. He needed him to leave, soon.

"I went where you sent me, Dennis. I spoke to a guy who knew all about me. He had my record on his desk, knew stuff I didn't even know myself. Why would I make that up?"

"Why would Freidman say you didn't show?"

"Because I didn't fucking see him. We've already done this, Dennis, and you know what, I'm bloody sick of it. Maybe you made the mistake."

"I didn't, Joey. I wouldn't send you to Gilmour House."

"Why, because it costs an arm and a leg, and the budget's already hammered?"

"No, because Gilmour House closed its doors to psychiatric patients twenty-five years ago. It hasn't been used or licenced since."

McNeil curled his lips into a sneer. "Yeah, well, I'm telling you it's open for business now, complete with fresh paint and new carpet. I can take you down there right now and prove it. You want to take a ride in the snow?"

Dennis shook his head. "It's after midnight, Joey. I think I'll pass."

"You don't believe me, do you?"

"I believe *you* believe it, and, at the moment, that will have to do. I have far more important things to discuss."

McNeil narrowed his eyes. He also had far more important things to discuss, and he needed Dennis out of the flat so he could begin. Nell was waiting.

"Like you said, it's after midnight. I think I'll pass."

"You don't get to pass, Joey. You get to listen. We got some additional results back, rushed through, in fact, from the labs. Mather has dipped into the budget in a big way. He's pulling out all the stops on this one."

"Oh yeah," muttered McNeil, "I wonder why."

"To bury you, Joey. I warned you to watch your back, but you didn't listen."

"Huh?"

"We ran the blood from Nell's room. One individual. It matched the orderly's."

"So?"

"We ran the blade. No prints, no blood. Clean as a whistle. Not a single trace. The lab guys are telling me that's not the weapon used to slit the orderly's throat."

McNeil shrugged. "That doesn't make sense, unless he took the real weapon with him."

"*He?*"

"Jacob."

Dennis nodded. "Sure, Jacob ... or Nell. Let's not forget Nell, and, of course, we only have her word that Jacob exists."

"So?"

"Then we tested the blade you brought in. It came up with a veritable smorgasbord of matches."

"Big word."

"I do a lot of crosswords."

"Go on."

"But not the matches we expected."

"Really?"

"One set of prints. Yours."

"Yeah, well, I did pick it up."

"Two separate traces of blood. Yours ..."

"I cut my hand." McNeil opened his palm. A sudden image of Nell's kiss sucked the breath out of him. The wound could barely be seen. He coughed to cover his confusion and clenched his fist tight. "And the second?"

"... the orderly's."

"That's impossible."

Dennis sat back and folded his arms across his chest. "That's what I thought. Would you care to explain it to me, Joey?"

"Someone is trying to set me up?" Now he did risk a glance at the bedroom door. He wanted to burst right in there and demand to know what was going on, but instead he focused back on Dennis.

"That's one option."

"Just ask the orderly. He'll tell you what happened."

"There's a problem with that."

McNeil's stomach twisted. "Shit. Don't tell me he's dead."

"No. He discharged himself an hour ago."

"I thought he was on ICU, at death's door."

"So did we."

"What does this mean?"

"For the case or for you?"

"Both."

"As far as the case is concerned, we're back to square one. We have two dead vagrants and a missing suspect – Nell. I have no idea what the drugs in her system mean, or what all the shit was at the hospital, but I suspect that you do. Until you decide to behave like a police officer should, I have no option but to place you on suspension. If it was up to Mather, you'd be answering questions under caution. You might yet. Mather wants you in his office at ten-thirty tomorrow. It's a meeting you need to attend, Joey. I can't stress that enough."

157

"That's a pile of shit, Dennis. I don't know any more than you do."

"Right, so what were you doing up on the viaduct?"

"I told you, I was checking out the crime scene."

"Yeah? It took you long enough."

"I ... I've been having some issues, you know I have. I took some pills." Dennis' brows shot up. "Prescribed pills, Dennis. Maybe I overdid it or under-did it, I don't know."

"Prescribed by whom?"

"Dr Richardson."

"The doctor who doesn't exist."

"Yes, he fucking does. He practises from Gilmour House."

"The conveniently resurrected funny-farm? Sure he does, Joey."

"Yes, Dennis, I'm telling you I was there. Richardson does exist. I was in the same room, as close to him as I am to you now. His receptionist is called ... fuck, I forget her name, and she wasn't there anyway, and the lights were dodgy ..."

"Joey, you're not making any sense."

"No, wait, Dennis, I can prove it ... I met him before at the hospital. Check the CCTV. He was there the day I first interviewed Nell, the day I blacked out. I bumped into him in the lobby. I was being an arse. He was being a smug bastard. I wanted to hit him. Check the cameras, Dennis. He was there and he was at Gilmour House. He knows things. He knew about Kit, about Nell, about me."

"What did he know about you, Joey?"

"He knew about what happened ..."

"When?"

"Before ..."

"And what happened ... before?"

"I ... I don't remember."

"Then I suggest you try very hard, or find somebody else who does."

Twenty-Six

I am stronger now, and so is he. Armed with the knowledge of his true love's survival, he is now a worthy foe and a far more valiant protector.

He has tasted the blood of battle, glimpsed the horror of defeat, and now it is time for him to step up, to show his true colours to all who play the game.

I will help him as, ultimately, he will help me. Honour is a much-maligned concept. Temptation on the other hand is so ... tempting. We were destined from the outset, our silken threads far stronger and more tangled than those that bind him to Kit, but, by their very nature, they are buried deep and only he can uncover them.

Smugness seeps gently into my belly, and I make no effort to dispel it. Finally, I see victory as a distinct possibility.

"Be wary, my dear."

Jacob's voice is in my head. He is never far away now. He lurks in dark corners, in the shadowy places where righteous people fear to tread. Even now, in this place of believed sanctuary, where the very essence of Kit and her love for Joe is held, I cannot keep him out. I shake my head and concentrate my mind on *my* goal rather than his, and yet his bitter laughter mocks me.

"Do not forget our agreement."

He blocks the moonlit window, his shadow depicted eerily upon the wall. I do not waste time wondering how he has tracked me, how he has stolen silently into the room. He is all-knowing. He is a step ahead, always, and I must focus solely on that if I am to bring about his downfall. I hug the covers closer, Joe's scent my protection against the beast, yet Jacob merely shakes his head at my perceived weakness. In some ways, he is correct: I am weaker, not stronger as I smugly proclaimed, my resolve, my single-mindedness, diluted by hope. Perhaps it is all part of the game, the double bluff. He invented the game, and, in turn, he is the keeper of the rules.

"All goes according to plan?" he continues, as he steps closer, drawing the cold of winter with him. He lowers his gaze to avoid the moonlight as he approaches the bed, but, in that brief moment, I see that he is pale, depleted, and I smile inside. As I fully expected, the wound at his throat is no longer visible, but he has nevertheless misjudged the effects of his outrageous theatre, and now he suffers the consequences. I load that knowledge, like silver bullets, in a gun. He has erred for the first time, and I will use it against him.

"He is alone. His superiors suspect him. He is reliant upon you, Nell, and you must now ensure our quarry is herded to the place of waiting."

I consider Jacob's request, accept that it is, in fact, a demand, but choose to debate a little longer. To concede too readily would merely alert his suspicion. "He is stronger than you imagine," I chide softly. "He will not bend easily to your will."

Jacob inclines his head in agreement and I lean away, seeking comfort beneath the downy cover with its memories of love. Soon, I shall have my own such memories to replace the horror that inhabits my soul.

"What have you told him?"

I hesitate, unsure what is safe to reveal and what is wise to hold back. But, when the mattress depresses under his weight, and I feel his breath at my cheek, I risk a desperate glance at the door. I have no wish for them to meet here in this place, and I venture Jacob reads my thoughts and agrees, for he leans away and lowers his voice.

"What does he know?"

"Merely that Kit lives."

"Does he believe you?"

I recall Joe's desperation, his insistence that I tell him more, and I incline my head in response to Jacob.

"You must resist his attempts to discover her location. You must ensure that he is led there by his own efforts. Do you understand?"

"That may prove difficult."

"Then I will assist you."

160

He smiles. The moonlight catches the whiteness of his teeth, and I press back further into the pillow to avoid him.

"He has the means to see the path clearly. His vision, at present, is obscured by confusion and denial." He reaches out and trails his fingers gently down my arm. "You must ensure that he uses what he has. The boy will lead him to me."

He grips my wrist, and I barely feel his bite, as if he is tiring of me and seeks a more challenging subject. Or perhaps he is merely tiring of the game. I hold onto that hope tightly, though even I know it to be false. Jacob will never give up the prize.

Twenty-Seven

"Wake up, Nell. We need to leave now."

McNeil peered through the darkened room, confusion at Dennis' revelation well camouflaged beneath his calm hushed tone. He was no nearer working out what was going on around him, or to him, but Nell obviously knew something, and there was no way he was giving her up, to Dennis or anyone else. He'd left her to sleep as long as he could, while he'd showered and changed and deliberated on his next step, but he couldn't leave her any longer. Dennis' suspicion and disbelief had been palpable. As a friend, Dennis had given him the heads up, the chance to explain and provide a logical explanation for his increasingly erratic actions, and he'd failed miserably. He'd made no sense, even to his own ears. Who would want to set him up? Who would have the imagination and energy to create an elaborate alternate reality so convincing that he believed it entirely? Who hated him enough to do that?

It was little wonder Dennis was questioning his account. If the situation were reversed, he'd have been way past the questioning stage. At the end of the day, Dennis was a copper, and knowing the way Dennis worked a case, McNeil reckoned he'd be standing back now and waiting to see what happened. He had to make sure Dennis didn't see anything.

He reached out, shook Nell gently, and she roused slowly, warm and scented. McNeil let his hand linger on her shoulder, seduced by his own need for sleep, comfort, the safety of the nest. She opened heavy lids and struggled to focus, her pupils dilated, the distinctive violet muted and dull.

McNeil recalled Dennis' comments regarding the lab results. Although expected, they'd disappointed him. He needed to believe everything she'd told him, and now he wasn't sure whether all she'd alluded to was merely a product of a drug-addled brain.

"Have you taken something, Nell?" he sighed. He shook her more roughly and she peered groggily back at him. "Come on, we haven't got time for this. You need to get dressed."

A secret smile played around her lips, and McNeil shook his head with frustration, uncertain whether she'd been playing with drugs or simply playing another game.

He pulled her to a sitting position, and, when he pushed back the quilt and swung her legs over the side of the bed, she flopped against him, her head on his shoulder, hair against his cheek. He took her face firmly between his palms and forced her to look him in the eye. For once he didn't avoid her gaze. He invited it. He needed to catch every reaction.

"Why are you doing this?"

"You think this is me?" Her words whispered against his skin, her hair caressed his cheek. He turned with a frown. The window was open, the curtains adrift. Coldness crept silently into the room.

"Jacob? Is this all Jacob's doing?"

He felt her sag, resisted the compelling need to hold her warmth against him, and lowered her gently back to the mattress. He checked each arm for fresh track marks, smoothed his palm against the soft skin at the crook of her neck, and, when he found nothing, he dismissed his own paranoia with a frustrated shake of the head. It was all part of some elaborate game – the Nell show. Roll up, roll up, and prepare to be amazed by the freakiest side-show on earth. Only he wasn't amazed, he was scared, scared that he'd be drawn so far into the game, he'd end up centre ring, the star attraction, the two-headed boy in the formaldehyde jar.

He crossed to the window. The fire escape was empty, no footprints to suggest there had been an intruder, but he knew someone had been in the room. He could feel evil creeping like a weevil beneath his skin. He closed the window, secured the lock, and turned back to the bed.

"Nell, I have to go, and I can't leave you here, it's not safe. I don't trust you, not in this state. You need to wake up now and help me."

She smiled sleepily, her eyes clearing slowly. "He is near. I feel his presence."

"No, you don't," he answered brusquely. "Snap out of it. I just told you we have to leave." He crossed to the wardrobe, opened the door, and was rewarded as each hanger released the last particles of Kit's scent like a puffball. He closed his eyes briefly as her love coated him, armoured him, and strengthened his resolve. *I hear you*, he murmured silently. *Not long now.*

He reluctantly pulled out some of her clothes and threw them on the bed. "Come on, help me, Nell. You need to get dressed." He struggled to dress her, forcing unwilling limbs into jeans and sweater, and socks onto tender feet. Like dressing a mannequin, her passive resistance was worse than the wriggling and twisting of a recalcitrant two year old. By the time Kit's boots were secured and laced, McNeil was ready to slip back off the wagon and hit the bottle.

"Sit there and don't move," he ordered. "I'll be two minutes."

He picked up Kit's jewel box, took out the bracelet and the photos, and slipped them into his pocket. Nell watched.

"You can't escape him," she said. "No one can. He bides his time and waits. He is inordinately good at waiting."

He slipped on his coat and pulled her roughly to her feet.

"You imagine you know me. I don't know why or how, but you don't and neither does he ... if he exists at all. I need to know the truth about everything. I have to find Kit, and you're going to help me, whether you like it or not."

He checked the street from the lounge window. There was no sign of Dennis. That didn't mean he wasn't lurking or that he hadn't left someone else to keep watch and report back. It was the logical thing to do with a suspect, and it seemed he was suspected of something, even if Dennis hadn't quite worked out what. McNeil got the feeling that Dennis hadn't quite decided about him, and he was being given the benefit of the doubt, at least until his meeting with Mather. It didn't give him long to find out what was going on.

"We have to leave, now."

"Where are we going?" asked Nell, as he bundled her down the stairs, out the door, and into the car.

"To find Kit, while I still can. Who knows, this time tomorrow I could be sitting in a cell carrying the can for this whole fucking business."

"I told you, it's not that simple. Searching is what Jacob wants you to do, and therefore the very last thing you should do."

"Then save me the trouble and tell me where she is."

"I can't tell you."

"Can't or won't."

He started the car and pulled out slowly into the night. He shot a quick glance at Nell when she failed to respond.

"You already know where she is," she sighed. "You don't need me to tell you."

"I have absolutely no idea where she is. If I did, do you think I'd be sitting here now listening to your fairy stories?"

"Yes, you do. You've just forgotten."

"What, you think I had something to do with her disappearance?"

"Yes."

McNeil shook his head. "You're wrong."

Nell closed her eyes briefly and drew in a soft breath. When she re-opened them, McNeil could see that the fog, whether real or imagined, had totally lifted, leaving the violet sharp, intense and calculating. "As I told you at the hospital, you are responsible for all of this. To understand, you must go back to the beginning."

He checked his mirror. There was very little traffic. The snow and the lateness of the hour meant anyone with any sense was tucked up at home in bed. All the same, he squinted at the lights behind, until they disappeared somewhere south of the Bedlam turn off. His lip twisted sourly. He was clearly the only person crazy enough to head into Bedlam in the middle of the night. The snow was thickening, and the wipers fought to clear the screen. It was unusually harsh weather for November, but somehow fitting. It suited his mood.

He turned off the main road and nosed the car down a darkened alley, a rat-run in the true sense of the word. Street lights had long since fallen prey to vandalism, vermin scurried between discarded rubbish bags – all-in-all a perfect place to get to the truth. He pulled in adjacent to a derelict warehouse, and left the car idling, unwilling to switch off the ignition in case the temperamental engine failed to re-start. Reaching into his jacket, he pulled out the photo.

"Okay, Nell, if it's so important, let's do that. Let's start at the beginning. What's the significance of the snake? You have a tattoo. Kit had a charm – this charm." He threw the photo into her lap. The image was distorted by the fold of the paper, nevertheless it could still be seen, particularly by one who knew where to look. Clutched tightly in her outstretched hand, barely visible through the mud and blood, was a small enamelled charm, a two-headed snake.

She picked up the photo carefully and smoothed out the fold with the heel of her hand. Her fingers trembled as she traced the outline of her own battered image.

"Is that how you found me?" she whispered.

"No, that's how the SOCOs found you, before I got there. They thought you were dead. Everyone thought you were dead."

"I was."

"And now you're not." McNeil shook his head. "Don't start with that, Nell. I'm done with the whole undead, vampire-trippin' thing. All I want to know is where you got the charm in the photo, and what the connection is with the tattoo."

She raised her wrist and stared at her tattoo as if seeing it properly for the first time. "I've always had it, for as long as I can remember."

"What do you mean, as long as you can remember? How long have you been with Jacob?"

"Forever."

"All of your life?"

"All of my lives."

"*Lives*? I don't understand. Is Jacob your father?"

Nell shook her head and confusion clouded her eyes. "No ... my creator."

"Nell, I just told you, forget the riddles. I don't have time for them. What about the charm? How did you get it?"

"The charm? I picked it up. It fell in the long grass and I wanted it back."

"*The long grass?* Were you there when Kit was taken? Down at the canal? Did you see what happened?"

"I saw everything."

"What did you see?"

She shook her head. "I don't remember."

"You're not making any sense. If you saw everything, you must remember."

"Another life, and the memories fade."

"Nell! Cut it out. I don't understand."

"You will. Soon."

McNeil shook his head. He tightened his hands on the steering wheel. He didn't trust himself anymore. Knowing she was withholding information and there wasn't a damn thing he could do about it caused his gut to cramp and the voices in his head to scream at him. He could make her talk. He could put his hands around her throat and squeeze the truth out of her. His hands itched to do just that – or he could hand her over to Dennis and let him decide whether she was crazy, or he was crazy, or both.

"You said you wanted the charm back. Was it yours to begin with?"

"No, not mine ..."

McNeil turned to look at her. "What do you mean?"

"It had served its purpose. I had to retrieve it."

McNeil frowned. He tried to think back. He couldn't recall where the charm had come from or how long it had hung from her bracelet, just that Kit was particularly fond of the snake with the purple glass eyes. "Did you give her the charm? Did you know her ... before ... before she disappeared?"

Nell smiled. "I knew her before. I know her now. I will know her again."

"Just stop!" McNeil yelled at her. In the confines of the car, the force of his voice, the vehemence in the two short words, threw her back in her seat, and her eyes widened. "You took her, didn't you? You and your fuckin' freak of a boyfriend. What did you do, befriend her, entice her to a spot at the edge of nowhere, and steal her away from the life she loved?"

He raised his clenched fist and felt something dark rear up and threaten to overpower him. The engine cut out with a shudder, and silence engulfed the car.

The boy sat where Nell had been, skinny arms raised to ward off the blow. One foot jerked with fear, hitting the glove-box with a rhythmic thud. Cheeks wet with tears and snot, lip burst and bleeding. T-shirt torn, spattered with mud and blood, one sleeve hanging from the seam by a single thread. Beneath, unwashed skin, a scrawny bicep, bruised and swollen, marred with angry finger marks, and, at the centre of the battered flesh, a twin-headed serpent coiled ready to strike. Fresh blood oozed from every pinprick. Ink bled from the image and stained the surrounding skin. McNeil heard the child's words in his head as they tumbled in a broken stream from his open mouth. "I'm ... sorry ... I'm ... sorry ... I'm ... sorry ..."

McNeil gasped and felt white hot pain smother the words and strangle his response. He dropped his fist, dragged in tepid, sickly, recycled air-con, and felt his stomach roll. Flinging open the door, he staggered from the car, boots sliding in the fresh snow, hands outstretched as he scrambled desperately to maintain his balance. He veered away from a pile of rubbish, painfully shouldering a brick wall in his attempt to avoid the seething mass of rodents that streamed angrily from the refuse. When his momentum finally slowed, he dropped to his knees and vomited.

I'm sorry ... I'm sorry ...

His chest was tight, his head pounded. Fear irrigated his system with every beat of his heart. He raised a shaking hand and wiped away tears and saliva with his sleeve. Eventually, he lifted his head. Nell crouched alongside him, one hand on his shoulder.

"I'm sorry."

McNeil blinked. Confusion slowed his reactions as he pushed her aside and hauled himself back to his feet. "What's happening to me?" he stammered.

Nell stepped back as he steadied himself like a drunk, swaying, frantically seeking a point of reference, something immoveable in a world of shifting images and altered reality. He fixed his gaze on the one working lamppost at the end of the lane, its solitary beam providing a halo of muted light, a beacon obscured by driving snow.

"If you want this to end, you must go back to the beginning."

"*The beginning*?" His palm tingled. He remembered her first touch. The tingling worked its way up his arm and he gripped his shoulder as the sensation turned to pain and his muscle contracted in response.

"You know how to resolve this," she continued. "You've simply forgotten."

"Forgotten what?"

"How this all began."

"And how do I remember?"

"You have the means to see things more clearly."

McNeil reached into his pocket and pulled out the bottle prescribed by Dr Richardson. The capsules rattled like live things trying to escape.

"Is this what you mean? Is he part of this?" He raised his hand, his first impulse to throw the meds as far as he could.

"You need to remember," Nell cautioned. "Memories are weapons in the liminal war."

"Memories? Repressed or implanted?"

"Only you know the truth."

That was the whole problem. He didn't know the truth. He shook his head wearily and looked away, aware that she watched him carefully, waiting to help or waiting to pounce. He focused on the driving snow, and the silence between them grew.

"Why can't you just tell me?" he asked eventually.

"Because, if you are to come to terms with what you did, the truth must be learned, not told."

A muffled noise at the far end of the alley reluctantly drew his attention, and he raised a hand to silence her. Hooded figures moved like a feral pack, crossing through the weak beam of light in the direction of the warehouse gates. He squinted and counted three scaling the metalwork. The heavy chains rattled dully as they climbed. As they released their hold and thudded to the ground inside the compound, he spotted a fourth who paused for a moment before reaching out and hauling himself up nimbly. As he swung over the pinnacle of the gate, his hood slipped, his green hair suddenly illuminated by the yellow light.

McNeil turned back to Nell. "Last chance, Nell." He stepped closer, ducked his head, and whispered hoarsely. "Tell me what's going on."

"I'm sorry ... I can't."

"Right. Get back in the car," he hissed. "Lock the doors and stay there until I get back."

Nell reached out and caught at his sleeve "Where are you going?"

"To do what I should have done all along. To look for real evidence."

"You're making a mistake. You need to stay with me."

"No. My mistake was thinking that I needed you at all. I never needed you. I'll find the connection, and I'll find Kit, and I'll do it my way."

Twenty-Eight

They must be kids, he decided, if agility was any measure of age. He was barely thirty, and as fit as the next guy, yet as he followed them over the gate, his muscles screamed at him and he heaved with the exertion. Then again, he couldn't recall when he'd last slept or eaten or done any of the usual prerequisites for maintaining life, things that had ceased to register importance since first laying eyes on Nell.

He dropped heavily to the ground, rose with a grunt, and peered into the darkened compound. There was no noise to indicate which way the youths had gone, but fresh scuffs in the snow pointed the way. He pulled out his phone, switched it to silent, then cautiously tracked the footprints to a door barricaded ineffectually with a corrugated iron sheet. The metal was bent out of shape, allowing access through a narrow gap. McNeil sucked in a breath and squeezed his way through.

The warehouse was a redundant mausoleum, a reminder of the glory days when Bedlam had been wealthy and the adjacent streets housed workers who'd kept the alleys clean and free from vermin. Now, along with its neighbours, decay oozed from the building like a bad smell. There was nothing to recommend the site to developers, and no money to regenerate. All those with an eye to a profit were snapping up real estate in the suburbs, while the arteries that fed the ischaemic heart of Bedlam were clogged with apathy and discontent.

Distant voices drew McNeil further into the darkness, and he followed the sound as it reverberated along corridors that reeked of damp and urine. He wondered at that, as he tried for shallow breaths, how dilapidated buildings always stank of waste, as if it was a necessary component in the process of decay. Old buildings, old people – both stinking of piss. There was a moral there somewhere, but his brain could only concentrate on one thing, the tattoo.

He had to know what it meant.

Because he had one, too.

Using his phone as an inadequate torch, he swept the graffiti-daubed corridor, stepping carefully over debris and crap, by-passing ancillary offices with no more than a cursory glance. Metal filing cabinets lay upended, desks smashed, anything of value long since removed. McNeil recalled many emergency calls to this neighbourhood, arson mainly, and this old building had suffered its fair share. The main roof had gone at the last call out, but only after it had been stripped of slate and lead. Vultures had pretty much picked the bones clean – recycling, Bedlam style. Now awaiting demolition, it was meant to be locked up tight for safety's sake. In reality, just like the underbelly of the viaduct, it was a haven for the feral and lawless.

He pushed heavily against a door at the end of the corridor, wincing as it creaked on rusted hinges. Everything was wet and cold. He paused to wipe his hand dry on his coat, and cocked his head cautiously to listen, but the raised voices ahead, laughing and jeering, more than covered any noise he made. He stepped into a cavernous space and stopped abruptly.

Above his head, a giant ribcage of blackened beams allowed the snow to enter the space from a heavy, laden sky. At the far end, high up and dead centre in the surviving brick gable, a circular fan light, as wide as he was tall, allowed weak moonlight access through the broken louvres. The fragmented beam projected onto the centre of the warehouse floor, where a fire blazed, fed by charred timbers. A ring of youths huddled around the pool of light, hoods raised, shoulders stooped.

Clearly intoxicated, they passed drinks and smokes between them, whooping and jeering at something in the centre of the ring. McNeil fully expected an illegal dog fight and braced himself for beasts scarred physically and mentally, bred solely for destruction and the entertainment of the ignorant.

Pocketing his phone he moved closer, keeping to the shadows, his eyes gradually adjusting to the dappled light. The iron posts that supported the remains of the roof were thick with graffiti – the usual tag names, blasphemy and profanity – but, as he looked more intently, he realised that the words formed artwork and each pillar actually depicted horrific images of slaughter and torture. On one, a grotesque man lay twisted, his belly split open in a hideous smile. The next showed the head of another exploded by gunfire. The red paint sprayed halfway up the height of the post and pooled on the ground beneath his feet. He lifted his foot gingerly. The paint was dry, the image old.

As he approached the inner circle, the raucous noise increased. Fighting had broken out between two of the youths, who scrabbled like rabid dogs as a loaded syringe skittered across the wet concrete in McNeil's direction. He ducked behind a pillar and held his breath. Weed, the kid with green hair, passed within feet of him, whooping loudly as he bent unsteadily and retrieved the drugs.

McNeil pressed his face against the cold iron pillar and exhaled slowly. His head began to swim, the images and the pungent odour of menace and decay contributing to his light-headedness. When he pulled his cheek away from the metalwork, his stomach contracted with a jolt.

"Fuck," he muttered as he looked up and realised he'd been resting against an image of Popeye hanging by his open throat; on the adjacent pillar, Jaimsey, complete with blood splatter and vacant expression.

He'd been the one to suggest that the murder of the vagrants was unconnected to the attack on Nell, but, if that were really true, it would by default also be unconnected to Kit's disappearance, and he didn't want that. In his head, they were all connected – they had to be – or he'd be back at square one with just a jumble of incoherent dreams, thoughts, and suspicions. He'd been led here for a reason, and, although unclear of the ultimate motivation, he accepted it as a necessary step in some purposeful game. He knew he needed to speak to Weed, but if the youths had been witnesses to what happened at the viaduct, then they weren't going to stand around politely answering his questions.

He pulled out his phone and punched out Dennis' number. "Come on," he urged impatiently. Dennis and the boys could round up the whole litter of miscreants, interrogate them to their heart's content, and he would grab Weed on the rebound. A night in custody might loosen his tongue about the tattoo.

He raised his head when the shouting turned to chanting, and the youths all looked up in unison. McNeil followed their gaze in horror. More hooded figures scuttled like rats along the remaining roof trusses. Ahead of them, balancing precariously, arms tied behind his back, a man was being prodded and taunted. When they reached a spot above the flames, a final lunge with a stick caused the man to topple.

His fall was broken by the rope around his neck.

The body jerked. The feet kicked violently. McNeil heard rhythmic thudding in his head despite the fact that the boots kicked impotently in thin air.

"Huh?" Dennis' grunt came harsh and heavy in his ear. "This had better be good. It's the middle of the fucking night."

"Dennis – Tavistock Road – the old Spillers warehouse." McNeil's words came out in a short staccato burst. *Kids, bloody kids!* He couldn't believe his eyes. "I think I have the little fuckers who did for Popeye and Jaimsey. Get some back-up down here pronto."

"*What?*"

"They've just strung up another one." McNeil inched forward. He heard heavy breathing in one ear, as Dennis struggled awake; in the other, he heard the anarchic cry of the mob.

"Where are you?"

"Inside the warehouse. It's like something out of a horror movie. There's at least ten of them that I can see, maybe more. Crack-heads in hoodies, drink, drugs, and fucking mayhem."

"I'm on it." Dennis was suddenly transformed, sleep cast aside, DI Todd reporting for duty. "Joey, keep out of sight. Wait for backup. Do not, under any circumstances, intercede. Do you hear me?"

"I'm going to have to do something, Dennis. There's a chance this one might still be alive."

He doubted it. He was sure he'd heard his neck snap, but he couldn't just leave him. He couldn't hide in the shadows while a man was murdered in front of him.

He thought of Nell and all her secrets waiting in the car. He thought of Kit, just waiting for him – somewhere. Then his gaze swung back to the man at the end of the rope. He'd seen him before, that very morning, on the front cover of the Bedlam 'Herald'. John Bales, the water bailiff, stared back at him with bulging eyes.

"Armed police!" yelled McNeil. "You're surrounded. Stop what you're doing. Now!" He was already running, the phone pressed to his ear. He wasn't armed, and they weren't surrounded, nevertheless the kids began to scatter, and Bales, at the end of the rope, twitched as if electricity were passing through him.

"Joey. *Joey!* Wait for bloody backup!"

McNeil kept running. Even when the youths were no longer in front, but had scattered sideways and behind him, he ignored the obvious danger and made for the man at the end of the rope. He stopped when his feet were kicked out from under him and he hit the ground with a thud. His chin hit the concrete. Air expelled in a rush from his lungs, and the knowledge that he'd made a reckless mistake was confirmed when he felt a heavy weight on his back.

"What we got here?" The voice, barely broken, grated in his ear and spittle sprayed his cheek.

McNeil twisted, struggled to his knees and tried to dislodge his attacker, but he clung like a limpet and another joined in, adding his weight.

"We caught us a copper." The grunt was accompanied by drunken laughter. "Play time, lads."

"Fetch another rope," squealed a younger voice.

The sound of running feet indicated the return of the pack. Many rough hands hauled him up, forced his arms violently behind his back, and he was frog-marched to the arena.

Above, John Bales had stopped kicking. His eyes were closed, his face blue with asphyxia. Flames licked at the soles of his feet.

McNeil lurched forward, heart pounding, muscles bunched, a final attempt to make a difference, but the collective weight of the mob held him back.

"Cut him down, for God's sake," he yelled desperately. "The whole place is surrounded. Cut him down while you can. Don't make this any worse than it needs to be."

He was answered by manic, drug-fuelled laughter, as another length of timber was thrown onto the fire. Sparks erupted, catching hold of Bales' trousers. McNeil struggled impotently, but when a redundant can of spray paint was also hurled into the flames, all he could do was turn his head away and hope for a speedy end, both for Bales and himself.

The first blow to his belly was an ineffectual punch from an immature fist, the stick poked tentatively at a captive animal, macabre curiosity or a litmus test. He gasped more through surprise than pain. Then the second blow, from a larger attacker, harder, with more intent, landed at his temple. His head snapped back, sharp white light fragmented his vision, and his knees buckled. He slumped and felt a boot at his kidneys, another at his shin. He clutched his phone tightly and tried to curl into a ball, but his tormentors prevented him, stamping at his limbs, kicking at his vulnerable belly, whooping at his grunts of pain. Someone grabbed at his hair and slammed his cheek against the concrete, back and forth. Pain exploded into his temple, his head was hauled back, and he felt rough fibres scrape his face as a rope was forced around his neck. He gagged at the stricture.

"String 'm up."

"Slit the fucker's throat."

"Wait!" The word struggled for life and exploded desperately. The last gasp, the long shot, and, when miraculously the pressure at his throat eased, McNeil heaved in a lungful of rancid air. "Don't do this ..."

"*Don't do this. Don't do this,*" they mimicked him, yanking the rope tighter.

"You're ... making a ... mistake," rasped sounds barely intelligible, and McNeil's eyes screwed tight with the effort.

"No, the mistake is yours."

The deep growl cut through the chaos and stopped the pack in their tracks, like a child's game of statues. Fists raised, boots in mid kick, his assailants all turned toward their alpha, and McNeil raised his head and tried to do the same.

He was dragged back to his feet and held upright by the mob as his knees buckled and muscles failed. Vicious fingers nipped at his skin, yanked his hair, twisted tight at his clothes and at the rope around his neck. He dragged his eyes open and tried hard to focus on the man standing before him, not a kid in a hoodie, but a man tall enough and broad enough to block the beam of light and cast a shadow that enveloped McNeil like a shroud.

"I warned you."

Like the first notes in a long-forgotten song, the voice taunted his memory. *I warned you. I told you what would happen. This is all your fault.*

He dragged in a desperate breath as shattered ribs joined the mob in further torture, stabbing from the inside. He felt terror bubble up and force its way past the stricture at his larynx. It exited as a feeble yelp, but in his head, it was a howl of pain and fear and anger.

"I ... I'm sorry ..." McNeil didn't recognize his own voice. It came out grated, disconnected, and his mind followed suit. Voices, real and imagined, jostled for supremacy. He swung dangerously between realities.

"Sorry isn't good enough. It's far too late for that."

McNeil's chin dropped to his chest, and blood and saliva drooled onto his shirt. He tried to concentrate, but his head spun, and consciousness crept stealthily away. He hung over the abyss, suspended by a single tenuous thread – a siren. It taunted him with its haunting faraway sound.

"Gut the fucker, Weed." An angry voice in his ear; hot, stale, cider breath on his cheek; cannabis smoke at his nostrils; and white-hot searing pain at his abdomen. He couldn't move. He didn't even try.

"Run. We've killed a copper. Run!"

And then they were gone, and all McNeil could hear was a jumble of sounds: the roar of the fire as it twisted, fed with human flesh; the distant wail of the siren; and Dennis screaming desperately from the phone still clutched tightly in his hand. All he could smell was piss, and this time, he was sure it was his own.

"I'm ... sorry ..." he sobbed, in his head or out loud, he wasn't sure. He no longer cared. His eyes drifted shut. The last rational thought in his head as his blood pooled around him was Kit, beautiful Kit, with her whispered smile and golden hair. And the fact that he had failed her, again.

The little boy reached out his hand across the void and waited. McNeil stared back in confusion, and the child's face dimpled into a gap-toothed smile. The boy's fingers were covered in mud; his own were slick with blood. They slid together effortlessly, and he was helped to his feet and led away.

His palm tingled. His chest hurt. His legs were numb, heavy and leaden. Nevertheless, he followed the child toward the light, squeezing through the gap in the hedge, scrambling over the dilapidated wall, sharp stones grazing his knees, and then on through the orchard, heart pounding, excitement bubbling, running, chasing. The sound of children playing – giggling, high-pitched, happy voices – distracted him and he slowed to a stop. Beneath the cherry blossom tree, two little girls skipped around and around the trunk, ropes turning, feet jumping. Petals showered them from above, and, as he neared, they paused, dropped the skipping ropes and joined hands, beckoning for him and the boy to do likewise. And then, all four circled the tree, around and around.

Ring a ring a rosy ...

A warm sensation spread throughout his body. His palm ceased tingling. His chest no longer hurt, and he felt like he could run forever on legs that were sturdy and strong.

Suddenly a shadow cast upon them all, and the game sped up until dizziness and nausea swamped him. He lost sight of the girls. The boy's small hand slipped from his. He tried to call out, but water flooded his open mouth. A sea-fret of loss clung to every fibre, seeping into his skin. A hand clamped over his mouth and nose, and he hadn't the strength or will to remove it. He felt searing pain jolt repeatedly through his chest, and then nothing but ice-cold, terrifying blackness.

Twenty-Nine

Noooooo ... I howl inside, bereft.

He cannot die.

Not now when we are so close.

My heart is torn asunder. I feel it bleed my sorrow, as his blood seeps from his broken form. Hope deserts me in dry flakes that mingle with the fallen snow. He is cold. He hovers in that liminal space I know so well.

Wet lashes on grey cheeks.

Forgotten kisses on blue lips.

He is battered, broken beyond repair, and I rage inside at the unfairness, at the madness, at the waste.

This is my fault – all my fault. Swayed by Jacob, I allowed need to skew the game. I fear his wrath, but even more than that, I fear eternal damnation, and it surely awaits me if I lose Joe.

All around the flames of hell consume. Burning rafters plummet and crash to the ground, showering sparks like a demon welder's torch. Masonry, now depleted of its timber skeleton, groans and warps beneath the intense heat. The smell of burning flesh coats my nostrils, and my stomach reacts at the abomination. Bedlam leaches its evil through my pores, and I raise my head and barter all I am for all he will be.

Regardless of the cost, I must make amends.

I place my lips to his and offer my life, for that is all I have. I breathe for him, into him, and his chest rises, but it is a futile gesture while his blood flows freely and life ebbs. Frantically I attempt to stem the flow, but it slips between my fingers, hot and slick.

"Hear me!" I cry desperately into the fiery maw. "You have won. Is that not enough?"

And, as if in response to my plea, the sky exhales its icy breath and the snow intensifies around us and upon us, until

Joe and I are cocooned in a soft white crystalline blanket, a fragile gossamer protection from the flames.

Hope renews.

I tear off Kit's jacket, ball the fleece into a tight wad, and force it beneath his blood-soaked shirt. She will assist. Together, we will save him, she and I. Kit must hold back the flow while I cradle his heart, gently, carefully.

I press my lips against his and breathe into him once more.

Help must come. I pray that it does, but it must be swift, before Jacob comes to claim his prize.

Thirty

The boy sat cross-legged at the end of the bed. Water dripped from his hair, wet clothes clung to his frame. Mud from his shoes stained the white sheets. Blood trickled from his nose, and he wiped it away with the back of his hand. Crying had long since ceased. Sobs had given way to an occasional hic which caused a shudder to ripple through his thin frame. He held out his hand, fingers outstretched. McNeil tried to reciprocate, but his limbs would not respond.

Light flooded the room, and the boy turned away, his hand taken by another who helped him to the floor and led him away. His reluctance was passive, a dragging step, over his shoulder a regretful glance, and then a final sad smile and a child's wave, fingers flexing tentatively. Solemn grey eyes held his briefly before shifting to a shadow in the corner.

As the door closed behind the boy, he glimpsed a second child pressed back against the wall. She sat amidst a growing pool of water, grazed knees drawn up, skinny arms wrapped tightly around them. A tiny bud starved of sun and rain, her outer layer was shrivelled and dry. She raised her head. Uncombed hair, twig-tangled and dusty, fell aside to reveal an unnaturally pale face. A broken daisy chain hung from her neck. She regarded him with striking violet eyes.

JoJo ...

He heard the whispered caress, felt the soft kiss brush against his cheek, but it did little to assuage the overwhelming pain of loss and regret as it swept through him. He shuddered, physical pain intruded, and a firm hand at his shoulder anchored him.

"It's about bloody time." Dennis' brusque voice pulled him back.

Harsh white light greeted him as he dragged sticky lashes apart. He squinted. "Dennis?" His throat was sore. He swallowed in an attempt to lubricate it.

"Where ...?"

"What ...?"

They spoke in unison, and Dennis conceded with a grimace.

"Where am I?"

"Hospital. And, pardon me, but this is getting to be a habit."

"Huh?"

"You, waking up in a hospital bed with a vacant expression on your face and umpteen stitches in your head. How do you feel?" asked Dennis.

"Fucked," replied McNeil.

"So you bloody should. I told you to wait for backup. Why do you never do as you're told?"

McNeil raised a hand to massage his brow. His head was thick. A dull ache fogged his ability to think straight, to speak in full sentences. An IV line restricted his progress. Oxygen tubes irritated his nasal passages. Adjacent technology bleeped and buzzed reassuringly. He was still alive. That was something.

"How long have I been here?"

"Two days. You've been out of it for most of that. You had us worried for a time."

Two days. That was far too long. He felt a familiar apprehension stir in his gut, but hadn't the wherewithal to process its origin.

"How long have you been here?"

Dennis snorted gruffly. "Not long. I haven't had time to sit and hold your hand. I've been out feeling collars, practising some good old police brutality." He laced his fingers and cracked his knuckles.

"Of course you have." McNeil smiled weakly. Sudden memories flashed in his mind – noise, laughter, pain, and fear. The fear settled deep inside. The smile slid from his face. "Did you get them all?"

"Four so far. Caught the buggers as they fled the scene. The rest will come in the next day or so. We're busy rattling cages, upending beds, and prying the little tossers from their mothers' ample bosoms. Bloody toe-rags come home covered in blood and stinking of God knows what, and the sad old cows still think their little Johnny wouldn't hurt a fly. Little gits are busy blaming each other and dropping names like hot shite."

"Did you get Weed?"

"Oh, we got more than weed. What wasn't already up their nose or in their veins, they tried to dump as they ran, but the dogs saw to that."

"No, I mean Weed, the kid with the green hair."

"Aka, Robert Jessop? Yes. He is *known*, as we say in the trade. A sheet an arm long, mainly juvenile stuff – robbery, possession, public disorder. He's going up in the world. Little Weed has just had a birthday, so he'll be paying for his crimes just like the big boys. Forensics linked him to the blade used on you. He used the same one on Popeye and Jaimsey."

McNeil twisted painfully as unwelcome images unfurled in his mind. "Just as well my Hep-B jabs are up-to-date, then."

Dennis studied him closely. "Do you remember what happened?"

"Enough."

"Good, then perhaps you can tell me why you were there, Joey, in the middle of the night in the toilet bowl of Bedlam, the last place anyone with any sense would choose voluntarily. Because, I can tell you, I'm having a hard job working it out. I left you ready to crash out. What made you turn your back on your bed and go back out into the night?"

"Kit." The word whispered from his lips. The soft sound alone brought him comfort as if she'd placed her hand gently on his brow.

Dennis twisted his face like he'd just bitten down on a lemon. "Joey ... Joey ... when is this going to end?" He shook his head wearily.

"When I find her."

"Yeah, well, in the meantime, and when you're up to it, son, I'll need a full statement," muttered Dennis.

When he was up to it? He needed to put all the pieces in the right order first. "What about Nell?"

Dennis took his time replying, as if he was making some effort to choose his words carefully. "*What about Nell?* That's a good question. I asked if you knew where she was. You lied to me, Joey. Why did you do that?"

"Because I needed her. I still need her."

"For what?"

"I ... I'm not sure."

"She saved your life, Joey, just like you saved hers. You're both even now. Forget about her."

He remembered her lips, her breath within him, her tears as they fell on his cheeks. He felt her pain as well as his own. He couldn't forget about her. She wouldn't allow it. *He* wouldn't allow it.

"Where is she?"

"Back where she belongs."

"What do you mean?"

"She's crazy, Joey, barking bloody mad. When the paramedics got there, she was covered in blood, your blood."

"I had a knife in my belly. I expect there was a lot of it."

"True, and most of it was on her. They had to wrestle her away, jabbering on and on about how you belonged to her and nobody else could have you. Bunny boiler – take my word for it."

"Where is she?" sighed McNeil. He was exhausted. He didn't have the energy for insistence or demand. He forced his eyelids to stay open and focused on Dennis.

"Back at the crazy house, safe in a padded cell. You don't need to worry about her anymore. Like I said, you're even. You don't owe her anything."

"Which crazy house?"

"Joey, just forget about her. I don't recall the name of the place. You don't need to know it. Some doctor picked her up, said she'd been missing for days, off her meds, not safe to be out on her own. She saved your life, but she could just as easily have taken it." He tapped at his head. "Like I said, crazy. You were lucky this time. Live and learn, Joey. Live and learn."

McNeil wriggled painfully to a sitting position, pulled the oxygen tube from his nose with a grunt and leaned in. "I have to speak to her. She knows about Kit."

Dennis shook his head. "No, she doesn't. She was stringing you along. Apparently, it's what she does, fixes on someone, burrows under their skin and into their head."

"She knows things."

"Like what? Joey, I'm sorry, I know how you want it to be true, but, let's face it, you bang on about Kit to anyone who'll listen. Why, even the night before we found Nell, you were making your mouth go at Minkey's. Your thoughts on Kit were plastered all over the front page of the 'Herald'. Nell doesn't know anything that she didn't pick up from elsewhere."

"I believed her." McNeil closed his eyes. *Did he? Did he really?* He still wasn't sure, but he was sure that he needed to see her again. Nell had told him they were the same, and now they were – once dead and now alive.

"Joey, come on, you'd believe Elvis was still alive if it meant Kit was too. I'm sorry if she messed with your head and raised your hopes, it was a sick trick, and you were ... are ... vulnerable, but try not to blame her. According to the doctor, she's barmy, always has been."

McNeil snapped to attention. *"What?"*

"Forget it, Joey. Just concentrate on getting well. I'm a man down, as usual. I can't have you lolling about in here getting waited on hand and foot. Mather is saying nice things about you for a change. The press is saying nice things about you, too. Clarissa What's-her-face has been camped on the doorstep, waiting for an interview. You're the poster boy of Bedlam. Make the most of it. Not satisfied with bringing bodies back to life, you're now being hailed as the copper who solved a triple murder. You'll be star guest on the 'One Show' before you can say 'Welcome to Bedlam'."

"It won't last, Dennis."

"Huh?"

"It won't last, because this isn't over."

"Joey, for pity's sake ... We have the youths, most of them, anyway. We have the kid who knifed you. They'll be going down for Popeye, Jaimsey, and Bales, and maybe a few more once we start digging. We've got forensic evidence. We have your evidence. What more do you want?"

"Motive?"

"Huh? They were kids, crazy feral kids. You said it yourself back in Mather's office. They did it for kicks."

"What about Curtis?"

"Curtis?"

"Archie Pollock's cousin. A latter-day Fagan. He's running drugs and kids from Minchem Road."

"And?"

"And he was there."

"If he was, the kids are protecting him. His name hasn't come up, and those kids are squealing like piglets at a hog-roast."

"He was there."

"There's no evidence, Joey."

"You have his voice on the phone. He was controlling the kids. He's behind this. He was there, Dennis. I saw him."

"Did you? The only voices on the phone are yours, the kids', and Nell's."

McNeil looked away. He tried to replay the scene, but it was corrupted by hindsight, blame, and regret. Had Curtis really been there, or had the voice been in his head, along with all the others, another figment of his warped imagination? He tried to separate his confused realities.

"Curtis knew Bales. They were both at Minkey's the night before we found Nell. Curtis threw the last punch, Bales helped to throw me out. Bales knew something about Kit."

"Joey, Curtis wasn't at the warehouse."

"Bales was."

"You're reading too much into this, trying to make connections that just aren't there. All roads do not lead to Kit."

"Okay, forget Curtis," grunted McNeil. "What about Dr. Richardson? I was there, in his office, talking to him just like I'm talking to you. Did you check him out?"

Dennis exhaled loudly and settled back in his seat. "I went down there myself, Joey. The place was boarded up. Padlocks on the front gates. Shutters on the windows. Maybe you dreamt it. Stranger things have happened."

"I was fuckin' there, I'm telling you." McNeil yanked at the electrodes on his chest angrily. The machines buzzed their response. "Did you check the CCTV at the hospital? I spoke to the guy. He spoke to me."

"Joey, I had the tape checked. Not personally, because I've been a little busy with a murder enquiry, as you know, but I had it checked and, yeah, you're on it, pushing and shoving your way through a lobby full of football supporters. There was nothing to see other than that. No weirdo doctors. Nothing."

"That's not right," murmured McNeil. "I know what happened."

"Look, you'd just had a ruddy turn or whatever you want to call it. You had concussion and enough stitches to start your own quilting club, so maybe, just maybe, you weren't thinking right. It's not a criticism, merely an observation."

McNeil shook his head slowly. Dennis was making perfect sense, but he knew that wasn't the case. "What about the orderly and the blood on the knife I handed in for evidence?"

Dennis shrugged. "Well, that's a bloody riddle if ever there was one. And, I can tell you, it's got me stumped. It turns out the personnel department had no record of the name he gave. The orderly didn't exist, Joey. He didn't work at the hospital."

"Maybe he was an illegal, an Eastern European who came into the country on the underside of a lorry?"

"Well, whatever. The guy had a miraculous recovery. One minute at death's door ..."

"Sounds familiar."

"... next, he's up, disappeared into thin air, and SOCOs have lost the knife. It's a bloody procedural nightmare. Mather's having a private coronary, but it's not your problem, don't sweat about it. We might never know what that was about."

"That's not all the SOCOs lost."

"What do you mean?"

"There was evidence removed from the viaduct crime scene, after the photos were taken."

"Evidence?"

"A charm. It linked Kit to Nell."

Dennis shook his head. "Look, I know you've had issues with Contrary Mary in the past, but I'm going to put this latest paranoia down to the meds currently running through your veins and the fact that, two days ago, you died in a derelict warehouse, and a freak from the twilight zone brought you back to life. So, naturally, you believe you have a connection, empathy. You don't, Joey. Believe me, you really don't."

"It was on the photo. It wasn't booked in."

"So why didn't you tell me about it when I sat in your flat and asked if there was anything you wanted to share?"

"I don't know. I wasn't sure. I hadn't worked it out in my head."

"And you're sure now?"

"No."

"Okay, where's the photo?"

McNeil faltered, "I can't remember. I had it ... before ... in the car with Nell."

"You gave crime scene evidence to a suspect?"

"Shit, Dennis, I can't fuckin' remember." His heart rate escalated, frustration and anxiety getting the better of him.

"Well, don't try too hard, Joey. You'll have a bleedin' coronary, and we'll be back to square one. You've just got things mixed up in your head, that's all. I'm not surprised your memory is shite. You've had a hell of a hiding, and, if that knife had been an inch lower, you'd have been pissing through a tube for the rest of your life."

"And if it hadn't been for Nell, I wouldn't even be here. She could have run, but she didn't. She waited with me, kept me alive."

"Yes, well, there's that. Like I said before, you're both even now. Forget Nell. Remember the good times with Kit, and, for pity's sake, Joey, move on."

McNeil scowled his response.

"Harsh, I know, but you've spent too long hankering for the past, Joey. You're a young man. It's time to look to the future."

"*The future?*" McNeil raised his head from the pillow and took in all the monitors and tubes that were currently feeding, oxygenating, and keeping his pain level bearable. "My future is with Kit, and, as soon as I'm out of here, I'll keep searching, with or without your help."

Dennis sighed. "You know I'll help you any way I can, Joey. I'm just not sure that helping you to prolong the agony of losing Kit is what a good friend should do."

"And you're a good friend?"

"You know I am."

"Then help me."

Thirty-One

Clarissa Temple thought she'd pulled a fast one. McNeil could tell by the way she offered a smug smile as she brushed past him in to the flat. In reality, it was the other way round, and Ms. Temple was about to work harder for her money than she realised.

"DS McNeil? Clarissa Temple. Pleased to meet you, honey."

McNeil shrugged his own greeting and stood back watching as she quickly scanned the hastily tidied room, processing, making assumptions, more than likely writing a by-line in her head while she spoke. She extended her hand aggressively, and he took it. Dry wrinkled skin, liver spots, and oversized rings. They could inflict far more damage than the skull ring worn by Curtis, should she ever have occasion to land a punch. Her grip was firm and self-assured. Judging by her journalistic reputation, he reckoned her for a scrapper, and that's exactly what he needed, someone who would do whatever was necessary to get to the truth.

"I do appreciate you granting me this interview, honey, but I have to confess to some curiosity." Her husky voice hinted at a forty-a-day habit and a touch more than the recommended units of vino.

McNeil reached out and took her coat, throwing it carelessly over the back of a chair. "I told you on the phone I couldn't discuss details of the current case."

"Yes, of course. Absolutely. That goes without saying. I fully understand." She was lying, but that was okay, he expected it. She placed her bag on the coffee table and pulled out a Dictaphone. McNeil eyed it suspiciously. "We wouldn't want to prejudice any court proceedings, but, of course, anything you might mention in error would be off the record. The public naturally wants to know what happened to you. You're a hero, honey, and, right now, Bedlam needs one of those."

"I wouldn't go that far. Right place, wrong time, that's all."

189

"Hey, take it while you can. Next week we'll be hounding someone else with a zoom lens."

McNeil nodded. "Yeah, last week you couldn't wait to stick the knife in."

"That's journalism for you, honey. It's nothing personal. Last week we did it verbally, this week somebody did it for real." She smiled shrewdly. "It makes for a damn good story ... when you're ready to tell it, of course. The human interest, what makes a good copper risk his career, hit the bottle and slide off the rails. Your story. Your words. If you don't, someone will just make it up, and you wouldn't want that."

"I told you ..."

"Yes, yes, you can't discuss the case. I'm not talking about the case. I have people sitting in on your department's press conference as we speak. I already have enough on the vagrants. I know there are currently four youths being held in connection with the murders and your attack. I'm talking about you, detective. About your life, what makes you tick, and why you continue to stand up against the establishment, and, more importantly, your friends? My experience suggests you have a story that will sell newspapers. My intuition leads me to believe that you want to tell it. I also assume DCI Mather warned you away from me completely, and that's why I'm intrigued."

McNeil shook his head. "No, he was the one who suggested I provide you with an update." That wasn't entirely accurate. The latest events had rather superseded Mather's intention to have him recite a specially prepared statement. If Mather knew that he'd invited the black widow herself into his home, he reckoned Mather would be a very unhappy DCI.

"Right, and you thought you'd meet me here in your flat, rather than at the station?" Clarissa's arched brow revealed that she was one step ahead.

He smiled. "It's more private."

"Detective, either you have an unhealthy interest in older women, or you're up to something you don't want your boss to find out about. Knowing your recent history, I'm staking my career on the latter."

McNeil decided he liked Clarissa. He wouldn't want her for a mother-in-law, or a boss, but reckoned she could probably keep order at Minkey's. "You could be right. Are you going to stay and find out?"

He gestured to the sofa, blinking away an image of Nell curled up in the corner, his football top pulled down to cover her knees, a cushion clutched to her breast. Four days since he'd last seen her, since she'd saved his life. It seemed like an eternity. He still didn't know where she was being held, which meant he was no nearer to finding Kit, and the pain of that was far worse than the pain from the knife.

"Can I get you a coffee?" he murmured softly, so easily distracted despite his resolve.

"Can you manage?"

McNeil's lips twitched. He could, but he chose to prolong the picture of the selfless cop cut down in the line of duty a little longer, so he made a big deal of limping to the kitchen, one hand pressed to his side, and Clarissa raised one of her pencilled-in brows sceptically and came to his aid.

He'd been up and about for a couple of days, albeit slowly and painfully, but physically he wasn't as wrecked as he could have been or, indeed, was making out to be. Weed, it turned out, was crap with a knife, and, although the blade had cost him a few pints of blood, it had miraculously missed all his vitals and the wound was healing. The broken ribs would take longer, and there wasn't a great deal he could do about that but grit his teeth and get on with it. He'd ignored medical advice and discharged himself the day before, and, once he'd done his deal with the self-appointed 'Queen of the Broadsheets', he was ready to hit the painkillers and the road, and find Kit.

She'd been notably absent since he'd got back to the flat. Not a breath or a whisper, and he worried at that. He missed her reassurance, her hand in his. Instead, it seemed her place had been taken by a little girl with violet eyes. He felt her anticipation, her held breath. She was there now, in the corner, waiting. He suspected she'd been there all along and he'd just failed to see her.

McNeil shifted his gaze to the photographer who'd accompanied Clarissa. He was sprawled in the armchair, surly expression, camera in hand. Was it the same man whose camera he'd broken? McNeil wasn't sure, but the man was itching to get a shot of him while he still had some visible battle scars to add drama to the article. He'd already had the police photographer taking snaps of all his wounds – the stitches, the abrasions, the colourful contusions, and the six inch abdominal knife wound, all neatly logged as evidence along with his blood-soaked clothes and his phone that had conveniently stayed open throughout his ordeal. He hadn't heard the recording of what happened after he lost consciousness. He didn't need to. He'd heard Nell's howl of despair and he'd heard her beg for his life. He wasn't sure which side he'd heard it from, but he'd clung to it like a lifebelt in a stormy sea. He would never forget either.

Now he needed information that would lead him back to her, back to the beginning, and finally back to Kit.

He inclined his head toward the man. "He can take his photos and then he has to leave. Our conversation is confidential and has to stay that way until I say otherwise. You understand that, don't you?"

Clarissa tutted loudly and nodded her agreement.

"I need to hear you say that or our deal is off."

Clarissa tapped at her nose conspiratorially. "Don't worry, honey. I've been in this business long enough."

He smiled. That was exactly why he'd chosen her and, similarly, why he didn't trust her.

The photographer subsequently took his fill of monochrome moody shots that made him look less like a hero and more like a villain, and left him with more than an inkling of the type of article Clarissa intended to write. He needed to ensure the balance of power between them was equal or run the risk of his flirtation with the press turning into a kiss and tell. "So, Clarissa," he said eventually, "what's the story with you and the DCI?"

Clarissa narrowed her eyes over the rim of her coffee cup. "I'm not here to talk about Frank. It's old news."

So it was 'Frank', not 'DCI' or even 'Mr. Mather'. Naughty Frank. It was always worthwhile having something on the boss. "My news is pretty old, too. Just like treasure, the longer it's buried, the more valuable it becomes."

"How valuable? We haven't discussed money, but I suppose we should."

"I don't want money."

Clarissa's surprise was quickly replaced by suspicion. "What do you want?"

"Merely your co-operation."

"Go on."

"Ladies first."

"Such a gentleman, but I'm afraid my history with Frank is nothing that would interest you."

"Try me." McNeil smiled, though he knew no amount of charm would work on the woman. Apart from the fact that she was old enough to be his mother, she could have read him chapter and verse on the art of prostituting oneself for one's art. The only thing that would turn her to putty in his hands would be the seduction of an exclusive. If she was willing to take a gamble, he would give her one.

She studied him for a long moment, and, although he recognised it as an attempt to unsettle him, he was happy to allow it. For the first time in over a week, he was focused. Physically and mentally he might still be a wreck, but there was something about coming back from the dead that gave him an advantage, he thought wryly. Maybe it was the acknowledgement that death wasn't necessarily the final step, not when there was business to finish up. Nell had given him a second chance. He had to make the most of it.

He met Clarissa's gaze steadily.

"Okay," she finally conceded. "Frank and I had a disagreement many years ago."

"Over?"

"Ethics."

"A journalist with ethics? Sorry, but I find that hard to believe. I'm a detective, remember. I interview and interrogate on a regular basis. I'm used to hearing all kinds of fiction, but that's a new one on me."

"I was young and idealistic at the time. We had an affair. It was ill-conceived and headed for disaster. It didn't last."

McNeil struggled with the image of Clarissa, woman about town, who was striking at sixty and would have been stunning at twenty, and Mather, the guy who needed a shoehorn to get out of his own chair.

Clarissa caught his look. "It was a long time ago. Not something I like to dwell on." She picked up her bag, rifled in it, and pulled out a flattened pack of cigarettes. She gripped one fiercely, and, when she sought his permission to light up, much to her chagrin, he declined with a shake of his head. He was in a delicate enough state without adding nicotine to the cocktail.

"Right. So you made out, then you fell out, and that's justification for a thirty year feud?" He was a little disappointed. He'd hoped for something he could use as a lifejacket when he started making waves in the department.

"There was more to it, as you might imagine. But that's none of your concern. You invited me here to write your story, not mine."

"I need to know I can trust you. You give up a few secrets and I'll give up some, too."

"Are you trying to get something on Frank?"

"Not especially."

"You're lying, detective. You blame him for mishandling the investigation into your girlfriend's disappearance, and now you want him to share some of your pain. It won't work."

"Why not?"

"Because Frank doesn't have a conscience, and he's adept at covering his tracks."

"It'll work if you help me."

"Honey, I rattle other people's skeletons, expose the dirty laundry of the masses. I keep my own neatly pressed and out of sight. I won't expose myself or my career to help you. Why would I?"

"Because I don't think the case was merely mishandled and, I think, secretly, you'd like to get one over on Frank, too."

"What do you mean?"

"Mistakes were made, procedures not followed, evidence lost. There are too many coincidences, and Mather is currently swinging between having me diverted or discredited by this kind of crap ..." He gestured vaguely to her reporter's paraphernalia on the table. "... the interview, the whole good cop / shite cop routine, or by direct threats to have me sacked."

"To be honest, and coming from one who's been riding the train to rebellion since before you were born," she paused for a hacking cough, "if your antics last week are anything like the norm, honey, I'd say you've been giving Frank every good reason to sack you. For a detective, you haven't been playing a very clever game so far. You have an almighty chip on your shoulder, and the weight has you bent in two, looking straight down at the gutter. You look at it long enough, you start to think you belong there yourself, and, let's face it, the law-abiding public, even here in Bedlam, prefer their policemen fresh, not pickled." She picked up her coffee and drained the last dregs before narrowing her eyes and leaning in toward him. Her voice dropped an octave, from lecture theatre orator to confidante. "Rumour has it you've also been spending time on the couch, and I don't mean the casting couch, honey. Psychiatric counselling? Are you sure this isn't all just a conspiracy theory playing hopscotch in your head? Love is a funny thing. Lost love isn't funny at all."

"I'm sure." He was far from sure, but the more he discussed it out loud, and the longer she listened, the more convinced he became that the events leading to his hospitalisation were not merely random acts precipitated by his own recalcitrant behaviour but connected in some bizarre way by Kit and Nell, the two women in his life.

"Okay, I'll play along ... for now." She looked wistfully at her cigarettes and McNeil ignored her.

"Go on."

"There was a child."

"What do you mean?"

"It's quite simple, honey. You're a man of the world. I guess you know all about the birds and the bees. Fulsome Frank had no desire to reap what he'd sown. He refused to stand by me, too scared of his wife, whose connections are worth far too much to him and his career. I was left to deal with the situation. I had an abortion. I'm not proud of it. I don't talk about it. If you talk about it, I'll deny it, sue you for slander and murder your career – and probably you, too."

McNeil smiled. "I don't die easily."

"So I hear."

"Do you blame him?"

"I blame myself. I could have said no. He bought me off. He promised me breaking news exclusives in exchange for my co-operation. I was young, determined, and greedy. I had my career ahead of me. I agreed and I've lived to regret it."

"Did he give you the exclusives?"

"For a while."

"Were they worth the life of a child?"

She winced at his words. "No."

"Do you want to help me save one?"

"I don't understand."

"Twenty-five years ago, another child was lost, and she may as well have been aborted because, to my knowledge, no one has missed her or grieved for her, or even attempted to find her. Something terrible happened. I don't know what. I need you to help me find out."

"Why do you need me? You have all the facilities of missing persons at your own finger tips. Why not use police data?"

McNeil shifted his gaze to the corner of the room. It was empty. "Because, on this occasion, Ms Temple, the Force is definitely not with me."

"Why not?" She leaned toward him, the hardened newshound sensing a story. "Do I smell cover-up?"

"I'm not sure, but someone is going to great lengths to ensure I don't succeed. I need you to check back through your records. Nineteen eighty-eight, something happened right here in Bedlam, and it was covered up. If anybody can uncover it, I think you can. You'll know it when you see it."

"This means a lot to you?"

"Yes."

"Are you going to tell me why?"

"Not yet."

Clarissa regarded him in silence for a moment. "Some things are best left in the past, honey."

"Like you and Frank?"

"Yes."

"But not the baby?"

"No."

"And if you had your time again, would you have done things differently?"

"Yes."

"Well, that's all I'm asking, the chance to go back and put things right."

"You might not like what I discover."

"I know I won't."

"And you still want to go ahead?"

"I have to."

"And what do I get out of it?"

"You get your exclusive, and, if we're lucky, we both get the chance to put the record straight."

Clarissa rose to her feet and began to gather her things. "Tell me, honey, has this got something to do with your girlfriend?"

McNeil sighed. "It has everything to do with her."

Thirty-Two

The last time McNeil had visited St. Bartholomew's Church was for the funeral of Aunt Mae, the woman who had brought him up. He couldn't recall a time before Mae, and what he remembered of his life with her was a rose-tinted canvas of cold winters, beach-combing summers, and the smell of home baking. It had been an idyllic apple-pie childhood, made all the more perfect because it was through Mae that he'd first met Kit.

He paused in the lane outside the arched stone gateway. In summer, it was covered in pale yellow roses. The remembered scent softened his tense expression. The graveyard was blanketed now in a thick layer of drifted snow, but he recalled it in springtime: irreverent games of hide-and-seek behind stones that had stood for centuries; stolen daffodils and bluebells hidden behind his back, when the Reverend was near, and hastily produced with a flourish and grin, first for Mae, and later for Kit. His heart ached with the memory.

His eyes strayed through the arch to the church entrance. The heavy oak door was ajar, and he was free to enter, as was every parishioner of the small hamlet of Eden, but, even so, reluctance dragged his step. His memories weren't all of Kit, and they weren't all good.

He ran his fingers over the rough stone that topped the wall and inhaled gently, stealing a moment of solitude before he took the next step. He needed to ensure that the paper he'd pasted over the cracks in his persona was secure.

He'd made a significant effort. His suit was pressed, his shirt fresh from the packet, his tie straight. He'd even dallied with the razor. But there was little he could do about the scars and bruising on his face. The pills he'd been given by Richardson had been taken as evidence with the rest of his things from the warehouse, and, true to his word, he hadn't had a drink since Minkey's, but that didn't mean it was easy or that he didn't need either. Inside, his mind played games with him and his gut churned with apprehension. He'd come for answers, though he had no idea what the questions should be.

He slipped into a pew at the back of the church and sat a moment in silence – remembering. This was where he'd first seen Kit, on Easter Sunday, nineteen ninety-three. He was ten years old, she an ungainly seven, with flowers in her hair and sand between her toes. With hindsight, he realised he'd loved her from the moment he'd laid eyes on her, but, that first summer, things had been very different, and she'd merely been the shadow that dogged his every footstep, the child who squealed at spiders, couldn't throw a ball or ride a bike, and insisted on holding his hand when he didn't want her to. A treasured child, she suffered terrible nightmares, was never let out on her own, and rarely strayed from the vicarage garden or church yard ... until she met him.

After a nomadic period, where they'd travelled the countryside together like gypsies and he'd changed schools as often as his socks, he and Mae had finally found Eden, and, a year later, the new Reverend and his family had arrived. Mae had encouraged their friendship, and it wasn't long before he'd taught Kit to ride a bike with no hands and climb trees fearlessly, and, before the first summer was out, they were inseparable. It was many years before their friendship developed further, but the love had been there from the outset. Was still there. Would always be there.

"Joey, is that you?"

A soft voice, delicately flavoured with melancholy, interrupted his thoughts, and he raised his head to the woman who stood at the end of the pew. He hadn't seen Kit's mother for almost a year. She'd aged far more in that time. She smiled, Kit's smile, and her tired washed-out blue eyes lit briefly.

"Have you come for the memorial?"

"*The memorial?*" His words, softly spoken, barely moved the frigid air.

"For Kit." She slid into the pew alongside him and twisted sideways to study him more closely. "It's a year today since she left us, Joey. Surely you know that."

He stared blankly at her, felt a strange tightness in his chest. The paper was beginning to peel. Was he really the only one who believed she was still alive? "Of course, I know that," he murmured. "It's been a long year ... the longest year."

He dropped his eyes as she took his hand and squeezed it gently. "I read about what happened to you. A terrible business. Sometimes I wonder what the world is coming to. You look awful. How are you, Joey?"

"I'm fine."

"Really?"

A ghost of a smile brushed his lips as an image of Kit racing down the cliff path to the beach slid into his mind. She was barefoot, her eyes screwed tight against the wind-blown sand, her hand clasped tightly in his as the momentum of the steep path hurtled them ever more quickly toward the crashing waves. He inhaled the salty tang of the sea and shrugged the image away. "I'm still searching, Audrey. I will find her."

"Don't, Joey," she sighed. "Don't keep putting yourself through the torment. It really doesn't help anyone, least of all you. She's with Jesus, that's what George believes, and I believe it, too. She was a beautiful daughter, a wonderful young woman. That's what today's memorial is for, to celebrate her life. I know how hard this is for you, Joey. I know how much you loved her. I'm her mother, it breaks my heart to think she's gone, but it will help me if you can stay and celebrate with us."

McNeil shook his head. "I came to speak with George. I'm sorry, but I can't stay ... I ..." He pulled back his hand, squeezed past her to the end of the row, and stood, one hand gripping tightly to the back of the pew, the other palm pressed flat against the wound dressing nestled beneath his shirt. He inhaled discreetly. If ever there was a time when he needed Kit's whisper in his head, it was now. As his eyes swept the interior of the church, the funereal flower arrangements and burning candles caused his stomach to recoil. He had to stay in control. He pleaded silently for Kit to help him.

"George won't want to speak with you, Joey, certainly not today. I'm sorry, but you know how he is. This has all been too much for him. Losing one child brought him to the church, losing the second has almost cost him his faith. It's been very hard for him, Joey. He ... he's not the same man. If you can't stay for the service, come back another day when you're less emotional, when we're all less emotional."

"I'm sorry, Audrey. I'm so caught up with Kit, in my head, in my heart, I can't think straight. Mae told me you lost a child a long time ago. Kit never spoke about it. How old was she when she died?"

Audrey's face softened and McNeil recognised that faraway look. Memories. At least she had those.

"Elizabeth was barely two when she passed away. Kit was inconsolable. They say twins have a bond. I don't know, but I know she retreated into a shell and didn't come out of it until she met you. I'm glad she had you, Joey."

McNeil smiled sadly. "I'm glad we had each other. What happened to Elizabeth? Mae never said."

Audrey looked away. McNeil heard the gasp as she armed herself with an extra breath. "A tragic accident. George has never forgiven himself."

"He was with her when she died?"

"Oh yes. He's been paying penance ever since."

"How did it happen?" The words were out before he realised how insensitive they sounded. He was so used to questioning those left behind following a traumatic loss, he'd slipped into detective mode without thinking, and instantly regretted it.

Audrey's face fell. "Not today, Joey. It's too much. My heart is in pieces. I don't think I can go through it again. She was such a beautiful child, old beyond her years. I know people throw out that statement and rarely mean it, but, in Elizabeth's case, she was so full of grace, she just had to look at you with those big soulful eyes of hers and that smile. They say God has a purpose for us all. I console myself with that thought, and so did George, until Kit was taken. Now he's full of self-doubt. He's a broken man, Joey. I'm sure you understand what that means."

McNeil knew all too well. "Where is he, Audrey?"

"Joey, it's not a good time ..."

"Where is he?"

She sighed, pulled out a linen handkerchief, and dabbed at moist eyes. He felt his own lip tremble as he witnessed her distress. He sucked in a ragged breath and tried to turn away, but, before he could, she had followed him, her arms were around him, and he had reciprocated awkwardly. He couldn't break down, not now and certainly not here.

"Joey, regardless of what George might say, you're not to blame for Kit. Just remember that."

McNeil put her aside and nodded. Of course he was to blame. He already knew that. "Where is he?"

"In the vestry. He's putting the finishing touches to his reading, weaving his memories of Kit into words of hope." She smiled wistfully. "I don't know how he does it. I open my mouth and all that comes out is sorrow."

McNeil stood in the open doorway and watched as the Reverend Foulkes stooped over his desk, pen in hand. The smell of old books and furniture polish made him smile. It brought back memories of Mae and the pride she'd taken in all her church duties. That was how he'd come to know Kit, helping out Mae as she cleaned for the Reverend and his family. From chance meetings they had become co-conspirators, inseparable. There was never any doubt that they would be together. But no one, not even he, could have predicted how things would end.

"It's time we had a chat, George." McNeil's request was barely audible above the hiss of the ancient gas fire in the grate, but the Reverend, as if in possession of a sixth sense, laid down his pen and spun his chair slowly to face him.

He leaned back, creaking the worn leather beneath him. His face was grey and drawn with lines of regret. "You think this is an appropriate time, Joseph?"

The use of his full name in the long-suffering tone reserved specifically for him put McNeil immediately on the defensive. He recalled the pats on the head, the reluctant acceptance, and, latterly, the simmering distrust. He pushed it all to one side.

"It's important. It can't wait."

"More important than Kit's memorial?"

"Kit isn't dead. So, yes, this is more important."

"Denial won't bring you peace. Believe me, Joseph, I know."

"What do you know?"

"I know you're not welcome here anymore."

"Tell me, George, why is that?"

"Because you took the most precious thing in our lives and you lost her."

"No, George. I fell in love with your daughter, and she with me. A madman took your daughter and I'm going to get her back."

The Reverend shook his head. "It's too late for that. She's at peace. Leave her be."

"I can't. I believe in her. I believe she's alive. I won't stop until I find her." He wanted to add, *and you shouldn't either*, but the man had clearly given up, and the evidence of desolation leached like sweat from his pores and gathered in the deep furrows on his brow. Had he always been like this? McNeil couldn't honestly remember, but he'd always sensed that George had suffered, rather than embraced, him.

"Why did you disapprove of our relationship?"

"You weren't good enough for her."

"I expect all fathers think that about their daughters' ... lov ... suitors."

George shrugged wearily. "I don't care about anyone else's, just mine."

"You're a man of the cloth. You're supposed to care about everybody. It's in your job description."

"Don't try and be clever, Joseph. This isn't the time or the place."

"Well, as it happens, I agree with you. I was never good enough for her, never will be, but she thought I was, and that's what counts, isn't it? Her happiness."

"All I ever cared about was her happiness. Protecting her, keeping her safe ..."

"Like her twin, Elizabeth?"

George shot him a wounded look and McNeil ignored it.

"What happened, George, to change your opinion of me? We got along when I was a kid. We got along when Kit and I first got together. You knew we were in love ... would always be in love, and then Mae dies and, suddenly, I'm the devil incarnate. What happened, George?"

"You took my daughter to Bedlam and you lost her, Joseph. What do you expect?"

"No, George, what happened before Mae died? I saw the look on your face at her funeral. Did she tell you something ... about me?"

The Reverend pulled himself out of his chair and tried to shepherd McNeil out of the door with an outstretched hand. "It's time you left. I have to get ready for the service."

"What did she tell you?"

"Get out."

McNeil stood his ground. "I need to know what my aunt told you. There are things I don't remember about my life before Mae. It's important that I do. It could help me find Kit."

The Reverend rounded on him with an expression that was not exactly fire and brimstone, but was enough to cause McNeil to take a step back. There was anger, but, more than that, there was hurt so intense, so all-consuming, that he wondered if there was anything else left inside the worn-out shell, and how the man had survived.

"Elizabeth is dead and I'll carry the weight of my sorrow and her mother's tears till the day I die. Kit is dead and I blame you for that, for luring her away from her family with your smile and your promise of better things. Regrettably, we lost one child, but Kit was ours to keep and you took her from us. I can't tell you what Mae told me, I can't break her confidence even if I wanted to, but I can tell you this for nothing. Mae was not your Aunt. She was not related to you in any way. You came to Mae from the devil himself, and, believe me, Joseph, he will claim you back."

Thirty-Three

Clarissa rang him as he headed back to Bedlam. He pulled to the side of the road and fumbled with the unfamiliar replacement phone. He was grateful for the distraction. His hands shook. George's outburst had broadsided him, the words of a man consumed with guilt and loss, but they were in his head now, and the voices were back. Not Kit's whispered smiles, or even Nell's soft taunts. Someone else stirred in the dark recesses, someone he recognised from long ago.

"I have something for you, honey."

He stared at the phone, took a moment to register Clarissa's words and then finally mumbled his response.

"Yeah, what's that?"

"Not a lot. Comparable, it seems, to your enthusiasm."

"Sorry, Clarissa, busy peeling onions. I can't see straight."

"Well, that's life, detective, and I'm guessing you have a few layers to go."

"Maybe. Go on ... what did you find?"

"To be honest, honey, I've had the office junior on this. Nineteen eighty-eight was a busy year, and I've got better things to do than loop through microfiche until my eyes scream for mercy. Despite a considerable amount of tragedy and mayhem as befits Bedlam, there was nothing that jumped out as being worthy of more than a few days' angst or particularly fitting the bill as per your remit. There were only a few front page items that may be of interest to you. The first was a bus crash that killed four passengers and one pedestrian. The bus collided with a removal lorry. The driver was drunk. It wasn't the first time, and he went to prison. He came out a few years later and hung himself."

"Was one of the passengers a child, a little girl?"

"Yes. Seven years old. Emily Parker. She was killed with her mother."

McNeil scowled. Sad though it was, that wasn't it, though he didn't know what *it* was meant to be. "Is that all?"

"No. Reports were circulated of a man driving a grey transit van who tried to lure a child. The usual 'Come see some puppies' kind of thing."

"Did he take a child?"

"No."

"Was he caught?"

"No, the story fizzled out. The kids were vague about what had happened. There was a suggestion that they'd made it up to cover up the fact they were late home."

"How old were the kids?"

"Eight and nine."

"Too old. Anything else?"

"More than a few murders – drug-related, domestic, the usual run-of-the-mill. There was one particularly gruesome discovery of two bodies that had lain undiscovered for a number of years, but you probably have more information than me on those."

"Any involving a little girl?"

"No. There was a drowning. Pretty tragic."

McNeil perked up. "A child?"

"A girl. Ball in the water, you get the picture."

"Where?"

"The lake at the town park."

"I didn't know Bedlam had a park."

"It did twenty-five years ago. Now I guess you'd call it a nature reserve. Basically, the money for maintenance ran out and it was left to run wild."

Yeah, that sounded about right for Bedlam. Society's nettle patch, complete with burned-out cars and leaking chemical waste. Maybe things were different twenty-five years ago. He couldn't remember.

"So, no reports of a missing child?"

"Nothing. Sorry if that's not what you want to hear, but I did my bit. We need to get together for your side of the deal. I need that exclusive. I'm holding the front page."

McNeil nodded distractedly, disappointedly. He wasn't sure what he'd expected her to find. "Sure. I'll get back to you in a day or so."

"Make sure you do."

"One last thing, Clarissa. The name of the kid that was drowned?"

McNeil heard scrabbling as Clarissa checked her notes.

"Elizabeth Foulkes, aged two. Tragic. Church picnic. Pony rides and merry-go-rounds. The story dragged on for a week or so, with petitioning by locals about safety. Apparently another child drowned there in eighty-six."

Tragic indeed. He felt the leaden weight of guilt sink to the pit of his stomach as he recalled the way he'd spoken to George. The man had taken his eye off his child, let her hand slip from his, and lost her forever. No wonder he was beside himself with grief. No wonder George hated him for doing exactly the same with his remaining child.

He ended the call, laid the phone on the dash board, and sat for a moment staring out at the snow. He wasn't sure what he'd achieved or where to look next. He was running out of options. Perhaps he should do as everyone else suggested and accept the fact that Kit was dead. But he knew he could never do that. He knew he wouldn't give up until he found her. Just like he hadn't given up on Nell beneath the viaduct, and she, in turn, had stood by him. He felt like an unwilling participant in a game of pass-the-parcel. Sooner or later, the last wrapper would come off and he was certain he wouldn't like the prize. He rubbed at weary eyes and refocused. He had to find Nell. She was the only one who knew what was really going on, and, crazy or not, he would make her tell him.

The scent of candy floss and toffee apples wriggled its way into his consciousness and drew his eye to the rear-view mirror. A red balloon bobbed against the roof of the car. The boy was back, and, for once, McNeil was almost relieved to see him, his paranoia providing a realm of almost comforting insanity. Their sense of connection was growing, their separation less bearable. Like a drug, he wanted more, yet feared the addiction and its consequences.

The boy sat in the middle of the back seat, feet pulled up awkwardly, one arm draped around a small huddled figure. He was soaked. Tendrils of pond weed clung to his hair, his lips were blue, his skin translucent, his grey eyes wide open and scared. McNeil absorbed his fear. It started as a tremor at his fingertips and, soon, his whole body jumped with it. The need to run, to scream, to fight, had his heart banging in his chest. He began to hyperventilate, dragging in oxygen in massive gulps as if in competition with another, and only one of them could survive.

The boy opened his mouth to speak and water gushed from it, spewing minnows and pond skaters. The little girl at his side held out her pale hand. In her palm, a tadpole wriggled, flipping tail and head in a frantic attempt to stay within the diminishing supply of water that dribbled between her fingers. The tadpole slipped from her grasp and the boy took her hand gently. They inhaled in unison, McNeil's heart slowed, and the children, entwined in each other's fragile embrace, turned to him and smiled.

Thirty-Four

He attracted some attention when he turned up at the station. The curious glances were mostly disguised beneath handshakes and choruses of 'Well done' and 'Nice one, mate', which was curious in itself because, as far as McNeil was concerned, he hadn't done anything noteworthy – yet. Regardless, he accepted the congratulations on his miraculous survival, which he reckoned had little to do with any prowess on his part but was nevertheless worth celebrating.

The squad was busy interviewing suspects, crossing Ts and dotting Is, to ensure a case that would ultimately meet the approval of the Crown Prosecution Service and stand up in court. The arrests now numbered twelve. Number thirteen, he hoped, was being reserved for king rat, Curtis. That, of course, was supposing he could either convince them of Curtis' involvement or the investigating officers were able to squeeze some youthful throats tightly enough so that his name popped out of its own accord.

McNeil scanned the squad room. Dennis was seated on the corner of his desk, phone at his ear, putting the world to rights as he lambasted the unfortunate on the other end of the line. He caught his eye, and Dennis frowned and gestured for him to wait. McNeil had other plans. Weed was still in the holding cells, awaiting a formal charge, and he needed to speak with him before he was shipped out elsewhere.

Dennis caught up with him as he waited for the lift. "Hey, what are you doing here? You're meant to be resting up and taking advantage of the Department's less-than-generous sick policy."

McNeil leaned a shoulder against the wall and smiled. "I was bored."

"Where are you headed?"

"I need a quick word with Weed."

"Sorry, Joey, I can't allow that. On this occasion, you're a victim, not a copper. You need to stay well away from all the little bastards. I don't want anything going wrong with this case."

McNeil reached out to call the lift.

"I mean it, Joey."

"So do I. Five minutes, that's all I need."

Dennis shook his head. "It's not happening, Joey. You go in there and start shouting the odds about Kit and Nell and God knows what, and we'll end up with the kid's defence buying you a bloody drink and the judge throwing out your evidence as unsound. We have to be smart here, Joey. Ultimately, you'll have the last word – just not here and not now."

"I thought you were meant to be helping me."

"I am. That's what I'm doing now. At the moment, you're a bloody hero, and the public loves you, Christ only knows why. The whole give-Bedlam-back-to-the-people brigade are holding you up as an example. While you were getting your vitals tweaked in hospital, the placard-carrying public were laying siege to the ruddy council about extra funding from central government for street lighting, drug rehabilitation schemes, extra bobbies on the beat, you name it, and they're chanting it from every street corner, cranked up, no doubt, by your new best friend and confidante, Ms. Clarissa, who's backing you like you're running for bleedin' parliament. I'm not even going to ask what all that's about, but if you go in there and start mouthing off about bloody ghosts and ghouls, and riding the ruddy dragon to enlightenment, where do you think we'll end up? I'll tell you where – with no bloody case."

McNeil's face twisted sourly. Dennis was right. Despite his current kerb appeal, he was essentially the weak link in the chain, as far as the case was concerned. In direct contrast to the Free Bedlam Brigade, the do-gooders would be tumbling out of the woodwork to find justification for the appalling actions of the mob, citing bottle-feeding, broken homes, missing father figures, and whatever else they could imagine. It would be madness to provide them with more ammunition by suggesting that he was less than perfect himself, or by illustrating that notion with an ill-advised interrogation. Public opinion was pivotal, and there was too much at stake to jeopardise the case. He would just have to get his information from elsewhere.

"I suppose when you put it like that ..."

"Good lad. Now, come on, let me buy you a cuppa. I've got ten spare minutes before I go bang some more heads together. I'd stand you a pint, but I don't think that would help matters, would it? So, on this occasion, Betty's twice-brewed will have to do." He steered him away from the lift and down the corridor toward the canteen. "Maybe there's something I can do to help you without rocking the love boat."

"Do you have the address?" McNeil asked, as he stirred his tea unenthusiastically. "That would help."

"The address?" Dennis had added a bacon and egg buttie to his order, despite the fact that it was long past breakfast time. He munched as he spoke. McNeil averted his eyes as a combination of grease and egg yolk made a bid for freedom down Dennis' chin. His stomach still hadn't recovered. He doubted it would until he had Kit back with him. He concentrated, instead, on Dennis' bulging notebook laid next to his plate, a virus-free pseudo computer that never crashed, but with limited storage capacity, hence the overstretched elastic band holding everything together.

"The address of the hospital, for Nell."

Dennis raised a long-suffering brow. "Are you still banging on about that? I told you. Leave it alone, she's barmy."

"You promised to help me." McNeil waited patiently as Dennis finished the last morsel and licked his greasy fingers clean.

"The wife's at her sister's," said Dennis, by way of explanation as he rose from his seat. "Might just get myself another while we're here. Save the gas at home."

"The address?"

"I have it somewhere on my desk. I'll check when we get back. Sunny Hill, Sunset Towers, Seventh Heaven, Psycho's Rest, something beginning with 'S' ..."

"Psycho doesn't begin with 'S'."

"Well, bugger me. I always knew that ruddy phonics malarkey was headed for disaster." He left the table with a grin and headed back to the counter.

McNeil waited until Dennis' back was turned before pulling a card from the notebook. *Serenity House, Bedlam.* He doubted it lived up to its name.

"Forget the address, Dennis," he called as he rose from his seat, one hand clasped to his side. "Maybe you're right after all. I came back too soon. Bloody wound is giving me jip. I'm just going to check something out and then I'm off home to rest up. You enjoy your fry-up."

Back at his desk, he logged onto his computer, resisting the lure of the on-going enquiry, the statements of the youths, and the crime scene photos of char-grilled Bales, and focused his attention instead on a little girl called Elizabeth, who, twenty-five years before, had slipped from her father's hand and disappeared into the darkness of a forgotten lake. Two years before that, the lake had stolen another child – three year old Jonathan Miller. What Clarissa had neglected to tell him was that neither child's body had ever been recovered.

According to the records, Bales, the water bailiff, had assisted police with both searches of the lake. His experience of all the local waterways, the gullies, and underwater currents, had proved invaluable to the search teams, and, within twelve hours, when it became evident that the toddlers had met a tragic end, they were downgraded to recovery teams. Divers had searched without success and it was accepted that the tiny bodies had either sunk beneath the silt at the deepest part of the lake, to be consumed in the fullness of time by water creatures, or been carried by underwater currents through one of the many channels that ultimately led to the sea or the sewer. It was little wonder that the Reverend Foulkes was beside himself with grief.

Bales, again. The man was everywhere. He'd been present at the scene of both Kit and Elizabeth's disappearances and assisted police in their search. He'd also been acquainted with Curtis, and now he was dead. Why had no one made the connection? McNeil used the mouse to position the last pictures of the two children side-by-side on the screen. Elizabeth's photo, presumably taken at the picnic prior to her disappearance, showed her clutching a red balloon. Jonathan's earlier shot was an evidential Polaroid snap of a battered child, who had evidently suffered physical abuse throughout his short life, ending his days, perhaps mercifully, in the cool waters of the lake. Statements from his parents, who were noted to be intoxicated at the time of interview, suggested the child had wandered away from them at the annual church picnic.

He zoomed in on the children's faces. Elizabeth was a picture of concentration, tongue poking between her teeth as she struggled to keep the balloon string from slipping through her fingers. Her eyes were downcast, her attention on the task not the photographer. Jonathan's eyes were also hooded, puffy, and red from crying. His face was dirty, his lip swollen, fresh sutures stood out starkly from a wound on his brow.

I warned you.

The oily voice slid into his mind as cold black water lapped at his feet. He gasped as the water flooded him, slowly from the bottom, as if he were a sponge filling up with regret and sorrow.

You wouldn't listen.

It bubbled in his gut, churning like a stormy sea, eddies and currents revealing dark things that had lain hidden in the silt far too long.

I told you what would happen.

It was up to his chest, tight and heavy, constricting his heart, filling his lungs. He struggled against it, his breathing erratic, his panic overwhelming.

Are you sorry now?

The water was in his mouth, on his tongue, and forcing its way between his teeth ...

Say it!

... up into his nose, stinging and sharp. He couldn't breathe. His lips were sealed tight. Cruel fingers pinched his nose. He felt a howl erupt from within, and the force of it ripped the hand from his nose and tore his lips apart. He ducked his head instinctively and Betty's twice-brewed white-with-no-sugar missed the computer screen and sprayed the waste-paper bin instead.

His heart pounded. His head was crammed to bursting with images that refused to budge. He wiped tea from his chin with the back of his shaking hand and inhaled. *Get a fucking grip.*

"Sorry ..." he murmured vaguely to those closest to him, who had narrowly missed the spray and now shared uncomfortable glances. "... I should probably go."

He stood unsteadily, one hand braced on the desk, and turned away from his judgmental audience. He could feel their communal alarm at the mess he'd made, at the mess he was.

"Fuck, Joey. Are you okay? You look like you've seen a bloody ghost." A friendly voice, full of concern, and it was almost his undoing.

He glanced back at the computer. The screen was blank, the power light off, but he could still see the children. Their eyes were no longer downcast, but open and focused intently on him.

I hear you, he murmured silently.

Thirty-Five

He called the lab from the car and requested a priority cross-check. He used Mather's authorisation, was sure it would be added to his long list of misdemeanours and come back to bite him, but was past caring. By the time he had talked his way past the officers on duty at Bales' house, he was on a roll, fuelled entirely by adrenalin. Better by far to be hung for obsession than impotence.

Bales' house was adjacent to the canal, an old lock keeper's cottage that would have had some rustic appeal had it been picked up and dropped in one of the privileged garden counties, or alternatively had it been adequately maintained, but, as with the lock and the waterway over which it presided, it appeared several decades had elapsed since the building had benefited from a lick of paint. Now, amidst the grey shroud of winter, even Mother Nature had shunned the place. Climbers were bare skeletal wood. Briars ensnared the unwary with thin lashes of barbed thorns.

McNeil avoided them with care, as he pushed his way through the ramshackle porch.

Inside, the place was a mess. Newspapers, stacked shoulder-height against the walls, restricted his passage through to the living room. Here, a single sofa, pulled close to an empty grate, filled the small room. Bales, a bachelor, lived alone, and, by the pungent odour which stung McNeil's nostrils as he entered, it was obvious that Bales had warded off his loneliness by keeping dogs – lots of dogs. They'd been removed by the RSPCA, but their smell was everywhere. It seeped its way into his subconscious.

The investigating team had been through the house already, looking for anything that might explain why Bales had met such a horrific death, a connection, perhaps, via his fighting dogs, to the hooded feral pack. So far, they'd found nothing: no drugs, no weapons, just dogs. At Mather's insistence, it looked as though they might just settle for that in an attempt to tie up the loose ends quickly, but McNeil knew there was more to it. Bales had been fed to the pack to stop him talking, McNeil was convinced of it. He was even more convinced that the answer to everything lay somewhere on Bales' property. He didn't care now how the man had died, but he did need to know why. He wasn't there to solve his murder. He was looking for something else, something much less recent.

He wandered through to the rear of the building, where he found a decrepit built-on kitchen, little more than a lean-to, with a leaking corrugated roof. Rotten food lay on the table, filthy dishes in the sink, spiked dog collars on the back of the door. The man was a slob, but that wasn't against the law.

Up the creaking, rickety stairs, he ducked his head at the sloping ceiling and stood at the doorway to Bales' bedroom, where ancient floral wallpaper covered the walls, damp-spotted and peeling, and curtains hung haphazardly from a metal rail, hooks missing, fabric stained and torn. There was a wooden unmade bed, part of a post-war set with mahogany wardrobe and dressing table. The mirror was cracked, and thick dust coated the surface. Above the bed, not a crucifix but a child's drawing, a naive crayon sketch in a cheap plastic fame.

A two-headed snake – one black, one white.

In the bottom right corner, barely visible now on the sun-bleached paper, there was a name scrawled in red, the letters jumbled and back to front.

JoJo x

Faint laughter curled like smoke from an extinguished match. The smell of cheap wax crayons teased his nostrils. The bed creaked, and a puppy wriggled amidst the tangled bedding, its tail twitching. The laughter turned to mischievous giggles, and McNeil backed slowly to the door.

Outside, the rear garden was over-grown, a mess of scrap metal and jerry-built dog runs. He stepped carefully to avoid the mounds of dog faeces and lengths of chain that littered the ground. The snow had been trampled underfoot into muddy slush by the investigating team, and he followed their footprints until they ran out at the rear boundary. Beyond the fence, a thicket of woodland screened his view, but he knew that if he were to force his way through the tangle of bushes and scrubby trees for a mile or so, he would emerge somewhere south of the industrial units, and, if he continued a little further and didn't watch where he stepped, he might easily tumble down the steep embankment and find himself in the mud beneath the viaduct.

He turned on the spot, shoved his hands in his pockets, and scanned the plot. Almost hidden beneath the hanging branches of a small copse was a dilapidated wooden building. It was apparent, by the tracks in the mud, that the investigators had not seen fit to check the contents.

McNeil pried the rusted hasp and padlock from the rotten wood, and pulled back the warped wooden door. It had evidently been barred for some time. The hinges had dropped, and it required a measure of lifting and heaving to gain entry. He winced as his stitches protested. The interior was dim, the windows shuttered with thick ivy. The light from the open door slanted a weak beam across a dusty floor. He pulled out his phone and used the display to illuminate the details of the cluttered interior. A jumble of rusted tools lined the walls. Long-dead mowers, a collection of empty bottles, a bench and lathe, and an ancient gent's bike contributed to the eclectic mess. Overhead, a wooden rowing boat hung from the rafters. At the centre of the building, partially cloaked in a dusty tarpaulin, was exactly what he'd expected to find, a grey transit van propped up on bricks, minus its plates. The bonnet was up, the engine long-since cannibalised. One rear door lay propped against the wall, the other hung awkwardly by one hinge, as though an unsuccessful attempt had been made to remove it. Inside, alone in the cold empty space, was a small boy's shoe. Scuffed at the toe, it hung by its lace from the rear-view mirror. As McNeil stepped up into the rear of the van, his weight rocked the vehicle and the shoe thudded rhythmically against the windscreen.

The boy sat crossed-legged on the passenger seat, waiting for him, a bright red lolly in his hand, sticky fingers dripping syrup onto grazed knees. Tinny music blared from the cassette player. '*The Wheels on the bus go round ...*'

The little boy clapped his hands in time to the music, and the lolly slipped from his grasp, bounced off his knee, and landed in the foot-well. His face fell, his eyes grew wide with fear, and his skinny arms came up reflexively to protect his head. McNeil followed his gaze, his breath held frozen in his throat as he, too, tensed in anticipation of a blow, but the driver's seat was empty, and, when he turned back, the boy had disappeared.

He felt a whispered breath against his cheek, and a steady cool palm at his heart, Kit and Nell both urging him on. A small sticky hand slipped into his and squeezed gently.

He was almost back to the beginning. He was almost too scared to proceed.

He phoned Dennis from the car.

"Hey, Joey, what happened to you?" Dennis railroaded the conversation before McNeil had a chance to speak. "I heard you had an accident with the waste-paper basket. Your mug-shot is now on the dart board in the cleaner's room. Just thought you should know."

"Thanks for that."

"Are you okay?"

"I'm fine, Dennis. Just got my recycling and wet waste mixed up, that's all."

Dennis snorted.

"I need you to do something for me."

"I'd say 'anything', Joey, but we both know that wouldn't be the truth, so spit it out, and, if it's legal, I'll think about it."

"I'm down at Bales' house."

"Why? You're supposed to be home with your feet up, playing the wounded hero."

"It's a long story. I don't have time to explain. I need SOCOs down here. There's a shed out back. Inside is a grey transit van. I need them to do the business on it. I've bagged a plastic lolly stick. It's on the dash board. It's old stuff, Dennis, and I hope it'll work. They need to check the whole interior – the kiddies shoe, the steering wheel, door handles, everything."

"Why?"

"A possible link to two drowning cases from eighty-six and maybe eighty-eight."

"You're kidding me. We're in the middle of a budget-busting triple murder enquiry and you want me to spend resources on a cold case from more than twenty-five years ago?"

"Kids, Dennis. Little kids."

"Yeah, tragic. But, Joey, be reasonable here. What can we do about it now? It's far too late."

"It's never too late, Dennis." McNeil paused to swing his gaze out through the window to the house beyond. "You see, I don't think they actually drowned."

Thirty-Six

I have failed. There is no doubt in my mind now, for he has not come to save me, and, once again, I must repeat and relive my existence. Now, though, it is a far crueller sentence, for I have glimpsed what might have been, what should have been, and had it snatched from my grasp. Of course, that is what Jacob had in mind from the outset. I have no doubt about that. The game plays on and Jacob continues to roll the dice.

Restrained, I lack the will to fight or free myself. Perhaps, if I were physically tied by straps or ropes or chains, nipping my skin or squeezing my flesh, I would feel more inclined to rally against my shackles, but, alas, Jacob is far cleverer than that. He binds me with such subtlety that I have no option but to sit and gaze blankly at my white-walled prison, my ever-shrinking domain.

He believes me to be totally in his power, under his thrall, but little does he realise that I have acquired, through much self-discipline, the art of internal rebellion. My mind will no longer close down at his command, but is free to wander and wonder and dwell on my misfortune, while he is free to plot and play.

He has switched me off.

I am back in my box.

And like the marionette that I have become, I await the puppet master ... and the final act.

Thirty-Seven

Latimer Street was a long brick terrace of two-up, two-down houses that stretched from the end of Canal Road to the very centre of Bedlam, front doors opening directly onto the pavement, concrete yards at the back. They would have been slums anywhere else, but here, in Bedlam, they were homes. Back in the eighties, they housed both workers and out-of-workers, the difference illustrated by the number of locks on the door. Those with anything worth stealing, held tight to their treasures. Those with nothing, left their doors wide open in the unlikely event that goods might conveniently fall off the back of a passing lorry, directly into their lap.

The boy must have brought him.

The smell hit him first, the penny-tang of blood that invaded his nostrils, travelled to his taste buds, and made him want to gag. Then came shouting, a man's belligerence, the drunken verbal swagger, so loud, so overpowering, it erupted onto the street and pummelled his mind as hard as a fist. The accompanying high-pitched banshee wail of a terrified woman made him wince. He raised his hands to protect his ears, and the boy did the same.

Ears covered to block out the sound.

Eyes screwed shut to censor the horror.

Lips sealed tight to keep in the scream.

McNeil watched like an impotent voyeur as the little wise monkey in the torn 'Star Wars' T-shirt slunk into the arena, cowed, tail between his legs, flattened against the wall. His small head snapped back with the force of the first blow, a cruel backhander that sent him spinning. The child wailed as his small body hit the floor with a thud, and McNeil reached out, scooped him up, and held him close, heart-to-heart, absorbing the pain, living the fear in great gut-wrenching sobs. The woman screamed as she fell. The man bellowed as he punched. The air was humid with hostility and neglect.

And then they were running, he and the boy, hand-in-hand, down the alley, feet thudding on the pavement, along the crunching gravel of the tow path, splashing through puddles, avoiding the briars that whipped at their cheeks and the nettles that stung their legs. Tripping, crying, gulping air. Unformed words held tightly inside, fears squeezed into small dark places. His heart pounded, his nerve endings sung, his lungs were fit to burst.

The wheels on the bus went round and round.

The van door slid open without a sound.

There were lollies and puppies with happy wet tongues.

And no more shouting.

Sudden banging kicked him back with such a start that it took a few extra heartbeats to reset his rhythm. A young PC peered at him through misted glass. He wound down the window and scowled back.

"DS McNeil, are you okay? You look like you had a funny turn."

McNeil looked past the PC. He was still parked up outside Bales' house. His mouth was dry. Perspiration coated his skin. He inhaled discreetly. "How long have you been standing there?"

"Just a minute or so. You were talking on your phone. I was waiting to ask if you'd seen enough of the house. I did a quick circuit of the property, and, when I came back, you were out for the count. Pardon me for saying, but you look like you've seen a ghost. Can I get you something ... a drink?"

A drink? McNeil could have murdered for a drink – or two, preferably – in a short glass, poured over ice, but when the PC held out a bottle of water, he took it gratefully, unscrewed the cap, and gulped it feverishly.

"Thanks," he muttered, as he handed back the empty bottle. He reached down painfully and retrieved his phone from the foot-well. The line was dead, Dennis long gone. Starting the car, he gave silent thanks when it kicked into life at the first attempt.

"You need to ensure that no one gains access to the shed in the back garden until SOCOs get here. Do you hear what I'm saying?"

"Well, yes, that's what I was just about to tell you. The reason I was knocking ... DI Todd is on his way down here. He said to tell you to wait for him, said your phone was on the blink."

McNeil grunted. "Tell DI Todd, thanks but no thanks. Tell him I had better things to do than wait around all day for him."

"But he said ..."

"I'm sure he did, but I'm saying no. You tell him *that* when he gets here."

"He'll want to know where you've gone."

"Serenity House. Tell him ... tell him I've gone to wake the dead."

Thirty-Eight

McNeil headed out via Bedlam's decaying centre toward the more leafy suburbs in search of the hospital. He yearned for pollution-free air to clear his senses and reset his chaotic mind. Negotiating the evening traffic with one hand on the wheel, he held the phone at his ear. The streets were busy, the roads slick with ice. He should have pulled over to make the call, but necessity won out over good judgment. He had a sense of momentum building exponentially, inevitability, and, the sooner he reached it, the better for all concerned.

"Audrey, it's Joey. I need to speak to George." Silence greeted him, and, as seconds ticked by without a response, he opened his mouth to repeat the request, impatient now, driven by urgency, fuelled by anxiety.

"The service went very well, Joey. Thank you for asking." The reproving tone in Audrey's reply stung him to the core. His attention slipped momentarily from the road and the sound of a blaring horn dragged him back with a start. While he'd spent the afternoon uncovering dirty secrets in Bales' back yard, Kit's family and friends had been gathered together at the church.

"I'm sorry, Audrey," he sighed. "I've got a lot on my mind. I'm glad the service helped you, I really am, but it wouldn't have helped me ... I can't change that. It's just the way I feel." He braked hard at a red light. The seat belt tightened and his ribs protested. He would have taken his chances and skipped the light if there hadn't been a car in front of him. He cursed the car and the traffic and everything else that seemed to be conspiring against him.

"I'm sorry, too, Joey," replied Audrey. He felt her virtual embrace as she continued. "I shouldn't have scolded. It's been an emotional day for us all. I know how much you loved her. I know how hard this is for you."

Not loved, *love* – present tense. He wanted to say it out loud, but was weary of having to continually justify his belief, his commitment. He took out his frustration instead by banging a hand on the steering wheel.

"Is George there?" he asked again, a little more insistent, impatience colouring his tone.

"He's not, Joey. He's at a meeting and won't be back until late. To be honest, I think he needed some time ... away from me. I've been a little tearful today."

McNeil cursed under his breath, both at his own insensitivity and the fact that George was unavailable. "Maybe you can help me instead. Kit had a charm on her bracelet, a snake. Do you remember it? Do you recall where she got it?"

"A charm?"

"I realise this isn't the best time, but it's important, Audrey."

"She had a number of charms. I don't quite remember where they all came from. Some were birthday gifts. Some signified a special event like her graduation or passing her driving test. The snake may have been one of those ..."

"An enamelled, silver two-headed snake, Audrey. It was quite distinctive. One black and one white."

He got through the lights and turned right onto a wide road, where it seemed some redevelopment was underway. Cars and builders' vans lined the kerb, double-parked between mounds of ploughed snow. Behind a mesh security fence, construction workers were closing down for the evening, switching off the arc lights one by one. An illuminated sign on a large wooden hoarding announced the future 'Serenity House Assisted Living Complex', a home for the elderly and infirm that was duly illustrated with smiling grey-haired residents and imaginative sun-drenched landscaping.

He pulled the car into a gap at the kerb and wound down the window. Placing his hand over the phone, he leaned out and yelled to an elderly man who'd stopped while his aged dog cocked its leg against the fence.

"Excuse me. I'm looking for Serenity House Hospital."

The man gestured over his shoulder. "That's it."

"Huh?"

"The new old folks' home is being built on the site of the old hospital." He accompanied his words with a toothless smile. "I'm hoping for a place when it opens. That's if Barney here has passed on by the time they finish building. They don't accept dogs, you see. None of these places do. What they expect you to do with a lifelong friend, I've no idea. It's a bloody disgrace, if you ask me, but what can we do when our brains turn to cabbage? We forget where we live, leave the pan on the stove, and our own families don't have time for us anymore."

McNeil raised a brow. He didn't have time for the ramblings of an old man either. "Right. So, when did it close down?"

"Bloody hell, now you're asking." The man dropped his gaze to the dog at his feet. "That was in Barney's dad's mother's time. Trixie, now she was a lovely old girl. She would only eat fish. Can you believe that? Parky madam! She had a beautiful shiny coat, though."

"How long?"

"Oh, mid-length, like a collie."

McNeil hid his frustration. "No, how long since the hospital closed down?"

"Must be thirty years or more. They moved the nutters over to the other place, and then, I think, that closed down as well. Not sure what happened after that. There's no room in the modern world for crazy people, eh?" He gestured to the site. "Care in the community. What bloody community? This is Bedlam, after all."

Once again, another wild goose chase, courtesy of Dennis. McNeil scowled. "What other place? You said the residents were moved to another place."

"I forget the name. The place where that psycho feller killed all his wives. You know, when I was a nipper, we used to dare each other to climb over the wall and run through the garden. Always been a creepy place, that. The dogs, they won't go anywhere near. Dogs know about these things. Trixie, now she was particularly clever. I reckon it was the fish. Brain food, they call it."

The old man shuffled off with a backward wave, muttering to the dog as it laboured along behind him. McNeil turned back to the phone. He'd forgotten about Audrey. She was still speaking and he caught the tail end of it.

"… she cried so hard for little Nell. She just wouldn't be pacified …"

"Nell?"

"They were barely two years old when they parted, babies really. Kit couldn't get her tongue around the name Elizabeth, so she called her 'Nell'."

Of course.

He closed his eyes and drew a breath as the image drifted in. Two little girls. One red balloon, one yellow. One hand held tight, the other not quite. Fingers slipping from a father's grasp. Red balloon flying free, caught by the breeze, bobbing and teasing as it led the chase. Excited, clumsy running, white leather sandals stained green with fresh-mown grass, laughing, squealing, crying – Stop! He was yanked back with a painful jerk. His stomach churned with unimaginable, sickening dread.

I told you.

I warned you.

Now see what you've done.

"And the charm?" He gasped, shaking his head to dispel the imagery. Heat flushed his face, his hand instantly clammy where he gripped the steering wheel.

"I just told you, Joey. You weren't listening. She may have got it from Leonard. He was so kind to her, arranging her sessions. In fact, I'm almost sure he gave it to her. He was so supportive after we lost Elizabeth. He came to the service this afternoon. We hadn't seen him for years. I wish you'd had the chance to meet him."

"Leonard? Kit never mentioned him."

"No. She stopped going for therapy after we came to Eden and she met you. I suppose all she really needed was a friend, and you were that, and more, Joey."

"Therapy?" McNeil's stomach tightened a further notch.

"Yes, she had dreadful nightmares, poor child. She would insist that she'd seen Elizabeth long after the accident. Wishful thinking, Leonard said. He explained it was quite normal for her to experience visions after such a tragic loss. Maybe, if we'd found Elizabeth and put her to rest properly, things would have been different. George wasn't comfortable with talk of visions. I think he was relieved when the therapy ended and things got

227

back to normal ... well, as normal as they could ever be under the circumstances."

Back to normal? Back to the beginning? McNeil couldn't believe he had been so blind. "Where's the meeting, Audrey?" He was making small talk now, while his mind raced back and forth, picking things up and discarding them just as quickly.

"Why, at the church."

"How long do you think George will be there?"

"Some time yet. I don't expect him back before 9 p.m. It's the fundraising committee for the church picnic. We're holding one here in Eden next summer. Since ... Elizabeth ... we haven't held a picnic. It just didn't seem right. But we have to move on, all of us do, you included, Joey, and, next year, as it's the double-centenary of this wonderful little church, we decided we should celebrate the occasion with a picnic here on the village green in memory of both our girls."

Kit and Nell sitting in a tree.
Which will JoJo choose to free?

McNeil checked his watch. It was just gone five. He'd delayed long enough. "That sounds like a good idea, Audrey. We all need things to celebrate." He smiled sadly. He was guilty of wishful thinking, too.

Gilmour House was exactly as Dennis had described it – padlocked gates and shuttered windows. It didn't look as if it were in the middle of redevelopment, and, when he thought about it, he hadn't actually seen any evidence of work in progress when he'd attended his appointment. Richardson had merely told him work was on-going, but then again, according to Dennis, Richardson didn't exist.

He rattled the gates, testing their security, their ability to keep folk out, or in, depending upon point of view. The padlock and chain were new, which was interesting, given Dennis' insistence that the place had lain empty for the last twenty-five years. The ornate, wrought-iron gates were rusted in places and much taller than him, an insurmountable barrier in his current condition, so he sought an alternative method of entry. Regardless of what Dennis might believe, or common sense dictated, McNeil now knew that Gilmour House held secrets.

The building was enclosed by a high brick wall where it fronted the street. One side abutted the grounds of a now-derelict residence that showed signs of stalled building work, with a skip on the drive, a digger dusted with fresh snow, and a half-hearted attempt at a mesh security fence. He placed his hand on the *'Hard Hats Must be Worn'* safety sign, and pushed the flimsy barrier aside.

Somewhere off to his left, a dog sounded out his presence, but McNeil was satisfied that it was at least two gardens away, and he trusted the old man who'd maintained that all dogs, if they had any sense, stayed clear of Gilmour House.

Halfway down the darkened rear garden, on an icy path that canted perilously to one side, he found what he was looking for. The boundary wall connecting the two properties had succumbed to the thrusting roots of an adjacent tree and had subsequently been reduced to a rough pile of fallen masonry. As he looked through the gap, he could just make out the rear of Gilmour House through an overgrown, snow-shrouded orchard. He was sure he could see a dim light from a second floor window.

Sharp stone scraped his palms, sutures tugged, and ribs complained as he clambered stiffly over the wall. He took a moment on the other side to catch his breath and control the pain.

The property was vast, far bigger than he'd realised from the front elevation or the interior, briefly glimpsed when he'd met with Richardson. The garden ran to an acre or more, the far boundary unclear as it disappeared out of sight in a tangle of overgrown hedges, trees, and gathering dusk. Extending back from the elegant façade was a series of extensions and additional wings, each one cobbled onto the other as successive owners had executed their own ideas for its use. The Grade II listing had frozen not only those bits of architectural merit, but also the ugly carbuncles, leaving the once graceful building deformed and asymmetric.

McNeil had empathy with the scarred bricks and mortar. His own building blocks were precariously stacked.

The boy was with him as he crossed the virgin snow, small feet lost in his larger footprints, arms outstretched, wind-milling for balance as he leapt the longer strides from one impression to the next. Together they approached the short flight of stone steps that led down to the basement entrance. McNeil felt the child's warm candy-floss breath at his ear as he stooped to check the lock. The door swung open with the merest of invitation, and the boy's hand slipped into his and squeezed gently. *Yes*, he acknowledged silently, he would be careful *this time*.

The smell slammed into him before he had taken a full step into the narrow passageway. A thick, pungent odour of morgue-like disinfectant, underpinned by a cloying cocktail of sweet, damp soil and rotten vegetation, it caught the roof of his mouth and seared the back of his throat. The urge to spit it out was overpowering, but his mouth was so dry he could barely swallow, let alone summon the required saliva. His eyes stung, nausea threatened.

The boy hesitated at the door, one hand on the frame, one leg raised ready for flight. The percussion in McNeil's chest began a steadily increasing beat as he absorbed the child's fears and made them his own. He took a shallow breath and held it while he listened for any sounds that might help to confirm that he was not alone in the building.

At first there was silence, then, gradually, into the vacuum came indistinct noises. He cocked his head, trying to establish their cause and location – knocking pipes, a distant dripping tap, the rustle of rodents in the walls, the patter of crane fly feet on the ceiling, all magnified to the point where, along with the escalating drum beat in his chest, they formed a macabre orchestra, a chilling soundtrack to his fear. The music built to a crescendo, filling his head, his whole body, until he felt the walls and floor reverberate with the din. And then, abruptly, the performance was ended with the cymbal clash of a door slamming on an upper floor.

He climbed the wooden stairs that confronted him with apprehension and a subconscious remembered step.

Step three, can't catch me.
Step five, still alive.
Step eight, full of hate.
Step ten, begin again.

He didn't realise her presence until he'd reached the top and glanced back to see the boy hopscotching behind him, lips silently working as he chanted the rhyme like a mantra of protection. He watched as the boy reached behind with an open hand. The little girl sat on the second step, refusing to move.

Step two, I love you.

Dim emergency lighting punctuated the darkness of the next floor. A wide utilitarian corridor stretched to his left; to his right, it disappeared around a corner. Water pooled the floor, reflecting his own rippled image back at him. He blinked to rid himself of the illusion, and, for an instant, his mind was clear of muddle and subverted imagery. The resulting clarity was just as alarming. It allowed more room for anxiety and foreboding. Both rushed to fill the space. *Inhale, exhale.* He hesitated, unsure. He called to Kit and to Nell to guide him, but both were silent. Behind him, the boy splashed in water, knee-high and rising.

A bright red balloon bobbed past him, drawing his eye and his attention, and he watched its journey detachedly, its progress halted by the little girl who waited at the corner. She reached out and caught the string as it teased its way through her open palm. Without a second thought, he followed her.

Up another flight of stairs, and now the faded grandeur of the old place was evident. Threadbare carpet runners ran the length of the hall, waist-high wooden panelling lined the walls, and massive polished oak doors, with glass lights above, punctuated the space like sombre sentries. White light spilled out through one and cut a swathe through the darkened hall.

Running feet, giggles bursting through tightly clenched fingers, a bouncing ball with a rhythmic thud, a stick dragging along uneven panelling ...

Clickety clack,
Step on a crack,
Clickety clack,
JoJo's back,

The boy's finger pressed gently against his lips. A soft cautionary breath whispered at his ear.

Shhhh.
Step nine, you are mine,

When he stepped through the open door, they were waiting. *All of them.*

Thirty-Nine

The room was crowded with people, both real and imagined. All those who whispered their torments and warnings had gathered together for the final act. They slunk in corners, shifting like over-exposures on a long-forgotten film reel. Their lives, their motivations, lay like transparencies placed one above the other, until all became a jumble of secrets and shadow.

Despite the spectators, despite the confusion in his head and the fear in his belly, McNeil's whole focus was reserved only for one. His chest tightened, his throat closed, and he struggled to swallow. Sudden tears pricked his eyes.

"K ... Kit?"

She turned from the darkened window, golden hair shimmering, sweet smile reserved solely for him. He couldn't believe, after all the searching, after all the disappointments, he'd finally found her.

"JoJo," she breathed. The softness of her tone caressed him gently, wrapped around him, and, for a moment, he was removed from everything, held cocooned and suspended above the maelstrom his life had become. "I lost track of the time," she continued. "I hope you weren't worried."

She stepped toward him, a graceful ethereal step, and he stumbled forward, pulling her into his arms in a tight desperate embrace. His heart thudded wildly. He inhaled in short sharp gulps. Her skin was warm and fragrant, her breath soft against him. She was real flesh and blood, not a dream or a figment of his imagination. Yet, even as he rejoiced, something stirred amongst the dark things deep in his gut, and it drew him slowly back. He would do anything for her.

He was about to find out exactly what that meant.

It was Kit, and yet ... it wasn't.

She'd been missing for a year, yet she behaved like she was merely late for dinner. He raised his head and angled back, moving his hands to cradle her face. Her eyes were lacklustre, just as Nell's had been when he'd woken her in his bed. His anxiety flooded back and the voices in his head began to snicker. He took a calming breath – *inhale, exhale* – and swung his attention to the man behind her.

"Dr Richardson? Or are we Dr Freidman today?"

"I prefer 'Jacob'. It's less formal, don't you think?"

The red balloon that had held his hopes aloft burst with a bang and McNeil plummeted back to earth.

"What have you done?"

Jacob's narrowed gaze slid to Kit. "Sit down, my dear. Joe and I have some catching up to do." Without a sound, she withdrew gently from McNeil's embrace, her fingers slipping delicately through his as their hands pulled apart.

"Thank you, Kit. We won't be long." And, as if Jacob had flicked a subliminal switch, she settled herself on her seat, exhaled with a soft sigh, and her eyes drifted shut.

It was only then that McNeil became fully aware of the others in the room, the uninvited guests, the indistinct shapes that hovered in the shadows just out of reach, the hecklers, the patrons, the voyeurs, all awaiting their turn in this, the final act of Jacob's bizarre theatre: Mather, puffed up with self-importance, Mary Cameron with her sly smile, Clarissa, lost in a cloud of nicotine, Bales, watching and waiting, the swinging corpses with bulging eyes and thumping feet, green-haired Weed, taunting him, daring him, willing him to fail. And, between them all, the slavering indigo beasts that leapt from Curtis' skin to snap at his heels.

He raised a hand to his temple as reality began to slide and the boy pulled him back with an insistent grip, small fingers nipping fiercely, eyes darting back and forth as he peeped out fearfully from behind McNeil's leg. He lowered a hand to reassure the boy, and, as his trembling fingers skimmed the child's tousled hair, his own frantic heartbeat slowed and his focus sharpened.

Nell was seated next to Kit. Had she been there all along? He couldn't recall, but she stared at him now with empty soulless eyes.

"Nell?" The word was barely a whisper. She gave no indication that she'd heard, but he knew she had. He felt her hand on his chest, her breath within him, and hope returned. His eyes lingered on her for a moment. His enduring image was of her tears falling through flames to cool his cheeks. *I hear you,* he murmured silently.

He slid his gaze around the room again. There was no one else present. The shadows were simply that, voices in his head, tormentors born out of fatigue and desperation. He had succeeded. The hard work was done. He had found them both alive. All that remained of his nightmare was Jacob. He turned his attention back to the man.

"Are they drugged?" A first question, though he had many others. They fought like recalcitrant children to be next in line.

Jacob leaned back, crossing one leg over the other, making himself comfortable in his leather club chair. He gestured, with a dip of his head, for McNeil to do likewise, but McNeil baulked at the offer, unnerved by the bizarre conviviality.

"I suggest you take advantage of my hospitality while you can, Joe. You need to save your strength for later."

"*Later?*" McNeil grunted. "Is that when you resist arrest and I'm compelled to use unreasonable force?"

Jacob smiled benignly. "Is that what you'd like to do?"

"I'd like you to answer my questions."

"For goodness' sake, sit down, Detective McNeil. You're not at the station now. I'm not one of your common low-life suspects ... and you're obviously in pain. How is the wound coming along?"

As if the man had pressed some unseen torture device, McNeil was speared with sudden white-hot searing pain and overwhelmed with the accompanying urge to curl up around it. He gasped, inhaling in frantic gulps, while heat and perspiration flushed his face. *Get a grip. This isn't real. It's some therapist's party trick, word association or subliminal messaging.* Jacob was just a man, a very sick individual, but nothing more, no matter what Nell might believe.

McNeil absorbed the pain and met his eye. "It's nothing. Just a scratch," he lied.

"Have you learned nothing?" continued Jacob.

"Huh?"

"My bite is far worse than my bark, as Nell will attest."

235

Jacob smiled and McNeil's pain sharpened. He drew in a sharp breath and re-focused. "I asked a question. I need an answer. What have you done to them?"

"I see you're still unable to do as you're told, Joe, to take advice, to heed a warning. Is it any wonder you find yourself in your current predicament?" Jacob shook his head reprovingly. "I'm disappointed in you, Joe. I expected to see you at the church this afternoon. I'd counted on it, actually. I had a wonderful surprise planned. But no, as usual, you go your own merry way and to hell with the consequences. Poor Audrey was in such a state, and George ... well, there's a broken man, if ever I saw one." He leaned forward and reached for a glass. "Would you care for a snifter, Joe? I expect your throat is very dry by now, although ..." His lip curled into a sneer. "... on second thoughts, perhaps not. You need to keep your wits about you, don't you?"

He poured a measure, and McNeil watched as the amber liquid taunted. His throat was getting dryer by the minute. He swallowed in an attempt to lubricate it, but, when that merely exacerbated the problem, he cleared his throat instead.

"It's fortunate for you that Kit is unaware of your pathetic attempts to find her. George always was a good judge of character, and he was right about you, Joe. You really aren't good enough for her, are you?"

"He's not that good a judge if he swallowed your line."

"Touché," Jacob smiled. "But then, he had a little help. You'd be surprised how therapeutic the occasional counselling session is."

"And, as for pathetic attempts," McNeil found his voice getting stronger, fortified by the dark things that twisted in his gut, "I found her. She's sitting right there."

"And who brought you to her? Let's face it, Joe, you're a detective, a good one, so I'm led to believe, and yet, it took almost a year and a nudge from me to encourage you to look in the right direction."

McNeil turned his head. Nell stared straight ahead, blank eyes, expressionless face, yet there was something in there, something inside that reached out to him.

236

"Nell led me here." His tone was softened by gratitude but wrapped in confusion. Both girls, alive – but not quite. The vibe he was getting from Nell was unsettling. He sensed her torment. It matched his own.

"No, Joe. Nell helped, I'll grant you that. She baited the trap, loaded the dart, and sweetened the pill. But, think again, who really led you here?"

Fear exuded from the boy and McNeil mopped it up.

No ... noooo ...

Don't tell.

Mustn't tell.

Never tell.

The childish whisper curled in McNeil's mind, awakening the others, the voices that waited their turn, sometimes silent but always there. They crowded, jostling for attention. Vibrant images and emotions fought their way out, hot tears on stained muddy cheeks, small fingers gripped tightly to soiled and pungent rags. The rancid odour stung his nose. Dogs barked, puppies yapped, men argued, low and menacing. A rough hand grabbed at his collar, and he was powerless and helpless, suspended above the chaos while the world carried on without him.

His heartbeat accelerated, and, although he craved the comfort of Kit's embrace, his eyes strayed instinctively to Nell. *Help me*, he pleaded silently. This time, there was nothing, as if she, too, awaited his answer with baited breath.

"Bales." The name burst from him and the boy shuddered at his side. He jammed his eyes shut, pinched the bridge of his nose with shaking fingers, and tried hard to concentrate. It was all in his head, building, swelling, gathering momentum, like water poised to burst the dam, with only one small boy to hold it back. "Bales brought me here," he stammered. "He dragged me from my family and gave me to you."

"Not quite." Jacob smiled indulgently.

McNeil's eyes shot open. "I remember. I remember it all."

"No, you don't, Joe. If you did, you'd know that all of this is your fault." He gestured with an open hand to the two young women. "Bales may have kicked the first stone, but *you* are responsible for the resulting landslide."

I warned you.
You didn't listen.
This is all your fault.

"*My fault?*" McNeil swung his gaze between Kit and Nell. He recalled Nell's words: "You are responsible for all of this." He still didn't understand.

"Think again, Joe. Bales didn't drag you from the bosom of your loving family, did he? Bales saved you. The only mistake Bales made was in thinking that he could keep you."

Sweet, milky puppy breath and soft, warm bodies nestled alongside him. Bales, in the kitchen, clattering dishes and humming out of tune. Baked beans and sausages, out of a tin, but warm and filling. Jam on his cheeks and mud on his knees. A rough hand, gentle on his head, as tears were wiped with a ragged cloth. But there was more, and it helter-skeltered in to scour away the warm fragmented memory.

Turning away, McNeil drew a harsh breath. His hands shook. His ribs ached. He eyed the chair, but rejected it with a scowl when Jacob raised his glass and the melting ice rattled tauntingly.

"Sit down, Joe. We have a way to go yet. The girls wouldn't want me to be inhospitable, and I'm sure they're just as interested as I am in your memories."

"What have you done to them?" McNeil's voice was forced past a parched throat. He ignored the lure of the glass and swung his gaze back to Kit. He wanted to reach out and touch her, to reassure himself that she was real, not just another of his distorted daytime nightmares. Ghosts and shadows, that's what Dennis would have called them. He'd have put the whole episode down to some jumbled consequence of drugs or alcohol, or both. Maybe he was right.

"I've kept them safe, safe from the horrors of the world, Joe. Just imagine if you could close your eyes and forget that any of the last twelve months had ever happened, that Kit had never disappeared, that you hadn't turned to the bottle for consolation, and you hadn't jeopardised your career and friendships. Imagine that, Joe. A new dawn, a new day, a new life. The ills of the world would be much improved if we didn't have regret and remorse weighing us all down."

"Is that what you've done to them? Wiped their memories? Is that what Nell meant?"

"Not just to them, Joe, and I prefer to call it editing. I've spent my whole career refining the skill. There were others, successes and failures, but the girls are something else entirely. I must admit Nell does lack discipline. She learns and adapts. She challenges my authority, and, although I find her efforts amusing, she is nevertheless outliving her usefulness. Good twin, bad twin – perfect material. It's such a shame I can't publish my work."

McNeil swept his gaze around the darkened room. He'd faced many dangerous situations in his career, but the sense of foreboding building within him warned of a far greater threat. "*Others?*"

"Benjamin Rath was so misunderstood. I've followed his research. He was, in fact, a genius, a man ahead of his time. He delved into the darkest reaches of the mind. He just needed a little longer to perfect his craft."

"Benjamin Rath was a murderer. A serial killer."

"The unhappy consequence of an enquiring mind. He discovered the elixir of contentment, but never mastered the recipe." Jacob smiled slyly. "Too hot or too cold but never just right, which was rather unfortunate for his many wives. He didn't murder them, Joe. He just failed to wake them up."

"You're mad. This is all crazy. Playing with people's minds, playing God. The days of the madhouse and lunatic asylum are over. You can't experiment on real people. You can't wipe the tape and record over it as if you were scripting a screen play."

He edged toward Kit. The man was clearly unstable. It was time to put an end to the bizarre performance and get Kit and Nell to safety, but he had no idea how, when both were currently held in Jacob's thrall.

"Erasing bad memories. Is that so terrible, Joe? Perhaps you would rather remember? You were there when Bales made sure your parents would never hurt you again, weren't you? Would you care to share the experience with us all?"

He heard the boy's howl in the same instant that the shadows moved, and then they were there, in the filthy kitchen on Latimer Street, he and the boy pressed together, the boy, his face hidden in McNeil's shirt, arms tight around his neck, small fingers tangled in his hair. So close, they were as one, hearts thudding wildly to a single beat.

Everything was red, as if a filter had been placed before his eyes. Blood dripped, feet kicked, the ever-present thud of boots against wood. His eyes were drawn reluctantly up beyond the table where they both crouched, past the overturned chair and shattered crockery, higher than the door handle that was just out of reach, to the knife that gleamed on the kitchen counter and the bodies that hung from the ceiling. Bulging eyes, blue lips. The man no longer bellowed or punched. The woman no longer screamed abuse. Silence, thick, heavy and malevolent, wrapped around and threatened to choke them. The boy whimpered, and he held him tight and absorbed the horror. And then Bales reached down, with blood-stained hands, and gathered them up with a smile.

Safe and sound, JoJo.

Safe and sound.

McNeil staggered back onto the chair. His heart pounded. He dropped his head into his hands and dragged in a breath. *Inhale, exhale.* He thought he heard Nell's soft taunting lilt, but, when he raised his eyes to look at her, there was no change to her expression.

He turned back to Jacob. "Why are you doing this to me?"

"Because, Joe, this is all *your* fault."

"No, it's not. This has gone far enough. You've had your games." McNeil pulled out his phone and punched out Dennis' number. "It ends here, Jacob ... Richardson ... whoever the fuck you are. Let a *real* shrink analyse you for a change."

"Who will you call, Joe? Dennis, the good friend who thinks you're mad? Mather, the boss who fears you might uncover his secret affairs and corruption? The magpie Mary Cameron, who steals trinkets from crime scenes? Or perhaps the devillian Clarissa, with her unrequited revenge? In my time, I've counselled them all. *Dr. Freidman, what a marvellous doctor you are!* Myself, I'd go with the journalist, if I were you. I favour the theatrical, and, frankly, the others are an insult to my intelligence."

McNeil ignored him and struggled to his feet. The phone was ringing. "Dennis, where the fuck are you?" he muttered, when it became clear that Dennis wasn't going to pick up.

Jacob gave a warning shake of his head. "End the call or you'll never find out the truth."

McNeil hesitated. "Your version or mine? Maybe I don't want to know ..."

"Oh, but you do, Joe. It's burning a hole in your gut, eating away at you. It has been since you brought Nell back from the brink. Admit it. You see, you have the knack, just like me. You could be so good at this if you just gave it a chance."

The message service clicked on, and McNeil listened distractedly as a monotone recorded voice stated that DI Todd was otherwise engaged and gave options to leave a message or call back later, or call the alternative number that McNeil knew was the station, or, in case of emergency, dial 999.

He crossed to the window and peered out into the darkness. Outside, the snow had continued unabated, quietly blanketing the world in a pristine white veil. It provided a surreal contrast to the evil in the room and the turmoil in his head.

"Bales initially took you in like a stray puppy. He kept you and nurtured you, and, when your parents awoke later from a drunken stupor and realised you were missing, Bales, the water bailiff, supported their heart-breaking story of the little boy tragically lost in the lake. He helped search for your pathetic little body, and, all the while, you slept warm and safe with the fat little puppies. Afterwards, he couldn't hand you back, even if he'd wanted to, because to all intents and purposes you were dead, so he went back and made sure your parents were dead, too. An eye for an eye. And that, dear Joe, is how this all began. Once dead – now alive."

McNeil turned his attention away from the window and the phone. Jacob was right, he did need to know. "And then what?"

"Bales butchered your parents, hung them up like carcasses, and sealed their house up after him. Do you know, Joe, they weren't discovered until two years later?"

McNeil's mind drifted back to his recent conversation with Clarissa. "The same year that Nell was lost. It was reported in the papers at the time."

"Imagine that. Two whole years before anyone thought to check on them. What does that tell you about Bedlam, about community, or the lack of it? The world is indeed a shocking place. Bales always did have a fancy for the macabre," continued Jacob. "He became a liability in the end. I couldn't allow him to keep you. After all, you were just what I was looking for, the perfect subject, a motherless child with horrific memories, just waiting for the slate to be erased. I offered a far happier prospect for you ... and Bales was convinced by the sense of it. I'm very convincing when I put my mind to it." Jacob grinned slyly. "He soon forgot all about you."

McNeil's mind began to wander as he calculated his chances of overpowering Jacob. The man was older and, under normal circumstances, he wouldn't have thought twice about restraining him physically. He cast about for a weapon that might offset his current handicap, and made a further effort to engage Jacob in conversation. The longer he could keep him talking, the greater the chance that he could pull this back. "So, I was handed over like one of Bale's puppies?"

"And you were happy here, Joe – for a time, at least. You had something about you. Still do. You sense things, don't you, Joe, and that's how I knew you'd find your way back ... eventually. Of course, for my purposes, you were perhaps too clever, too stubborn for your own good. You wouldn't sleep."

McNeil still couldn't sleep, but he knew Jacob didn't mean the natural sleep that comes at the end of an exhausting day. He glanced at Kit, eyes downcast, soft dusty lashes on peachy cheeks, and at Nell, eyes wide open and staring, but her mind elsewhere, lost to the world.

"And sleep is good for you," continued Jacob. "Wipe the slate clean ... and begin again."

"So, this ..." McNeil gestured to the young women. "... this is just an experiment, a mind control game?"

"No, *you* were my experiment. They were yours."

McNeil shook his head. "You've lost me. I don't understand. I don't remember any of this ... of you. Just Bales and his puppies, then Mae."

"Oh, you do remember, Joe. Try a little harder. You wanted a play mate ..."

Carousels and candy floss.
Goldfish in plastic bags.
And bobbing red balloons.

A game of tag, laughter and excitement, the boy running ahead, the girl following with clumsy steps, the balloon just out of reach ... always. Then small hands clasped tightly, feet slipping in the mud, wet reeds under their feet and ice cold black water over their heads. They couldn't breathe. The weeds held them fast. Frantic splashes, silent screams. Hands held tight.

McNeil shuddered. A solitary tear slipped silently down Nell's cheek.

Don't let go.
Mustn't let go.
Hold her tight.
Keep her safe.
Save her!

The voice distorted as they sank deeper.

Mustn't let go.

Silt at his feet, soft and inviting. Lightness above and darkness below.

Save her.

And then, large, strong hands pulling him back, while small desperate hands pulled her. Together, he and the girl with the red balloon, dragged back to the light ... back to life.

Like a babe's first breath, McNeil inhaled desperately, and, in that instant, he realised that Jacob was right.

It was his fault.
It had always been his fault.
He had taken Nell.

Forty

Jacob smiled.

"So you see, Joe, I am not the monster, and neither was Bales. Bales plucked you from a life of neglect and abuse. I dragged you and Nell from the depths of the lake, and you were both re-born. Once dead – now alive, again.

Nell and JoJo.
Sitting in a tree.
Nell and JoJo.
Meant to be.

Nell's eyes swung silently to meet his. McNeil felt her pain, and was devastated at her heartache. He felt the boy's howl of despair deep inside, where it had lain buried for so long.

"I only ever wanted what was best for you, Joe. You wanted her. We kept her, and, in time, she, too, became an excellent subject. And then, you ruined it all by leaving us, by leaving her. Love is a wonderful thing, Joe. Obsession is something else entirely. You shared a beginning. You were meant to share a life. Nell has loved you always, from that very first moment when you took her hand. Yet you chose her sister instead. How could you, Joe?" Jacob's amusement rippled through his words and cut through McNeil's shock.

"You've kept Nell all this time?" Guilt washed over him. "You used Kit, bringing her here as a child, letting her believe this was all a vision, a product of her grief?"

"Don't sound so appalled, Joe. I did it for you, so you could have a normal childhood."

"*Normal?* You have no idea what *normal* is. What did you do, wake them up, get them out of their boxes, down off the shelf like toys, so I could play, and you could test out your bizarre experiments?"

"They were interesting subjects – twins. You chose well, Joe. You see, I told you, you had something about you."

"But that wasn't the end of it, was it? I got away. I found Mae. I had a life. That must have really screwed with your plans."

A crying child at the side of the road.

A childless woman with open arms.

His heart jolted, his chest tightened painfully, and, for the first time since he'd entered the room, he felt real tears threaten. Mae had saved him. Mae had kept him sane. He wasn't sure whether he'd ever be sane again. His attention drifted back to Nell. *I'm sorry.*

"You were a reluctant guinea pig, Joe. You continually resisted my techniques, drugs, and hypnosis. I designed the snake especially for you, as a trigger, but the charm was ineffective. You were a very stubborn child. So I used the bite of the tattoo, and it worked a little too well. It wiped you clear of everything, and there you were, little JoJo, mind a blank and running scared, looking for a mother who never really existed. As luck, or fate, would have it, you ran straight into the arms of a woman with secrets of her own. And so began your next life."

McNeil had only good memories of his time with Mae. He didn't want them tainted, but he needed to know, he needed to know everything. "How did you find me again?"

"Mae was cunning, fuelled by her own desire to save a lost little boy and keep him for herself. You see, Joe, everyone wants to save you. It's a pity you're so hell bent on self-destruction."

"Mae was a good woman. I had a good life."

"You did, Joe, and, all the while, poor little Nell awaited your return. Fortunately, she was a good sleeper. She had Kit for a while, but then, even those visits stopped, and now we know why ... When we discovered where you were, who you were with ... you and Kit. Dear me, Joe, and you call me a monster. You couldn't have hurt Nell more if you'd tried. But, as far as the experiment was concerned, bravo, Joe, it was an unmitigated success. You connected with Kit as you had with Nell. You may have forgotten the times you all played in the orchard together but, deep inside, both girls were imprinted. It was just a matter of time, and of course my timely intervention, before you found your way back."

"I asked how you found me."

"Mae knew she was dying and she couldn't meet her maker without confessing her sins. There were a few. Did you know she was a nurse? No, I don't expect you do. She worked in a maternity hospital, delivering welcome babies to happy mothers. In her spare time, she relieved unhappily pregnant women of their unwanted offspring."

"Clarissa?" the name whispered from his lips.

The game was almost over, all players poised for the music to stop, only one wrapper left on the parcel.

"She carried the guilt of all those lost souls around with her, and then she found you, and her life was changed. She had a chance to make amends. She'd witnessed terrible nightmares where you'd scream of slaughter and dark things. She was a God-fearing woman. She believed you'd been sent to test her faith. Melodramatic, perhaps." He smiled. "And that was the cruellest irony of all. She made her confession to the Reverend George Robinson Foulkes, who was, of course, beset with dilemma and indecision. He had the devil's spawn, not only in his midst, but courting his one remaining daughter ... And who did he come to for advice?"

"His favourite therapist?"

"And so began our little project, Nell's and mine, to bring you back to the fold, back to the beginning. I promised her freedom in return for Kit, and she delivered."

"Huh?"

"Down by the canal, with our good friend, Bales. Of course, he didn't know then who Kit was, or who you were. It was only later, when you sought him out and he manhandled you out of Minkey's. He once told me that he never forgot one of his puppies, that he could recognise them anywhere, even fully-grown. And he recognised you, Joe – that terrier tenacity of yours, that dogged determination, the refusal to give up or back down. The minute he touched you, he knew little JoJo was back. He wanted to save you again, Joe, and I couldn't have that. You belong to me."

"You had him killed?"

"In a roundabout way. The feral pack had already cut their teeth on the vagrants who'd witnessed Kit's abduction. The tramps would have escaped unscathed if Bales hadn't sought them out himself, doing your job for you, Joe, trying to help you, but making things worse. Once the pack had a taste for blood, there was no stopping them, until you came along, of course. They would have killed you, too, if it hadn't been for Nell. You're connected. You always were. You always will be."

He shifted his gaze. She was watching him. He caught a glimmer amidst the violet, a sharpening of focus that betrayed her intent, and he felt the coolness of her touch, the splash of tears on his cheek. Jacob might imagine she was under his control. McNeil wasn't so sure.

"So, what now?" he asked. "How do you imagine this will end? You can't keep us all here and you can't escape. It's over. Dennis will soon work out where I am." He held his phone aloft. "It's all on here, Jacob. Everything. Every sick detail on Dennis' answer phone. He's not as stupid as you seem to think. But just to be sure ..." – he smiled and brought the phone to his mouth – "... Gilmour House, Dennis, and don't forget to bring the troops." He pocketed the phone and stepped towards Kit. It was time to take control of the situation.

"And if he doesn't?"

"Doesn't what?"

"Pick up his messages. I expect he's delayed down at Bales' house. That's where you sent him, didn't you, to dig in the dirt, to uncover your past, to follow false leads? He's already been round here once, checking out your story, testing the locks. He has no reason to think this is where you are."

"Even if he doesn't show, this is over. I could overpower you now, if need be."

"Could you?"

McNeil was immediately dropped to his knees as pain lanced through him. He clutched at his belly. Fresh blood coated his hands.

"You forget, Joe. I am the master of this game."

"Fuck," McNeil cursed. "What do you want?"

He tried to stand and was felled again, landing heavily, jarring his ribs, tearing at his sutures. His heart thudded wildly, his belly was on fire. He scrabbled impotently for something to hang onto or something to wield, but, each time he raised himself up off the floor, Jacob smiled, and he was dropped again until he could do nothing else but submit. In his head, the boy's whimper was drowned out by something far more sinister, a whisper that grew louder by the second. *Hear me!* The voice demanded. Nell had risen from her seat.

"I want you to complete the experiment, my life's work."

"And how do I do that?" muttered McNeil. The shadows were gathering, the audience crowding the space with baited breath. The whisper became a shout that reverberated throughout his prone body. He shut his eyes in an attempt to shut out the images.

"Don't you know? Haven't you guessed? It's time to choose, Joe – Kit or Nell? You can only save one and, I sense, you have a fancy for both."

Yin or yang?
Sugar or spice?
Good or bad?
"Which is it to be?"

Forty-One

Did I really expect anything else?

Joe loves Kit. He has always loved Kit, and I have always known it.

He could never be mine, for he belongs to her, and she will not give him up. Her sweetness is deceptive, her strength far greater than mine. I am, as I have always been, the afterthought, the also-ran, the shadow. My mind debates gently, for I no longer have the will for combat, and can no longer trust my own beleaguered judgment.

He loves me, he loves me not.

Propelled by hope and sunk by reality, my sweet dreams have soured, my heart is broken, and I have finally accepted the end.

I am betrayed.

Not by Jacob, the man who took the child and moulded a monster in his image. He stole my life, but he promised me freedom, and I will have that soon. It gives me a small measure of satisfaction that I, not Jacob, am master of my own finale. The stage is set, the curtain all but closed, and Jacob has taken his final bow.

Not by Kit, who stole my reason for living, my one true love, though, I confess, I covet that sweetness and gentle beauty that has allowed her to enthral him, to blind him to the truth, to what was meant to be.

I am wrong, I know this, and I have always known this. I am an aberration, the blank page amongst vibrant colour, the single note in a rhapsody of sound, but so is Joe, and, in his heart, he knows this, too. We were meant to be. We are meant to be. He is mine, but sadly I will never be his.

I am betrayed – by Joe.

The blade hangs heavy from my hand, swinging gently back and forth as I walk. Blood, hot and slick, leaves a chilling trail on the snowy ground. I smile at the irony. Finally, my monochrome life is stained with colour. I am Gretel on my final journey to the gingerbread house. There is no one to save me – no Hansel, no woodcutter, just the inevitable encounter. I have taken control of my own destiny, and I do not fear the outcome. Freedom must be savoured. After all, I have sought it time and time again, only to have it pulled out of my grasp. I survive, regardless, and I continue. This time, I shall not.

The snow is cold beneath my feet, between my toes. I feel its chill creep up my legs, but I do not hurry. I am already numb, frozen from the inside out. Through the dormant winter orchard, happy voices taunt me as I weave silently between the sleeping trees.

Nell and JoJo.
Sitting in a tree.
Along came Kit.
And then there were three.

My smile betrays my conflict. My hand tightens on the blade. The blood flows faster.

I know the secret paths that meander at will through knee-high scrub, through the secret copse of silver birch and hornbeam – all naked, skeletal, winter wood that reflect the moonlight and illuminate my way. Had it been the pitch black dead of night, I would still have found the path unerringly, for I have followed it every night in my dreams. I know every step, every stone on the ground, every depression in the soft earth. I have trodden it in springtime, when primroses perfume my way, in summer, guided by the flit of butterflies, and in autumn, with the crunch of fallen leaves beneath my feet. But this is the first time my path has been carpeted in snow, and I decide it is fitting.

And now, I am here at the end, at the edge of the final abyss. This time, I do not choose the dizzying height to launch myself into Bedlam's open maw, I do not balance precariously at the edge of nowhere. Instead, I seek the silent oblivion of cold black water. It has waited, as I have, and now we are ready to be re-acquainted. Wet reeds guard the outer bailey of this enchanted castle of my dreams, clinging to my bare legs as they try to slow my progress. I cross with light foot and heavy heart. Frozen grasses sway and rustle with alarm, their noise soft in my ears, loud in my head. Roosting birds take to the air and the forgotten, slumbering, weed-choked lake is suddenly alive with apprehension and warning. I calm the rushes with a gentle hand and step through a thin film of ice into the water.

I am back to the beginning.

Forty-Two

"Joey! Joey! Come on, lad, open your eyes."

Dennis' urgent demand and rough hand at his shoulder dragged McNeil back, and he came awake with a jolt, adrenalin pumping, ready to strike. But with no discernible target, he pulled back his fist, and remembered.

He'd been offered a choice.

Nell had made it for him.

The distress of the boy he once was swelled inside, until his whole body was wracked with regret and shook with remorse.

"What the bloody hell has happened here?" continued Dennis.

McNeil accepted his help and struggled to his feet, swaying, leaning heavily. His head spun as he narrowed his eyes and scanned the scene.

The room was full, but this time there were no spectres, no images created from dark imaginings. This time the horror was very real. Police and paramedics jostled for space. Jacob lay slumped on the floor, the whine of a charging defibrillator alerting McNeil to the fact that his nemesis might yet survive, despite Nell's intervention. His head was flung back, and a paramedic fought to insert a tube for ventilation, while another clamped a gloved hand firmly at his gaping throat. Blood soaked his chest and pooled around him.

"Kit ..." He scanned the room desperately, relief stripping him of his last layers when he spotted her through the mêlée, held safely in George's desperate embrace. The man caught his eye. The slight nod, the cheeks wet with tears, said it all, but he voiced it anyway.

"Thank you," he mouthed, and McNeil dropped his gaze. He didn't deserve thanks. Jacob was right: *this was all his fault.*

His eyes grew heavy, nausea crept over him, pain bullied and chided. He should be elated. He had succeeded. He had found Kit, the love of his life. But his elation was defused by the echo of a whispered kiss, a hand on his chest, and a tear on his cheek.

"Where's Nell?" he murmured.

"Buggered if I know," replied Dennis. "I told you she was crazy. I've got men out searching. She'll not get far."

"No, you don't understand. Have you not checked your messages?"

"*Messages?* You think I've had time to check ruddy messages? If it wasn't for an old man and his dog, we'd never have found you at all. Don't worry, we'll catch her, and, this time, she'll be under lock and key for good."

McNeil's gut tightened, and, deep inside, down amongst the black things, the boy howled his despair.

No ... noooo.

Find her.

Save her.

Hurry.

McNeil stepped past Dennis and pushed his way through the crowd of emergency personnel. He reached for Kit's hand and took a slow breath before speaking. The feel of her hand, her fingers threaded between his, was almost his undoing.

"I love you, Kit. I always have, and you know I always will, but I'm not good enough for you. I never was. I doubt I ever will be. So, for now, you need to stay with your father." He focused on George. "Look after her, George."

He turned away and George stopped him with a hand on his arm. "I was wrong about you, Joseph. So wrong," his voice quivered with emotion. "You believed when everyone else did not. Don't leave. Keep the faith. What could be so important that you'd give up now?"

"Yes, where the hell do think you're going?" interrupted Dennis.

"I have to find Nell."

"Nell?" George and Dennis responded in unison, but it was to George he directed his reply.

"She's alive, George, little Elizabeth, the child you thought lost. She's out there somewhere, alone. I have to find her. She saved me. I have to save her."

George's knees gave way, and the big man would have toppled were it not for Dennis and Kit. "You found her?" he gasped. "You found our baby? It's been twenty-five years. I let go of her hand ..."

"And I took it," McNeil replied sadly. "George, if it weren't for me, you'd never have lost either of them."

Dennis swung his gaze from one to the other in confusion. "What on earth are you talking about?"

McNeil shrugged. "I don't have time, Dennis. Listen to your messages." He reached out a hand and gently cupped Kit's cheek. She leaned into him with a soft smile, and pressed a kiss in his palm.

"Go and find her, JoJo. I'll wait for you, just like you waited for me, no matter how long it takes." Her gentle whisper soothed his sorrow.

This would not end well. He knew that deep inside.

"Joey, you're not going anywhere," Dennis muscled in, sweeping aside the emotionally-charged atmosphere.

"I have to, Dennis. She's in danger."

"In danger from whom? She's a knife-wielding maniac!"

McNeil pushed past. "From herself. I need to save her from herself."

"Joey, just look at the state you're in."

McNeil dropped his gaze. His shirt was soaked in blood. "It's nothing," he muttered, suddenly aware of the pain from a wound wrenched apart. It was nowhere near as bad as the pain in his heart. "Look after Kit."

The boy was with him as he took the wide stairs two at a time. He gripped his hand tightly as they ran the length of the darkened corridor and stumbled together down the rickety basement stairs ...

Step eight, don't be late.

Step seven, hell or heaven.

Step four, evermore.

Step one, almost gone.

... and out into the cold night. *This way,* whispered the boy, and they ran together, McNeil's feet seeking out her prints in the snow, the boy following so closely that gradually they became one.

Hurry.
Find her.
Save her.

He pushed desperately through the overgrown orchard and squeezed through the gap in the fence that led to the wasteland beyond. His ribs hurt. He heaved in frantic gulps of frigid air. His blood began to flow, dripping, mingling with the drops in the snow that guided his way.

Wet reeds skittered beneath his feet, sharp icy fronds caught at his limbs as he battled his way through them.

I hear you.

Cold black water beckoned. She was there in the moonlight, waiting for him, drifting like a nymph in the weeds, violet eyes, inviting smile.

He stepped into the water and stretched out his hand.

He felt her hand on his chest, her breath on his skin, her tears on his cheek, and his heart jolted one last time. She drifted away, hair swirling, weeds entangling, pulling her down beneath the surface.

Nooooo! He and the boy howled in unison and, together, they followed her into the depths of the lake.

Cold black water closed over their heads. Soft black silt cushioned their feet. Velvet silence wrapped all around.

I hear you.

He grasped her hand and pulled her close, arms wrapped tight in a final, sad embrace. His eyes closed. Her eyes closed.

And the boy inside finally fell silent.

Then, splashing and shouting, and the winter lake drew back with a gasp. They were not forgotten, not forlorn. They were not damned. The weeds released their tangle and the water its icy hold.

Together. they floated to the surface, guided to the shore by unseen currents. Strong hands hauled desperately at his collar, dragging him back. His hand clasped hers tightly, fingers entwined as she, too, was pulled from the inky blackness.

His breath within her.
Her breath within him.
Once dead and now alive.
Again.

Forty-Three

The sun shines on the righteous. McNeil wasn't sure about that, but the sun had certainly blessed the small community of Eden with its presence. It glinted on Kit's golden hair as she strolled ahead of him, and McNeil watched and counted his good fortune. He caught her hand and fell into step beside her as she wandered between the stalls. The picnic was a success. Audrey and George had both their daughters back. All was right with the world.

A child ran past, squealing with laughter, and McNeil tightened his hold on Kit's hand. He watched, transfixed, as a string slipped between the child's chubby fingers and a red balloon bobbed free. Caught by the playful breeze, it skipped ahead, teasing, past the merry-go-round, where smiling children rode shiny motorcycles and airplanes, dancing above the carousel, where painted horses pranced, floating free as a bird above the church yard and onward toward the rectory.

McNeil followed its progress with a fascinated gaze, until the trailing string snagged on a climbing rose and the balloon bounced gently at the attic window.

Nell stood by the glass, looking out. Violet eyes met grey and held them fast. A soft smile brushed her pale lips.

He felt her hand on his heart, her breath within him and her soft tears on his cheek.

I hear you.
I love you.
Always.

Also by B.A. Morton